Promoting the Cowboy Billionaire

A Chappell Brothers Novel: Bluegrass Ranch Romance Book 5

Emmy Eugene

feel good fiction
FLANA JOHNSON

ISBN-13: 979-8709503373

CHAPTER 1

L awrence Chappell sighed as he stepped up to the mirror in the bathroom on the second floor at the homestead. He'd just showered for the second time that day, and he wished it was so he could go to bed clean.

Instead, he'd trim up his beard, splash on plenty of the cologne Olli had made for Spur, and get dressed in his best pair of jeans.

As he looked into his own pair of dark eyes, he could see the text from Mariah Barker. He wasn't sure how to label her, though he'd like to say she was his girlfriend. They'd been out several times this summer, but he'd never kissed her.

They went to her work events and held hands, talked, and laughed. He knew the women she sat by at work, and they knew him. To everyone outside the relationship, Lawrence and Mariah were a couple, and they'd been dating since June.

To Lawrence, though, who lived inside the relationship, he knew they were one-hundred percent *not* dating. Though Mariah acted interested, Lawrence could no longer decide what was pretend for her and what wasn't. Thus, he sighed again as he picked up his razor. He trimmed his beard, his unrest growing by the second. When he finished, he rinsed his face and splashed on aftershave so his skin wouldn't break out in tiny bumps. He seemed to be just one shade below the rest of his brothers, and the aftershave proved it.

His skin was fairer, and he had to wear sunscreen when he went outside. He'd learned through some recent painful encounters to spray it on every time, no matter what.

He still had the dark hair, though his wasn't nearly black like Spur's or Duke's. He'd definitely inherited more of the feminine qualities from his mother, and he turned away from his reflection at the thought of her.

Lawrence had struggled the most out of all the brothers to talk to women. Even in high school, girls had scared him, and somewhere along the line, Mom had decided it was her life's mission to set Lawrence up with every woman she deemed pretty—and Mom literally thought every woman was pretty.

He'd gone on several of her blind dates, but she wanted to dish with him afterward. She wanted all the details, down to exact lines said during conversations. If Lawrence didn't like one of her choices, she'd demand to know why.

After a while, Lawrence's embarrassment over being set up by his mother became too much, and he'd told her he didn't want her to keep doing so. They'd argued, of course. Everything with Mom turned into an argument.

As Lawrence went back across the hall to his bedroom, he told himself he wasn't being fair. Mom had come a long way this year, and he knew he needed to get down the lane and make his peace with her. She'd been trying hard, sending out memes and links to articles she thought he'd like. She had not invited him to come to the house where she and Daddy now lived out their retirement from the full-time work at Bluegrass Ranch.

Daddy had recovered well from his hip replacement surgery last year, and he went out into the Chappell stables almost every day. He cleaned equipment and brushed down horses for anyone who wanted him to. He'd been back on a horse in the past month, and only Lawrence knew.

If Mom knew... Lawrence chuckled as he shook his head. He dressed in his pressed and clean clothes, his mind moving forward too fast for him to keep up. No matter what else was in his head, he kept coming back to one thing: He needed to end things with Mariah.

The Summer Smash had concluded three weeks ago, and once upon a time, they'd agreed to keep their relationship "professional" until the inaugural race at Bluegrass had finished. She'd been the marketing executive assigned to the ranch, and Lawrence could admit she'd done an amazing job. Everyone thought so, and even Cayden—perfect, polished, and expects-perfection-and-polish-in-return—said he'd definitely use her again.

"*I'm* tired of being used, though," he muttered as he

bent to put on the pair of cowboy boots Mariah had actually bought for him. A rush of humiliation pulled through him, and he stalled in the movement to dress himself the way she wanted him to.

"You're such an idiot." He stood up, bootless, and strode out of the bedroom. Duke had finally moved into the homestead too, and his bedroom sat just down the hall from Lawrence's. He went that way and banged on the door. "Duke," he called. "I need your help."

"Comin'." A few seconds later, Duke opened the door, his headset still on. "Sorry." He reached up and took it off. "They're in the middle of a share," he said. "I have to be muted and off-camera, but the professor could come back on any second." He'd started taking some classes in ranch management just about a week ago, and Lawrence did like listening to him talk about it.

Duke was always so animated. He did tend to talk too much, but he also had the ability to know when he'd let his mouth run away from him, something Conrad and Ian didn't possess.

"It won't take long," Lawrence said. "I just need a yes or no answer."

"Okay, shoot." Duke glanced over his shoulder and then focused his full attention on Lawrence.

"Say the woman you've been going out with starts making excuses for why she can't see you if the two of you aren't going to a work party. For her. A work party for *her*." He cleared his throat. "Then she's available, and by the stars in heaven, you better be available too."

Duke started to narrow his eyes, but Lawrence plowed forward. "She says your boots make you look dirty, and she actually buys you a new pair. She texts you what she's wearing and makes suggestions for what you should wear. She doesn't let you come pick her up, but she arranges a meeting place so you can arrive at the party together. You haven't kissed her, but it's been months of this."

"I know where this is going."

Lawrence was sure he did. Duke went out with a lot of women, and he had no problem getting random strangers to come sit by him at weddings, dance with him, or attend any number of family parties and events with a simple smile or a cocked eyebrow.

"Should you break up with her?" Lawrence asked.

"The real question is: Are you even dating this woman?" Duke put both eyebrows up, the question clear.

"Let's say you thought you were. She might even think you are."

"Yes," Duke said. "If it's yes or no, Larry, it's yes."

Despite the nickname he hated, Lawrence nodded, his gaze suddenly finding something so much more interesting to look at over Duke's shoulder. "Yeah, I think so too. Thanks." He turned and started back to his bedroom, his heart heavy and his feet feeling like wooden blocks he could barely lift.

"And don't wear those boots," Duke called. "Be who you are, Lawrence."

Lawrence waited until he was back in his room, the door closed, before he said, "Easy for you to say, Duke. You went out with one blonde last night and have a date with a different one tonight."

He paused in the middle of the room and looked at the boots lying beside the bed. Nope, he wasn't going to wear those. He kicked them under the bed and went to his closet to get out a pair of sneakers. Mariah would hate these, but he put them on anyway.

She'd texted to say she'd be wearing a flowered sundress in navy and white, and wouldn't they look so cute if he wore a red shirt? *Like the flag,* she'd said with a smiley face.

"So cute," he muttered sarcastically, stripping off the red shirt he'd already put on. He didn't even like the color red, because it made his skin look pinker than it really needed to look, ever.

He pulled on a black plaid shirt that had big boxes of white in between the black ones. Faint yellow pinstripes ran down and across the white parts, and he felt more like himself instantly.

He skipped brushing his teeth, because he wasn't going to kiss Mariah anyway, and he went downstairs to find Ginny standing in the kitchen, a wooden spoon in one hand while she licked something off her fingers on the other.

She grinned at him, a bit of color coming into her face. "Heya, Lawrence."

"Evening, ma'am," he said. He was used to seeing Ginny Winters in the homestead. She and Cayden had been engaged since the Smash, and she loved to cook until he came in from the administration building.

Then whoever was around would eat, and she and

Cayden would spread out their wedding plans on the dining room table and talk and talk and talk.

"Going out with Mariah again?"

"Again?" he asked. "We haven't been out in weeks."

Ginny lowered the wooden spoon. "Oh, I thought... You're right. You left last week, but then you came back." Her dark eyes fired questions at him, but Lawrence couldn't even answer the ones already swimming in his own mind.

"I'm sorry," she added, turning back to the bowl she'd been stirring.

"No, I'm sorry," he said with a sigh. "I'm just in a mood, because I'm going to break up with her tonight."

Ginny didn't turn back to him, and he appreciated that. "You are? Things aren't going well?"

"I think she's only using me to go to her company parties."

Ginny did face him again then, her eyes wide. "Have you asked her to confirm that?"

"We sorta talked about it a while ago," he mumbled. "At Blaine's wedding, we *did* agree to use the relationship as a way for her to get to her boss's parties, but in my head, the agreement ended once the Smash did. Then we'd become a real couple, because she wouldn't be working for us anymore." He watched Ginny absorb the information, her mind obviously working much faster than his ever had.

"She had some sort of personal policy against dating clients," he finished.

"Now she doesn't want to go out," Ginny said.

"Doesn't seem like it."

"Maybe she's really busy?" Ginny guessed. "When Cayden first asked me out, I was so busy with the Harvest Festival at Sweet Rose. I put him off."

"I don't know," Lawrence said, but he seriously doubted it. Mariah seemed to have plenty of time to go for coffee with friends after work, or get her nails done, both things he'd seen on her social media this week.

He gave Ginny a small smile and reached up to touch his hat. Mariah had tried to get him to not wear it once, but he'd done it anyway. She hadn't said anything again, and Lawrence wondered how she'd react if the tables were turned.

He couldn't even *imagine* texting her and telling her what to wear for their fake date that night—to an apple-tasting party, of all things.

No wonder she wanted him to wear red. When they'd gone to an event over the summer, she'd known the theme was country chic, but he hadn't. She'd suggested he wear a red and white checkered shirt, and no less than twenty people had commented on how he and Mariah had really played up the theme.

In fact, she'd gotten the biggest client of the party because of it.

Guilt pulled through him as he left the homestead and walked over to his brand-new truck. None of his brothers had said anything, because he had his own money to spend, and if he wanted a two-ton truck, he could have a two-ton truck.

He didn't like thinking that he'd bought the huge truck to make up for how small he felt inside his own life.

Think about it he did as he navigated across town to the spot where he'd met Mariah several times in the past. A parking lot at an all-night doughnut shop. Lawrence didn't understand the point of Doughnuts After Dark, but they did have an amazing cake doughnut with maple frosting and a crumb topping.

Sometimes, if he was early, he went inside and got himself a tasty treat.

He wasn't early tonight. If anything, he was late. He tried to care, but he was having a hard time with all of it.

When he pulled into the parking lot, Mariah's white SUV already waited on the outside row of spaces, and Lawrence eased his truck next to it. She always rode with him, and tonight was no different.

She smiled at him through the glass, and Lawrence started second-guessing himself. It honestly was probably a third- or fourth-guessing.

"Hey," she said.

"Hey," he responded. He had the urge to tell her he was sorry he was late, but he bit back the words. She did look amazing in the flirty sundress, and she'd paired the dark dress with white flowers all over it with a pair of bright pink sandals Lawrence really liked.

He really liked *her*, and he didn't understand what had turned cold between them since Blaine's wedding. He pulled out of the parking spot and eased back onto the highway to get to her boss's house.

They drove along, and Lawrence waited for her to ask him something. He often started the conversations with questions about her day, or a client, or a co-worker.

"How's the ranch?" she finally asked.

"Good," Lawrence said, hating the false quality in his voice. He sighed again, and added, "Listen, Mariah, we need to talk."

"About what?"

"About what we're doing," he said, glancing at her. "I thought we were going to become a real couple after the Smash, but every time I ask you out, you have something else to do." He swallowed, but he'd started, and he couldn't stop now. "Which is fine. Maybe you're really busy at work right now. Ginny said she did that; she was so busy, and she couldn't date Cayden."

He stopped to shake his thoughts back into some semblance of order. He also needed to breathe. "Anyway, that's neither here nor there. I just want to know what you want *this* to be." He gestured between the two of them, his frustration obvious.

She gaped at him with wide eyes, and Lawrence felt the same shock moving through him.

"I..." she said. "I don't know." She looked out her window, and Lawrence had his answer.

"I don't think we should see each other anymore," he said. "I'll go to this party, and I'll be exactly who I've been all the other times." He shifted in his seat, his mouth so dry. "Then that's that. Okay?"

She didn't answer, and when Lawrence looked over at her, he found her nodding.

"Okay, then," he said, and a cloud of awkward silence draped over the two of them. *Idiot*, he chastised himself. *You should've waited until after the party to break-up with her.*

Now he had to attend the party as her fake boyfriend when he was exactly that. At least before, he'd had some hope of a real relationship with her, which had made the pretending easier.

This was going to be torture.

CHAPTER 2

Mariah Barker woke up to the scent of pumpkin pie spice and cream, and she groaned as she rolled over. She fumbled for her phone to check the time, and it couldn't be too late yet, because hardly any light came through her blinds.

Someone making coffee down the hall in her kitchen meant her sister had come over, and Mariah rolled onto her back and stared up at the ceiling. She'd managed to find a reason why she hadn't been able to make the family brunches, but Dani had the nose of a bloodhound, and she'd been texting Mariah for over a week now.

She didn't want to tell Dani about Lawrence; she didn't want to tell anyone about Lawrence. She'd been cursing her luck, the stars, and any cracks in sidewalks she'd somehow stepped on since the middle of July.

With only a week until the Smash, Dr. Biggers had called her into his office and said he thought she'd been using

Lawrence to get better jobs. Her heart thumped harder in her chest even now.

She'd denied it, and thankfully, Dr. Biggers had thought she meant she'd been mining the Chappells for more clients. She hadn't been; she'd simply been able to network with a lot of people while she'd worked on their event. She'd met a lot of people at the event, and she'd learned to carry her business cards everywhere with her.

Dr. Biggers had cautioned her not to mix business and pleasure, and Mariah didn't know what to do with that. She didn't know how to separate Lawrence from her life when he was the reason she got to go to the events that kept her working with the clients she wanted to work with.

She'd tried explaining to Dr. Biggers, but he'd flat-out told her not to ask Lawrence for clients if she was going to date him. *If you break-up with him*, he'd said. *Well, that's a different story. Then he's not a personal contact, but a business one.*

Mariah felt trapped between two plates of steel, and she had no idea how to slip out. She'd made a mess of things by trying to put Lawrence off in a fun, flirty way, hoping he wouldn't notice that they weren't going out for real.

"I want to," she whispered. "I just don't know *how*."

That was the story of Mariah's life, and she'd endured the apple extravaganza a couple of weeks ago, and she'd told no one that she and Lawrence hadn't spoken since that night.

Dani would get the story out of her, because Mariah couldn't put her off forever. She finally got up and shimmied into a pair of leggings to give her sister the appearance that she was going to work out today.

She wasn't, because Saturdays simply weren't for working out. They were for sleeping in and sipping pumpkin spice lattes, and Dani understood that.

Mariah padded out into the kitchen, where she found Dani pouring raw scrambled eggs into a muffin tin.

"It's about time you got up," Dani said. "I was going to slide these in and come see what was going on."

"What's going on," Mariah said as she overturned a mug her older sister had put on the counter. "Is that it's Saturday and barely eight a.m." She smiled at her sister as she poured her coffee and reached for the container of pumpkin spice creamer. "You are a Godsend, though. I've had a horribly busy week, and next week is going to be worse."

"You shouldn't have—"

"I know," Mariah said, giving her a glare. "Okay? I know."

Dani held up one hand in acquiescence and slid the muffin tin into the oven. She leaned one hip into the counter and asked, "How does your boyfriend feel about your busy schedule?"

Mariah tucked her messy hair behind her ear and shrugged.

"You broke up with him." Dani's voice carried shock.

"He broke up with me," Mariah said, and Lawrence was right to do so. Mariah wouldn't want to only go out with him so he could have an in with his boss. The fact that he'd kept doing it for almost a month after the Smash was a testament to him, and Mariah wished the situation was different.

"What happened?" Dani asked.

"I don't want to talk about it," Mariah said. "That's why I didn't text you back or come to the last two brunches." She cocked her left eyebrow at Dani. "Can we not talk about it today?"

"You liked him so much," she said. "I could tell."

"This is the opposite of not talking about him."

"Hey, I came and made coffee and breakfast," she said.

"Yeah, because your husband is out of town, and you don't know what to do with yourself if you're not mothering someone."

A pinch of hurt crossed Dani's face, and Mariah added her pain to the guilt that had been collecting in her stomach for a while now. "Sorry," she murmured.

"It's okay," Dani said. "What are you doing for Halloween?"

"Halloween?" Mariah chuckled. "It's almost two months away still."

"You make elaborate costumes, though." Dani smiled at her. "I know you have a plan. Just tell me."

"I was thinking about, I don't know. A Smurf or something."

Dani laughed and shook her head. "You're impossible." A dog barked, and she straightened before walking over to the back door to let in her dog. "You're not supposed to bark," she said. "You and that little dog next door need to learn to get along. Your relationship is dysfunctional."

Mariah laughed, because the idea of the two dogs having a dysfunctional relationship was hilarious. Dani's black dog with the big white patch on his chest caught sight of her and came running over.

"Whoa, whoa," she said, still giggling. "Not so fast." Phantom skidded to a stop just in time, his doggy face so happy to see her. "Yes, it's good to see you too. So good." Mariah scratched the dog's back and that white patch, his fur so soft. "You've been to the groomer recently, haven't you, bud? Yes, you have. You have."

"So, are you looking for a new boyfriend?" Dani asked, stepping over to the stove to check on the baked eggs.

"No," Mariah said. "I have plenty of clients right now. Let Dr. Biggers overwhelm someone else for a few months." She picked up her coffee and took it to the couch. Phantom followed her and jumped up beside her.

Mariah relaxed into the couch and closed her eyes. She could get used to someone taking care of her while she relaxed, as that hadn't happened in a while now. She'd been gearing up to ask Lawrence to come to her house for dinner, as he'd never been here to pick her up before. She hadn't wanted him to cross into her personal space while he was her client.

Dr. Biggers didn't have a problem with that, only with her using him to get more clients. All at once, Mariah realized why she'd gotten in trouble with him. *He* liked to be the one to bring the heavy hitting clients to his people, and he did not like her bringing her own companies to The Gemini Group.

"I need to quit my job," she said.

"What?" Dani asked, spinning from the stove. "You love that job."

"I hate my job," Mariah said, finally speaking the truth. "I *need* the job, and it's far better than anything else I've ever had. There's a difference."

Dani came toward her, and Mariah knew what she was going to say. She held up her hand. "Don't. I don't want to live in your basement."

"What about Dad's—?"

"I can't believe you even said that," Mariah said, getting to her feet. "I'm not moving back in with Dad. I'm thirty-seven years old." She'd had quite the disastrous decade in her twenties, and she'd been paying for it since. She crossed into the kitchen, ready to dump her sister's coffee down the drain.

She stalled though, because she was thirty-seven years old, and she didn't need to act like a petulant child. "I liked Lawrence. Like him. I like him."

"Then go out with him," Dani said, her voice coming from clear across the room. At least she was smart. "Who cares what your boss says?"

"I just don't want to give any of the wrong impressions," Mariah said. "To anyone."

"You worry too much about what other people think."

"Yes," Mariah said. She wondered when that would disappear. Dani was three years older than her, and she and her husband hadn't been able to have children. They had their dog, and they had each other, and most of the time, that was enough.

Mariah knew there was an ache deep down inside Dani's soul, though. It came to life when it wasn't enough to have a husband and a dog, but she'd stopped talking to Mariah about it after Mariah's miscarriage and divorce, the filed bankruptcy, and the temporary protective order.

"I don't want Lawrence to know about my past," she whispered.

Somehow her sister heard her, and Dani joined her in front of the kitchen sink. "If he's the one, Mya, he won't care."

Mariah leaned into her sister, who put her arm around her. "How do you know if a man is the one?"

"You just do," Dani said. "Unless you won't go out with him."

Mariah's smile came quickly at the teasing in her sister's voice. "Thank you." She turned into her and hugged her. A few moments later, the timer on the eggs went off, and Dani cleared her throat. "Okay, let's eat. I have some news for you."

"Lay it on me, Short Stack."

Dani giggled as she got the muffin tin out of the oven. She'd hated Mariah's nickname for her growing up, but it seemed to endear them to each other now. They got along well, as they did with their younger sister, Alicia. The three of them only had one another—and their father—and Mariah suddenly felt bad for canceling on the last two brunch dates the four of them went on every Sunday.

"Doug and I might be getting a baby," she said, her eyes filled with hope but her voice calm and casual. "I'm not saying we are. We've got a meeting Monday morning at the agency, and Isaac says he's had a birth mother ask about us several times. He's going to put us in touch with her."

Wonder and amazement filled Mariah, and she hurried around the counter to her sister. "I'm so glad."

The strength with which Dani clung to her told Mariah that she was glad too, and her hopes were as high as they could go. "No promises," Dani said. "We've had birth moms ask about us before."

"Right." Mariah cleared her throat. "It's still exciting. Congratulations." She stepped back and ignored Dani as she wiped her eyes. She served her sister a couple of the omelet muffins and took two for herself too.

"How do you think I can get Lawrence to go out with me?"

"Just call him and ask."

Mariah shook her head as she split open her muffin and steam came pouring out. "That's not how it's done these days."

"No? Women don't ask men out? You wait for him to ask you?"

"No, you don't just call and ask." Mariah shook her head as she sprinkled salt over the eggs. "I need to, I don't know, run into him somehow. Like it's a mistake."

"That's ridiculous," Dani said.

It might be, but that was what Mariah needed to do. "I don't think he leaves the ranch much," she mused. Alicia would probably have some great ideas for how to "accidentally" run into Lawrence. She seemed to have a new date all the time—at least before the man she'd been dating for a while now.

"Then I guess you've got to get out to Bluegrass Ranch," Dani said.

She did... Now she just needed to figure out *how*.

* * *

A week went by while Mariah planned the perfect staged attempt to run into Lawrence Chappell again. She'd driven along the road that ran in front of Bluegrass Ranch a dozen times, hoping her old SUV would break down and he'd conveniently happen by in his truck to help her.

The vehicle just kept running and running, though, and all Mariah did was rack up a higher gas bill that week.

Still, she thought she'd give it one more try. Inspiration had struck her so many times out at Bluegrass that she was sure it would one more time.

"Just one more time," she begged as she got behind the wheel and started the pilgrimage to Bluegrass. It was a long way for her, but the time passed quickly under the cogs and wheels of her mind.

She was no closer to a solution when she approached the curve in the road where Bluegrass sat, up on the hill to her right.

A sign now sat there that hadn't been there before. *You Pick Peaches and Apples.*

It had a giant arrow pointing left, and Mariah knew from working with the Chappells on the Summer Smash that one of them actually lived down the road at this other ranch.

She hit the brakes and put on her blinker, though there was no one behind her. After making the turn off the highway and onto the white gravel of a long driveway, Mariah took a deep breath. "This is crazy," she said. "You don't have time to pick fruit."

She did adore peaches, though, and if she could get even a half-dozen of those, she'd have breakfast for a week.

A man rose from a chair positioned underneath a portable and collapsible shade, and Mariah recognized him. Not Lawrence, or Cayden, or Spur, whom she'd actually worked face-to-face with.

But Conrad Chappell, the brother who'd brought a giggly blonde to the family table during Blaine's wedding.

He came out a few steps, a clipboard in his hand and a smile on his face. "Good morning," he said, simply grinning at her like she was the one person he'd wanted to meet. "Welcome to Triple T Ranch. Do you want to pick apples or peaches?"

"Is there a price difference?"

"Yes, ma'am," he said, flipping something on his clipboard. He took off a stiff piece of plastic and handed it to her. "The peaches are at their peak right now, but we've had a lot of people out here in the past couple of days, so you have to climb up to get them. They're a bit more expensive. The apples are Liberties, and some of them need a few more weeks. Again, we've had a fair bit of traffic out here recently, and you'll have to hunt for the apples."

"Hunting and climbing," Mariah said. "Sounds like hard work." That she was going to pay to do. It made no sense, and yet, she found herself studying the plastic sheet. *This is the closest you've been to Lawrence in three weeks. Don't blow it.*

"We've got guys out there that can help you," he said.

Mariah looked up, her hopes climbing too as an idea occurred to her. "Do you recognize me, Conrad?" She handed him the plastic sheet back, his eyebrows furrowing down as he took it and reattached it to his clipboard.

"Should I?"

"Yes," she said. "I ate with you at Blaine's wedding. I sat next to Lawrence."

"Oh, right," he said, but his eyes didn't light up. He still had no idea who she was, and her stomach clawed at itself. "I was one of the marketing execs for the Smash."

That got him to really glow. "Of course. Mariah...Barker." He snapped his fingers, obviously proud of himself. Lawrence didn't talk about his private life with this particular brother, or he wouldn't be smiling at her like that.

"Yes." She returned the smile, wishing she wasn't quite so far into her professional voice. "Listen, I haven't heard from Lawrence for a while. Is he one of the guys out in the fields?"

"Yes, ma'am," Conrad said, looking at his clipboard. "He's on peaches this morning."

Perfect, Mariah thought. "I think I want to pick some peaches," she said.

"Great." He started telling her where to go, and where to park once she got there. He said he'd radio ahead to "the guys" in the peach orchard and let them know they had a customer coming in.

Mariah employed every ounce of patience she had while he went on and on, finally taking the tag with a peach printed on it and tossing it onto her dashboard like he'd told her to. She went down the lane he'd indicated, and she found the parking area easily.

Only one other car sat there, and Mariah prayed with all the sincerity of her heart that Lawrence wasn't out in the orchard with that customer. She wasn't exactly dressed for picking peaches, as she'd done her hair and makeup, and put on a cute pair of khaki shorts and a bright pink camouflage-patterned blouse that morning.

"The goal is the same," she muttered. "Get Lawrence's attention." She'd wanted to look good should she happen to run into him, and that would still be achieved.

She got out of the car, pocketed her keys and phone, and started for the fruit stand where they'd give her a basket and then weigh her out when she picked all the peaches she wanted.

As she approached, she met Duke's eyes—another brother she'd met a few times as she worked with the Chappells on their big event several weeks ago.

"You're up, Larry," he said, his eyes glued to Mariah.

"Fine," Lawrence's voice said from inside the stand.

"Then I'm goin' home. I'm on mowing tonight, and—" He froze as his gaze moved from Duke to Mariah.

Keep going, she told herself. *Keep going. Don't stop. Dear Lord, don't let me stop.*

"Mariah," Lawrence said, his voice grinding through his throat in the next moment. He reached up and adjusted his cowboy hat. She smiled at him, because he was so sexy in that hat, and when he spoke in that Southern voice, she wanted to melt right into his arms.

He glanced at Duke, but Mariah only had eyes for him.

In what felt like a rush of time, Mariah closed the distance between them and put her palm against his chest. His heart beat steadily beneath that handsome blue paisley shirt, and she felt completely outside of her head as she said, "I'm so sorry, Lawrence. I got all inside my head, and my boss said some things that confused me, and I didn't want to hurt you."

He blinked at her, his surprise evident. "Okay," he said.

Mariah couldn't go back now, so she might as well keep going. "What does *mowing tonight* entail? Would you have time to go to dinner?"

He fell back a step as if she'd hit him with her words. "Uh..."

Mariah didn't like the sound of that. She looked at Duke, who stood there watching them without any embarrassment at all. Plenty of it heated her face, and she dropped her gaze to the dirt at her feet.

The silence hanging in the air felt like poison, and Mariah shuffled backward. "Never—"

"He can't take you to dinner," Duke blurted out. "The mowing means he works all night mowing the hay."

She looked up at him as he moved between her and Lawrence.

"Duke," Lawrence said.

"He can take you to lunch, though," Duke said with a bright smile. "Right after y'all finish picking your peaches." He turned sideways and looked from Mariah to Lawrence and back, nodded, and went back inside the fruit stand.

Lawrence stared at her for another moment, a smile finally touching his face. He took a step toward her. "Are you free for lunch, Mariah?"

She grinned at him, nodded, and took his hand when he extended it toward her.

CHAPTER 3

L awrence steadied the ladder, really pounding it down into the ground. Thankfully, the sun had been shining for a few hours, softening up the dirt. Every nerve stood at attention, because Mariah's eyes had barely left him.

After he'd led her to the golf cart with the two bushel baskets for peaches on the back seat, his throat had somehow closed off. His brain had shut down. He couldn't think of a single thing to say when it should've been easy to find something to talk about. He hadn't seen her in a little over three weeks, and certainly she had a story or something to tell.

She always had, even when they'd seen each other all the time. When they'd been on texting terms, she related anecdotes about things that happened around the office, or the antics of her sister's dog.

Now, though, she seemed just as frozen as he was.

"There you go," he said, gesturing to the ladder.

"You just climb up and start picking?" she asked.

"Yes, ma'am," he said, treating her very much like the last customer he'd helped. He didn't want to be at The Triple T at all, working for Trey and Beth for pennies. He supposed it was a bit better than sitting around the homestead, wishing someone would make him a hot breakfast.

Maybe his life had taken a serious backward slide since he'd broken up with Mariah. Even as he thought it, he knew there was no maybe about it. He'd jumped at the chance to help Beth and Trey get their orchards picked, because Beth fed him like a king after every shift. In fact, her quaint, white farmhouse always had food pouring out of it.

The kitchen at the homestead did too, at least when Ginny was there. She didn't live with Cayden yet, but she seemed to be there a whole lot. Lawrence didn't mind, though he did wonder if the two of them would want him and Duke living upstairs once they got married.

That conversation hadn't been had yet, and Lawrence wasn't looking to move back to the house with Ian and Conrad. He'd lived with them before, along with Duke, and out of the four of them, Lawrence was definitely the quietest. The meekest.

The weakest, he thought, frowning at the course of his internal thoughts. No one had ever called him weak. He simply felt like he was, way down deep in his soul.

Trey swaggered around two ranches as if he owned the world and could do no wrong. He possessed a lot of talents, and he really did do a lot right. He seemed to know how to handle TJ, the now-six-year-old he'd become step-father to upon his marriage to the boy's mother, Beth.

Spur, as the oldest brother, definitely never exhibited any weaknesses, as he'd been running Bluegrass Ranch for several years now. He knew every in and every out that happened on the sprawling horse ranch, and Lawrence was eternally glad he wasn't the oldest.

"Okay," Mariah said dubiously, breaking Lawrence out of his introspection. He could go on and on about his brothers and his hidden place among them. He didn't like going into that cave, though, so watching a pretty blonde woman climb a ladder and reach for a peach actually brought a ray of joy to Lawrence's life.

Not only was Mariah here, but she'd worn a tight pair of khaki shorts that climbed halfway up her thigh, along with a bright pink T-shirt with a gray and white camouflage pattern on it that seemed fitted to her skin. She had incredible curves, and with her tennis shoes, she looked like a woman about to have a grand adventure out in Kentucky's horse country.

If she didn't fall off this ladder and kill herself.

Lawrence didn't usually stay with the customers, but he'd already told Duke he'd be leaving after helping this last one, and he wondered if he and Mariah would go to lunch today or a different day.

She tipped up onto her toes, really reaching out for a peach, and the muscles in her calf tightened and tensed.

Lawrence needed to stop staring. "So," he said, really

loud. Too loud. He cleared his throat. "You really came to pick peaches?"

"I only want a few," she said, putting the fruit she'd just snagged into the basket. Beth had bought special ladders for peach-picking this year, with platforms for the bushels to sit on. It made the you-picking easy as pie, and they'd had a lot of people out to the ranch in the past week since she and Trey had opened up the orchards.

Lawrence could admit he'd taken home apples that made his mouth water, and Ginny had made an apple crisp on Sunday that he still dreamed about. She'd been experimenting with Dutch oven peach cobbler, and Lawrence had been all too happy to be a taste-tester.

"I love eating a fresh peach with a lot of cream for breakfast." She smiled down at him and focused back on the branches and leaves. "I don't suppose you eat fruit, right?"

"Why wouldn't I eat fruit?"

"Doesn't seem like something cowboys do."

"It depends on how it's prepared." he said.

She giggled, the sound completely new for Lawrence and yet extremely familiar. He'd heard her laugh like this at the parties and events he'd attended with her over the months. This one sounded real, though, and a smile crossed his face without him thinking about it. "You just eat fruit," she said. "You don't need to prepare it. It's prepared already."

"I disagree," he said, falling into easy flirting with her. Finally. Gratitude rushed through him that he'd made it through the ice fields. "Fruit should be prepared—into cakes, pies, cobblers, crisps. Heck, I'll even take a fritter."

She burst out laughing then, a steady peal of happiness filling the sky around them. "I bet you will," she said, still giggling.

Only a few minutes later, she descended the ladder and looked from her bushel to him. "I got about twenty. That's going to be way too many for me, but my sister makes this amazing dessert she calls peach delight."

"Sounds delightful," he said.

"You didn't meet Dani," she said. "Only Alicia."

"Dani must be older," he said, not sure why he thought that. When Mariah had spoken of her sister in the past, the words had been tinged with annoyance. Now, she sounded happy and content, so he assumed Dani must be older.

"Yes," Mariah said. "She's three years older than me."

"And Alicia is three years younger."

"I am smack dab in the middle." Mariah smiled and tucked that pretty blonde hair behind her ear. Lawrence's eyes dropped to her mouth, and he wasn't even sure why. He hadn't kissed her during their previous relationship, because that one hadn't been real.

Was this one?

"Where do you...?" He trailed off, because he wasn't sure what he needed to know. "Do you want to go to lunch today?" he asked. "Or another day?"

"Mowing hay all night sounds horrible," she said. "You tell me."

"You're still working at The Gemini Group, right?" He took down the ladder and carried it back to the road, placing it on the ground parallel to the tree she'd just picked from.

That way, when Duke brought the next customer out, he'd know where to start them.

"Yes," she said.

"So weekdays are out," he said. "We're having a big... thing. Lunch. Something tomorrow at my parents'," he said. "Otherwise we could go tomorrow."

"We can go today," she said, training those bright blue-green eyes on him. "Unless you don't want to."

He didn't know what he wanted. He nodded and got behind the wheel of the golf cart. Just as he did, his radio bleeped, and Duke said, "Larry, come back."

Mariah giggled again. "He calls you Larry."

"I hate it." Lawrence gave her a dry look he hoped said, *Don't you dare start calling me that.* All of the younger brothers used the terrible nickname, but none of the older ones did. He wasn't sure why they'd divided themselves up that way, but they had.

"Duke must be younger than you," Mariah said with one of her gorgeous smiles. All those straight, white teeth, and those full lips.

Lawrence nodded, his face heating. He wished he had more experience with women. Then he might know what to say, or how to say it. He might know when to kiss her, or how to do that. As it was, he hadn't been in a serious enough relationship to warrant kissing for years now. Many years. Too many years.

"Yep," he said into the radio.

"The Millers are done out there. You want to swing by and get them?"

"I'll bring Mariah in first," he said. "There are four Millers."

"True, true," Duke said. "Okay. I'll let them know you'll be a couple of minutes."

"Roger that."

Mariah laughed again, and Lawrence pressed his eyes closed for a long moment. *Roger that?* He shook his head at himself, but at the same time, he didn't want to have to change who he was to be with her. He should be able to wear his dusty boots and whatever shirt he wanted. He should be able to say the little catch phrases he always had without embarrassment. He was thirty-five years old, and he wasn't an idiot.

"So you've got the seven brothers," she said, her voice almost musing.

"Yes," he said. "You have two sisters." Was this seriously what they were talking about? He'd thought their interaction couldn't get much worse, but it sure did seem like it could.

"Yep."

"And your dad...let's see." Lawrence zipped down the dirt path toward the fruit stand. "I think it's just you guys and your dad. Your mom..." He glanced at her. "I can't remember. I'm not sure if you ever told me what happened with your mom."

He hoped he wasn't opening old wounds or unstitching years of careful work for her to keep her emotions in check. He glanced at her, catching the tail end of a look on her face that sure seemed like...disgust.

His heart flopped in his chest, and Lawrence squeezed the steering wheel. "Sorry," he said. "You don't have to tell me if it's hard to talk about."

"It's hard," she admitted. "But it shouldn't be." She sighed. "My mother left when I was thirteen. Only a couple of days after my birthday, in fact." She flashed a smile that didn't hold any happiness at all. "She ran off with our next-door neighbor. They'd been having an affair, and as far as I know, they're still together."

Lawrence swallowed, his disbelief coursing through him. "Wow," he said. "I'm sorry. That's terrible."

"He left his wife and everything. They had three kids, just like us. Two boys and a girl." Mariah cleared her throat. "I maybe started dating the one boy close to my age after that. We just...both got it."

He wondered why she was embarrassed about that, but he didn't ask as he pulled up to the fruit stand. Duke took the bushel out of the back seat and turned to weigh it.

"I'll go get the Millers and be right back," Lawrence said, and that prompted Mariah to get out of the golf cart. He zoomed away, his face heating when he realized they'd never really nailed down plans.

Had he nodded when she'd suggested they go today? Would she be gone by the time he returned to the fruit stand with the Millers?

Lawrence muttered under his breath as he sped through the orchard. He dang near missed the turn into the left section, where Duke had taken the Millers. He swung the golf cart fairly violently, and he swore it came up off two of the tires.

Adrenaline pumping, and his heartbeat flailing through his veins, he slowed down. If he crashed, his day would get a whole lot worse. He eased to a stop where the family of four had gathered on the side of the road, and he helped them put their bushels of peaches on the floor in the back. The kids rode back there, with the mother in the front with Lawrence, and the father on the row of seats facing backward in the far back of the cart.

"Everyone in?" he asked, telling himself to go slow. With Mariah, he wanted to go fast. Everything else in his life had to go slow.

He'd tried to make plans and schedules quickly, and that never worked. When he did, he ended up having to redo large portions of the work. He made mistakes that resulted in a dozen phone calls.

He'd learned to go slow. Work meticulously, to make sure all the owners, trainers, and horses would be happy at Bluegrass Ranch. He sent out reminder emails, texts, and phone calls only after double-checking them. Heck, he probably triple-checked them, because he hated sending out invoice and payment reminders for people who didn't need them, or if they had the wrong amounts on them.

Both of those only caused more work for him—and a giant headache.

Back at the fruit stand, he noticed Mariah's little white SUV still in the lot, though she wasn't around that he could see. Tension stretched across his shoulders. He helped Duke weigh out the Millers, and he picked up his water bottle and the jacket he'd worn that morning before the sun had made a full appearance.

"I'm headed out," he said to Duke.

"Beth's expecting you," Duke said, shielding his eyes from the sun and looking past Lawrence.

His hopes fell to his boot tips. He'd forgotten about Beth. How, he didn't know. He'd literally just been thinking about her.

He waved to Duke, said, "Yep," and turned around too. Mariah stood at the back of her SUV now, and Lawrence smiled at her as he approached.

"I realize we never really made plans," he said, taking the horse by the reins. She'd directed so much of their previous relationship, and he wanted to feel a little bit in control. He also needed a few questions answered.

"No," she said. "We didn't."

He kept going even as he neared. He stepped right into her personal space and dropped his water bottle as he took her into his arms. "My sister-in-law always feeds me after a shift," he murmured, his voice a complete opposite to the way his pulse rammed through his whole body. "What do you think about stopping by over there for a bite to eat?"

Surprise flitted across her face, but she nodded and said, "Sure, okay."

Lawrence searched her face, feeling every pinprick of her touch where her palm sat against his chest. His skin super-heated, and he felt like he'd swallowed fire as her body heat mingled with his. He couldn't quite remember how to kiss a woman, but he thought he needed to take his cowboy hat off first.

He did that with one fluid movement, and then threaded his fingers through her hair in another. "I just..." He needed to know how she really felt, and he needed her to know how he did.

He moved slowly. So slowly, she could've stopped him.

She didn't, and the next thing Lawrence knew, he'd touched his mouth to Mariah Barker's. He kissed her, pure flame and heat rushing through him. He suddenly knew exactly where to put his hands, and precisely how to show her the things he felt for her.

CHAPTER 4

Mariah kissed Lawrence back with the same vigor he'd initiated. She hadn't come to this ranch to kiss him, but she wasn't complaining either.

The man held magic in his touch, and he spread it through her whole body with every stroke of his lips against hers. She hadn't been kissed with this level of care in quite some time, and her brain screamed, *Never! We've never been kissed like this!*

That was probably true, but Mariah was so wrapped up in the scent of Lawrence Chappell—fresh air, leather, musk, pine, peach—and so consumed with the taste of him—cool mint—and the rough touch of his hands along her neck, in her hair, and down the side of her face—that she couldn't think clearly.

He finally drew in a long breath through his nose as he pulled away. Mariah swayed on her feet, because the whole earth had been knocked off its axis with that single kiss.

She pulled in a lung full of oxygen too, her heartbeat right up in the back of her throat. The sun burned merrily behind her still-closed eyes, and Mariah hung onto the moment for a little longer, trying to box it up and put it in the storage of her memory to access it later.

Lawrence finally chuckled, the sound deep in his chest, and Mariah opened her eyes. "Okay," he whispered, dropping his head to nuzzle her neck too.

Mariah clung to his broad shoulders, all of the control she usually needed in a relationship gone. Wiped out. She'd given it all to him, and her stomach shrunk and squeezed in panic.

He stepped back and laced his fingers through hers, stooped to pick up his cowboy hat and settle it on his head with his free hand, and said, "You can drive us to the farmhouse, or I can. Which would you prefer?"

Just like that, and whether he knew it or not, he handed a measure of control right back to her. Mariah seized it. "I'll drive," she said, still leaning against the back of her SUV. She straightened and put her true weight on her legs. Thankfully, they didn't give out. "Which brother is Beth married to?"

"Trey," he said. "He's third oldest."

"And you're the third youngest."

"That's right," he said. "Do you say that, though? Third youngest?" He shot her a smile, and the mood between them lightened. "I'm third *from* the youngest."

"Who's younger than you?" She held up her hand. "Wait. Let me guess. Conrad and Duke."

"In that order, even." He grinned at her and went

around the SUV to the passenger side. When she arrived at the driver's side and opened the door, he was moving the front seat back.

"Sorry," she said. "The only other person who rides in here is Jane."

"Ah, Jane," Lawrence said. "How is she? Did she end up going out with Julian?"

Mariah gaped at him. "I can't believe you can remember that."

"Are you kidding?" he asked. "All of your friends over there at The Gemini Group totally used me as a male expert."

She burst out laughing for the second time that day, and it felt so good. Her throat might be a little dry, but laughing was so much better than crying. Or moping. She'd definitely been moping for the majority of August.

She backed out the spot where she'd parked and headed toward the farmhouse she'd seen earlier. Conrad still sat at the entrance, and he looked up as they motored by. He waved to Lawrence, who waved back. "He's dating Karla Rhodes," he said. "And Yvonne Churchill."

"At the same time?"

"He likes to keep his options open." Lawrence rolled his eyes and shook his head. "Him and Duke are the worst."

"Duke's better than that," she said.

"Is he?" Lawrence looked at her, curiosity in those dark eyes. "What makes you say that?"

"He wouldn't go out with two women at the same time."

Lawrence smiled and shook his head. "Wrong-o. The night we broke up?" A horrified look crossed his face, and Mariah watched him try to swallow. "I mean, I don't really know if we broke up. I'm not even sure we were dating."

She hated this sudden awkwardness, as well as the fact that he hadn't known what they were. His kiss back there suddenly made so much sense. He'd said, "I just..." before kissing her, and she realized that he'd wanted to know if there was still something between them.

Even she could admit the exchange out in the peach orchard had been a bit stilted. He'd say a witty thing, only to pull back a moment later. For the life of her, Mariah's brain seemed to have gone on vacation.

"Anyway." He ground his voice through his throat. "That night, he went out with someone. I don't even remember who, but he'd been to lunch with someone else that same day." He reached for the door handle as Mariah brought the car to a stop. "Conrad at least goes out with them on different days."

"Duke," she said, getting out of the car too. "Who knew?"

"They're so unpredictable," Lawrence said.

"Right," she said with a touch of dryness. "Because you're such the picture of routine."

He looked at her across the hood, his eye blazing with something hot and sharp. "I am, actually."

"Really?" she teased. "What does that look like for you, Lawrence?" She almost called him Larry, but that felt really mocking to her—not just a fun, flirty tease—and she was so glad she didn't.

Before he could answer, someone yelled from the front porch, and a child ran down the steps, calling every inch of the way. It took Mariah a moment to understand he was saying Lawrence's name, until the cowboy scooped up a miniature version of himself.

"What's goin' on, TJ?" he asked, glancing at Mariah.

The boy pressed one hand against Lawrence's shoulder and looked down at him. "Momma said I could get a dog."

"Don't you already have dogs here?"

"But like, a real dog," TJ said, pure excitement pulsing from him. "One that lives in the house and sleeps in my bed and everything."

"Wow," Lawrence said, glancing up to the house. "What made her change her mind?"

"I couldn't stand the begging," a woman said, and Mariah's attention swung from Lawrence and TJ to a pretty, blonde woman standing at the top of the steps, leaning one shoulder casually into the pillar there. She folded her arms and looked at the pair of boys with a small, slightly crooked smile.

When her eyes switched to Mariah's, she nearly wilted under the intenseness in her blue eyes. Still, Mariah had worked with plenty of high-rollers, businessmen, and the worst chauvinist on the planet. She could handle Lawrence's sister-in-law.

Just as she started to step that way, Lawrence beat her to it. "Morning, Beth."

"Lawrence." She gestured for something. "Come on, Teej. Let him come inside."

Lawrence reached for her hand, and sparks flowed through her system like slow-moving lava, popping and crackling all the way to her scalp. She very nearly shivered but controlled it at the very last second.

"This is Mariah Barker," he said. "Have you met her?" He led her up the steps to the front porch dreams were made of. It ran the full width of the house, complete with the white, picket-like railing. On one end of it, a swing shifted slightly in the breeze, with pillows bearing pumpkins, apples, and even an early ghost.

It looked like a scene straight from a best-of country living article, and Mariah felt the peace and quaintness of it oozing from the very boards on which she stood.

"I don't recall," Beth said, extending her hand.

"My sister-in-law, Beth," he said. "Her son, TJ."

"Nice to meet you." Mariah smiled her professional smile, wishing she wasn't wearing shorts and a T-shirt that had seen better days. But Beth wore a pair of dirty jeans, work boots, and a camouflage T-shirt with a chicken on the front of it, so perhaps Mariah fit right in here.

Beth led the way inside, and the scent of rising dough and dare she believe chocolate? met Mariah's nose. She found chocolate pastries on the kitchen counter and a man who clearly belonged to Lawrence flipping eggs at the stove. "The eggs are almost done. Rubber soles," he said, doing a double-take when he saw Mariah. "Hey."

He quickly looked at Lawrence and back to Mariah. "Who are you?"

"Give him five seconds to introduce her," Beth said, swatting at her husband's chest. "You have no tact."

"I have no tact?"

Lawrence's hand in hers tightened, and he said, "This is Mariah Barker. My somewhat blunt brother, Trey."

"Third oldest," Mariah said with a grin.

Trey blinked, clearly surprised by her assessment of him. She was too. In fact, she had no idea what she'd even meant by such a statement.

"There's sausage too," Beth said, nudging Trey further out of the way and bending to open the oven. She produced an entire sheet tray of sausage links, and Mariah's mouth watered.

Lawrence said, "Bless you, Beth," and reached for a plate.

Mariah's sentiments exactly, and she smiled at the woman and added her own, "Thank you."

* * *

An hour later, she eyed a gray and black horse like it would rear up and trample her at any moment. "I don't know about this," she said.

"It's fine," he said. "You put your foot here and swing up."

"Swing up?" She'd never swung up onto anything, ever.

"I don't have great body awareness," she said. "I've never been able to do flips on the trampoline or anything."

He simply looked at her, obviously trying to decide if she was kidding or not. Time slowed to that moment, and she realized that she knew very little about Lawrence Chappell. He knew very little about her.

Their previous relationship had been fake. Fabricated. They'd played parts in a pretend life neither one of them actually lived. She'd never shared personal things with him about her family, the things she was afraid of, or little tidbits like the one she'd just told him.

Therefore, he had no idea if she'd kid about this or not.

"For real," she said.

"I'll help you," he said.

"How long have you been riding a horse?" she asked, cocking one hip. One quite plus-sized hip.

"I think Daddy put me on a horse when I turned three."

"You have horses in your blood," she said. "I don't. I can't even name the last time I rode a horse." What had she been thinking? When he'd suggested they go for a ride, she'd simply said yes. She'd wanted to spend more time with him, that was all.

He'd brought her to a stable on the outskirts of dozens of other buildings, calling it "the family row." Ten minutes later, he had two horses saddled, and now he wanted her to "swing on up" there.

"I'll get a step," he said, and pure humiliation filled Mariah. Still, getting into the saddle was easier with the step, and she managed to do it without embarrassing or hurting herself. Lawrence swung right into the saddle as easily as taking one step after another, whistled through his teeth, and said, "Ho, Draco."

"Draco?" she asked.

"That's my horse's name," he said. "You're on Reid."

"Reid? That's so...human."

Lawrence grinned at her, and after a few more seconds of the steady *clop-clop, clop-clop* of the horse's hooves, Mariah slipped into a state of relaxation. "I see why you like this."

"Mm." Lawrence didn't look at her, but kept his face turned right into the sun. His eyes drifted closed, and Mariah did the same.

The earth moved again, and while Mariah didn't like the side-to-side motion nearly as much as she had when Lawrence had kissed her, she still felt like her life had finally slowed down enough to enjoy.

"I do have a question," Lawrence said, his voice soft yet full.

Mariah's eyes popped open again. "Okay." She hated questions, and she started a quick prayer in her heart that this one would be no big deal.

"What do you think has changed between us?" he asked. "To make things work this time?"

She blinked, because men didn't normally ask such blunt questions. "I...don't know."

"I'll be real honest with you," he said. "If nothing all that much has changed for you, then I'm not super interested in starting up again."

Again, she stared at him. He hadn't really talked like this

before. She didn't mind the conversation; she just hadn't expected it from Lawrence. He was the boy next-door. The cowboy looking to please. The man who wore the boots she told him to, with the shirt she'd actually purchased for him.

Humiliation filled her when she realized she'd been viewing him as her...subordinate.

Hot tears pressed against her eyes. No wonder he'd broken up with her, and this line of questioning was completely valid.

He didn't seem to have a problem with long, awkward silences, because he said nothing while Mariah struggled to come up with something that had changed between them that would convince him things would be different this time.

CHAPTER 5

Lawrence was *not* encouraged by Mariah's long silence. He regretted the question for only a few seconds before the indignation and a touch of anger started to tap against his heart.

"Let's go back," he said after another excruciating minute. A full minute, and she couldn't come up with a reason she wanted to be with him?

Not interested, he told himself.

He thought of the kiss they'd shared in the parking lot, and pride swelled in his chest. He'd done it without crashing and burning, and that deserved a victory lap all by itself. He'd thought the kiss was simply spectacular, but there had to be more than that for a relationship to work.

Lawrence hadn't personally experienced such a thing, but he'd seen two of his brothers get divorced, and two more break off engagements. He wasn't completely blind to women, nor did he have no opinion on the kind of relationship he wanted to have.

Open, honest, caring, and long-lasting all sat at the top of his list.

"What would you say?" she asked. "If the tables were turned. What would you say has changed between us that will help a relationship work?"

"First off," he said, a bit of bite in his tone. "It's not fake. I'm not going out with you just to impress your friends and your boss. When I call you at work, it will be for something real, not so I can drop the word 'boyfriend.'"

He cleared his throat, because he wasn't quite used to standing up for himself like this. "Secondly, because it's not fake, we can start to share our real lives and our real selves with each other. Like the fact that you adore sausage links but don't like sage. That's fascinating to me, and I want to know all your other quirky food things." He told himself to stop talking, but somehow his voice kept on going.

"So being able to share real things, not just surface stuff you need to know so it doesn't look like we're fake-dating, is completely different than last time. Third." He looked away from her, because if her eyes got any wider, they might take over her whole face. "I get to be myself. I won't have to wear what you tell me to wear, or try to match some theme at your parties, or pretend I like coconut in my soda when it's literally the most disgusting thing ever.'"

His chest heaved, and he did manage to get his voice to shut off. Finally.

Relief roared through him, followed quickly by an

intense wind of pure panic. What in the world had he just said? And why had he sounded so bitter saying it?

"Wow," Mariah said, and Lawrence finally dared to look at her. She blinked and reached up to wipe her eyes.

Great, he thought. *You made her cry, you idiot!*

"I had no idea you were so upset about the boots or the shirts."

"I guess I didn't either," he said quietly.

"You should get to be yourself."

"As should you."

"I'd like to share real things about myself with you," she said. "That was a good one."

Lawrence nodded, his teeth gritting together so hard his jaw ached. Why had he opened his mouth? He should've just enjoyed the ride, put her in her car, and waited for her to call or text him.

He thought of her mouth against his, and his blood ran hot again. He tasted the coffee on her lips, and he wanted to do it again.

There has to be more to this than you think she's pretty and you want to kiss her, he told himself. He had to like the woman for who she was too. He reminded himself he'd had fun with her at those parties, but along with that came the realization that she'd been pretending too.

In every single way, pretending. He didn't know her. Not really.

"Here's what I'm thinking," he said. "We start at square one. First date status. We get to know each other, the way a real couple would. Maybe I'll kiss you goodnight on the fourth or fifth date, the way I normally would. Maybe you'll let me. Maybe you'll introduce me to your father at some point, the way you would a real boyfriend when he's become serious." He glanced at her, beyond relieved the stable had come back into view. "What do you think?"

"I think that sounds nice," she said.

"So I'm mowing tonight. Church and family stuff tomorrow. I'm mowing tomorrow too. I get Monday off. Tuesday night?" He looked at her, his eyebrows up and his hope dancing somewhere up in the atmosphere. "Dinner? The two of us?" He watched her smile start to curve up. "At a real restaurant. No brothers or sisters-in-law or nephews in sight."

"Okay," she said. "You've got yourself a deal."

* * *

The following day, Lawrence sat next to Duke during church. He'd let Duke drive them to the chapel, and he let him drive him back to Bluegrass Ranch.

"Do you think I should call Louise?" Duke asked as he parked in front of the homestead.

"You went out with her last night, right?"

"Yeah."

"Did you say you'd call her?"

"I mean, isn't that what everyone says?"

"Duke," Lawrence said. "No, not everyone says that unless they're going to call."

Inside the homestead, noise nearly made Lawrence turn

and go right back out. He followed Duke down the hall to the expansive kitchen, where it sure seemed like he and Duke were the last to arrive.

Duke stepped over to a cheese tray and picked up a handful of crackers. Almost instantly, Mom shooed him away, a frown on her face and her hands swatting at him. He simply laughed, the way Duke did about everything.

Lawrence stood next to the fridge, out of the way.

"All right," Spur said, lifting both arms. "All right, we're all here. Quiet down."

It took several seconds for everyone to truly settle down, and then Spur put his arm around his wife, Olli. "Thanks to Cayden and the others who live here for hosting us this afternoon. This is the biggest place we've got for all of us."

They had a pavilion on the property, but the end of August still saw plenty of heat and humidity in this part of Kentucky.

"Real quick," he said. "Olli and I wanted to announce that we'll be havin' our first baby right before the end of the new year."

A hush fell over the group, and then a roar went up as congratulations went around. Lawrence smiled for all he was worth, because Olli had happy tears in her eyes. He hugged them both too, and he'd just released Olli when Mom said, "I think Cayden and Ginny are going to announce their wedding date too."

"Are we, Mom?" Cayden asked without a smile in sight. He looked at Ginny, who simply shrugged. Cayden sighed, and Lawrence knew the feeling of being backed into a corner and hating it. "Fine," he said. "Ginny and I have chosen December twenty-third to be married. Right before Christmas."

"That's so soon," Olli said.

"It's four months," Cayden said. "How much is there to do?"

Olli looked like he'd suggested he might elope with Ginny, and Lawrence stifled a laugh. He met Cayden's eyes, and they shook their heads in tandem. Yes, Mom could be really pushy, and no, Lawrence had no idea what took four months to plan for a wedding. Especially since Cayden and Ginny had literally been talking about everything for about a month now already.

"Let's say grace," Dad said, swiping off his cowboy hat. "The steaks aren't getting any warmer." He glanced around the room, and Lawrence didn't have to look down or away to avoid his eye. Dad wouldn't see him anyway. Sure enough, he said, "Cayden, would you?"

"Yep."

Lawrence swept his hat off his head too, ran his fingers through his hair, and listened while Cayden asked for a blessing on the ranch and the food. With that done, people surged toward the line-up of food on the table.

Lawrence stayed where he was, as if the refrigerator needed his support to stay standing. Mom approached with a small paper plate filled with veggies and dips. "There you are," she said. "It took me a minute to find you."

"Here I am," Lawrence said, watching her.

"So I met a woman at the library guild meeting," she said.

"No," Lawrence said. "I'm not going out on another blind date."

"Why not?" Mom demanded. "You're not seeing anyone, and she's new in town."

"I don't want to," Lawrence said. "You agreed to let me find my own dates."

"I could just give you her number."

Lawrence pinned Mom with a look. "Mom. Really?"

"Then you can set something up yourself," she said. "If you want. Or not, if you don't want to. That's all. *I* wouldn't be arranging anything." She looked so hopeful, and Lawrence still wasn't entirely sure what would happen with Mariah.

"I'm not telling you if we go out," Lawrence said.

"Of course not." Mom smiled at him. "I'll just send you the number. That's all. You can decide what to do with it." Her fingers flew across her phone, and his chimed in the next moment. "There you go. Her name is Nancy."

"Nancy?" Lawrence almost burst out laughing, only managing to pull it back at the last minute. With a name like that, she sounded far too old or more refined than he'd like. "Okay, Mom. Thanks."

She bustled off when Ian called her name, and Lawrence just watched her go. Maybe he would call Nancy. Maybe he was ready to get out of the waiting game and into the dating pool. The horseback ride with Mariah yesterday hadn't been great, but they'd at least parted on solid ground. He did want to know more about her. They did have a date scheduled for Tuesday.

He kept all of that to himself, though, finally joining the line to get food after nearly everyone else had already gone through it. He found a seat next to Duke, who told a story about a horse breeder Lawrence had heard a dozen times before.

It was still funny, though, and he didn't have to talk, so Lawrence listened and laughed with everyone else. That kept him out of the spotlight and in the conversation, and Lawrence was comfortable there.

The crowd started to break up as Mom got out peach ice cream and Beth brought in a vanilla cake. Lawrence didn't quite have room for dessert yet, and he glanced at Cayden as he sat in the spot Duke had vacated, a bowl filled with cake and ice cream.

"I hear you have a date on Tuesday night," Cayden said, scooping up a huge bite of his treat.

Lawrence glanced down the table, but no one was really paying them any extra attention. "Yeah," he said. "I do."

Cayden nodded, and he never did make a big deal out of things. "That's great, Lawrence. I hope it goes well." He smiled at him and glanced up as Ginny sat next to him. "Hey, sugar."

She grinned at him, and Lawrence watched as they shared a quick kiss. "So," Lawrence said so he wouldn't have to talk any more about his date. He'd told Ginny he was going to break-up with Mariah a few weeks ago, and he didn't want to have to explain anything right now. "What are you guys going to serve for dinner at your wedding?"

Ginny's face lit up as if Lawrence had asked the magic question, and she leaned forward. "I'm going to make the most *delicious* baked mac and cheese," she said with a huge grin. "It's going to be *amazing*..."

CHAPTER 6

Mariah hung up, a sigh gathering in the back of her throat. She didn't want to let it out, because June sat only a few paces away. Mariah didn't want to explain her frustration with this particular client, so she rubbed her fingers across her forehead and toward her temples, releasing her breath slowly so it couldn't quite be classified as a sigh.

"You okay, Mariah?" June asked.

Mariah lifted her head, her smile watery and weak on her lips. "Yes," she said. "I just have a headache." And a mountain of work to complete before she could leave for the day. She hated leaving a ton of unfinished tasks for the next day, because then she woke up drenched in sweat and wondering what day it was, usually way before her alarm.

She straightened and reached for the mouse. "I'll get up and make some tea in a few minutes. Do you want some?"

"Only if it's the orange blossom," June said with a smile.

She looked past Mariah's desk toward the entrance to the floor, where all of the marketing executives shared the workspace. "Swordfish, he's here."

"Who?" Mariah halfway stood up to check in the direction June was facing.

"Wish me luck," she hissed out of the corner of her mouth, and she tugged on the bottom of her blouse before striding away. June possessed a great walk in heels, something Mariah knew she practiced at home.

She approached the reception desk and touched Zoey's shoulder, leaning down to say something quick before she faced the extremely handsome man standing there. Mariah watched his reaction, and he sure did seem happy to see June.

His face lit up, and his smile stuck to his mouth, warming as June stepped into him and gave him a hug. She gestured to the right, toward the conference room, and she moved that way without a hitch in her step. She didn't look in Mariah's direction at all, and that alone told Mariah how important this client was to June.

She quickly sat back down and flipped over her phone. If June needed her, she'd get a text, and she wanted to be able to help her friend if possible. She'd sent June several texts over the years, and they came to each other's rescue if necessary.

Mariah opened the file for Tobin MacGuire, the man she'd just gotten off the phone with. She needed to send over the contract and the confidentiality agreement, which she did with a few clicks and the typing of an email address.

With that done, she opened her bottom desk drawer and pulled out the file for the MacGuire Conglomerate.

She'd worked with them in the past—a simple company anniversary party that had hit the media with a splash, thanks to her. They'd been in business for a decade at the time she'd planned their party, and she got Tobin in front of local papers and magazines, and even all the way to the state level, as she'd gotten the telecommunications company featured on the front page of the government website.

According to Tobin himself, MacGuire's holdings had increased by fifty percent after the anniversary and the features. That was all due to Mariah's efforts to shine the light on the company as much as possible.

Now, he wanted her to do something similar. The problem was, the ten-year anniversary was only a year old, and she couldn't replicate what she'd just done. Tobin didn't seem to understand that concept, and no matter what she'd said to him, he hadn't heard her.

"Mariah," someone said, and she looked up from the files she'd pulled from the drawer.

"Zak." She leaned back in her chair and took hold of the end of her pen with her other hand. "What can I do for you?"

"Dr. Biggers said you got the Botanical Gardens grand reopening, and he wanted me to follow-up with you on it."

Mariah's first instinct was to clutch the account to her chest and deny Zak the opportunity to do what their boss had asked him to. But Dr. Biggers liked team players, and the last thing she needed was to get called into her boss's office for another lecture.

Dr. Biggers always made it seem like it wasn't a lecture, but a "life lesson," and that was also something Mariah didn't want. She didn't really respect Dr. Biggers, so she'd avoid him if at all possible.

"Sure," burst from her mouth. She went back to her computer and added, "I've got the transcript from our initial call done through WeHear, and I've done a rough timeline."

"Can you send all of that to me?"

"It's on the way."

"Great." Zak knocked a couple of times on Mariah's desk, gave her an annoying grin, and walked away. In the past, Mariah would've thought Dr. Biggers was trying to take this client from her. Even now, she thought that.

She simply didn't care, because she had too many clients as it was, and she hadn't gotten the botanical garden herself anyway. She had plenty of her own clients, and she would not be relinquishing them to others in this office.

But the grand reopening at a botanical garden? She could give that up.

She typed in Zak's email and sent him the files he needed, and then she started leafing through the file for MacGuire again. Her mind wandered a few times, especially when her phone buzzed.

But none of the texts came from June, and after the third one, Mariah realized she was actually hoping the messages would be from Lawrence.

Their date only lay a few hours in the future, and Mariah's heartbeat picked up speed just thinking about it. Things between her and Lawrence had been somewhat...stuttered.

That was the perfect word for their relationship, and Mariah wanted to smooth it all out. She stared down at the file, letting the black letters blur in her vision as she thought about the handsome cowboy.

She let herself return to the moment she'd met him face-to-face, and she'd been instantly attracted to him physically. Not only that, but he'd been extremely kind to her in one of her weakest and most horrifying moments. He'd gone to the lamest work parties and barbecues with her, and she had led him to believe they could have a real relationship once Bluegrass Ranch wasn't a client of The Gemini Group anymore.

"There's nothing keeping the two of you apart," Mariah whispered to herself. "Except you, Mya. Get out of your own way."

She picked up her phone and started tapping. *Should I wear anything special for tonight?* she asked, sending the text to Lawrence without thinking too hard about it. *Just regular dinner attire?*

He didn't respond right away, and Mariah put her phone down and started flipping pages in her files. Her phone buzzed, and she practically lunged toward it, only to find June's message on the screen, not Lawrence's.

007 sat there, along with *Maxwell Magnate*, and Mariah bolted to her feet as her device vibrated in her hand. Lawrence had texted, but he would have to wait.

June needed the tactics of a highly trained MI6 agent, and Mariah was the only one who could help her. She bent and grabbed as many files as she could carry, picked up her phone, and dialed the top number there.

Lawrence.

"Hey," he said as she strode toward the conference room.

"You're going to play along with me for a few minutes," she said. "I'll explain everything after, okay?"

Silence came through the line for a couple of seconds, and then he said, "I'm confused, but okay."

"No, that is not going to work for us, Mister Adams." She burst into the conference room and kept on going. "That's not how we do things at The Gemini Group. You can't just sign the contract and then change things according to your own whims."

"Mariah," June said, getting to her feet.

Mariah almost dropped her files, but she managed to make it to the table. She met June's eye, frowning for all she was worth. "I need this room. Our biggest client is on his way." She plunked the files on the table. "And, no, I don't mean you, Mister Adams. Believe it or not, we've got clients who respect the way we do things around here."

The man stood up, buttoning his suit coat as he asked, "What's going on here?"

Mariah pulled the phone from her ear and said, "One of our biggest clients is coming in today. Maxwell Magnate? Are you two almost finished?" She looked from Maxwell himself to June, whose eyes were a little too wide, though she'd called for this performance.

On the other end of the line, Lawrence chuckled and

said, "Maxwell Magnate? Don't they own that fencing company?"

Mariah honestly didn't know. Maxwell wasn't her client.

"I'm Maxwell Magnate," the man said, rounding the top of the table to stand next to June. "And Miss Beaumont is doing a great job with my case." He swept the files Mariah had brought in. "I don't even know who you are."

"I'll call you back." Mariah ended the call and folded her arms. "You're Maxwell Magnate?"

"Yes," he said, drawing himself to his full height and pulling his shoulders back.

"June?"

"He's Maxwell Magnate," she said, barely hiding her grin.

"Did he sign the contracts?"

June tapped the table. "I just got them inked a few minutes ago."

"So you don't need these examples?" Mariah indicated the files.

"I think we're good," June said, glancing at Maxwell. "I think Max now knows that if he wants to change things in the contract, we just need him to sign an addendum." June grinned at him and then Mariah. "That was the part I was just getting to."

"Noted," Max said, his eyes barely leaving Mariah's.

"Well." Mariah started to gather up the files. "I guess we don't need these then. We do like punctual clients here at The Gemini Group." With all the folders back in her arms, she nodded to Max, then June, and got out of the conference room.

With everything back in her drawer, she tucked her hair and dialed Lawrence. "Hey," she said.

"What in the world was that about?" he asked. "You sounded *quite* intense."

"Oh, June and I have this little system worked out," Mariah said almost under her breath. She giggled, and it felt so good. "She's got this client that was giving her some trouble with a contract, and she texted me the double-oh-seven. When that comes in, I go in there and put the beat-down on him about the contracts and how they work here."

"Mm, I see," Lawrence said, and Mariah heard something behind those words.

"What do you see?"

"Can I tell you tonight? I've got a bit of a scheduling emergency on my hands." A yell came through the line, and while Mariah wanted to ask him what could possibly cause a scheduling emergency on a horse farm, she sensed he needed to go.

"Sure," she said.

"Great. Pick you up at six."

"Six," she said, but Lawrence called over the top of the single-syllable, and it sounded very much like, "Duke, don't you dare swing at her!"

Mariah pulled the phone from her ear as the line went dead, and she held her breath for a moment. Then she burst into giggles that didn't go away until June returned, her heeled power walk more impressive than ever.

CHAPTER 7

Duke Chappell balled his fists at his sides, his chin lifted as he stared at the maddening woman in front of him.

Lisa Harvey.

She sure knew how to push his buttons, and Duke wasn't sure if that was a bad thing or not. The way Lawrence flew between him and Lisa like Duke might start jabbing told him Lawrence thought it was a bad thing.

But Duke's elevated pulse could've come from the brunette's pretty face or her curves, both of which had intrigued Duke in the past.

Too bad you get along like oil and water, he thought as Lawrence asked, "What is going on?"

Thankfully, Lisa said, "Nothing," so Duke wouldn't have to. "I was just telling your brother that King Arthur has no slots in his breeding schedule. He didn't believe me."

"That's because I called yesterday," he practically spat.

"And your brother said I could have any slot I wanted."
Duke did take a step toward her then, and Lawrence actually
threw up his hand, palm out, warning Duke back.

"She's being catty on purpose," Duke said, almost like
he was tattling on Lisa. He looked at Lawrence, who swung
his attention back to the woman.

"I am not," she said indignantly. "Bruce just doesn't
know what he's talking about. All the scheduling goes
through me when it comes to the Harvey studs."

"And I'm asking you," Duke said. "To put us on the
schedule, because all the covering scheduling goes through
me." He loved his responsibilities at Bluegrass Ranch,
because he got to take their horses and business forward each
year. He worked tirelessly to get the best studs in Kentucky,
and he knew the reproductive schedule of literally every
mare the ranch owned. All Lisa needed to do was name a
date next spring, and Duke would match King Arthur—
their best stud—with one of his mares who'd be in heat.

Easy. The end.

But nothing with Lisa Harvey was easy, and he swore she
made it that way on purpose.

"It's seven months away," Lawrence said. "Is he really
booked solid?"

"Of course not," Duke said at the same time Lisa said,
"Yes, he books a year in advance." Her words ended after his,
and Duke just rolled his eyes at her pretty little twang, the
remnant of which hung in the barn air.

"I'm sure there will be a cancelation," Duke said. In
horse breeding, there were always cancellations. He had to

deal with them too, because sometimes his mares didn't take kindly to the studs he'd paired them with. That meant they didn't get covered, and he still had to pay the stud fee for nothing.

Horse breeding was a delicate dance, and one that Duke had gotten very, very good at underneath his father's tutelage. And one thing that Dad always said was that any stud could be had for the right price.

"What's his fee?" Duke asked. "I'll add fifty percent to it if you'll put me at the top of the cancelation list."

"You think you can throw your money around and get what you want," Lisa bit out. "That's not how it works."

"How many people are on the cancelation list?" Lawrence asked.

Lisa hesitated, which was an answer all by itself.

"There is no cancelation list," Duke growled. "So put us on it, Lisa. It's not rocket science."

"I'll have to consult my calendar when I get back to the farm," she said, taking a step away from Duke and Lawrence. She glared at Duke. "Stop calling Bruce." She lifted one perfectly manicured finger toward him, pointing it straight at his chest. "He's not in charge of the studs. *I* am."

"Fine," Duke said. "Maybe you should pick up your phone when a client calls."

"When a *real* client calls, I do." She tossed her hair over her shoulder and marched out of the stable row.

Duke growled with every step she took, his blood running hotter at the sway in her hips—or maybe that was from the near-perfect insult she'd thrown at him.

"What in the world, Duke?" Lawrence asked. "You're worse than me."

"What does that mean?" Duke said, throwing his frustration at his brother instead of where it really should go. "I didn't touch her."

"You looked like you were about to start throwing punches."

"That's ridiculous," Duke said. "She was ten feet away from me." *Too far?* he wondered. *Or too close?*

"Why'd she stop by?" Lawrence asked, picking up a pitchfork and digging into the stall Duke had been cleaning before the Harvey heiress had graced them all with her presence. "Just to say no?"

"About that, yep," Duke said, pressing his fingers together to make sure his gloves were all the way on. "She doesn't like how often I call, but to get on the Harvey stud schedule, you need to call six months out. I'm actually a little late this year."

His adrenaline wore down, and Duke sighed. "She gets me all...bothered."

"I can see that," Lawrence said dryly. He tossed Duke a look filled with questions. So Duke wouldn't have to answer them, he turned away and repositioned the wheelbarrow for Lawrence. Then he could pitch the sawdust and straw into it easier.

Duke pushed his hat forward and found another pitchfork. Working together, he and Lawrence got the row cleaned out and restocked for the horses that boarded there. During good weather months, the horses spent most of the day out in pastures and fields. They were trained when their trainers came and looked after by vets the owners sent. People constantly came and went from Bluegrass Ranch, and Lisa Harvey could drive onto their property any old time she wanted.

March right into the stable row where Duke worked and chew him out some more.

"All I was trying to do was schedule King Arthur," he muttered. "Why does Lisa Harvey have to have one of the top three studs of the year?" He looked up toward the ceiling, not really expecting an answer from Lawrence or the Lord. "Surely they don't need all that money. Can you give the best studs to more agreeable people, please?"

Down the row, Lawrence chuckled, but Duke ignored him. "I'm done here," he called to Lawrence. "Thanks for your help. You headed back to the office?"

"Yes," Lawrence said. "I'll check off when I follow you out." He came back out of the last stall. "Where will you be?"

"I've got a class in twenty minutes," Duke said, the load on his shoulders getting heavier with the words. "I'm going to catch a quick shower before that. Then I'll come find you in the office so I can go over my notes and figure out who to call tomorrow. I want my stud schedule full before October."

Lawrence nodded from where he leaned against his pitchfork, and then he went back into the stall. Duke left the clipboard hanging by the rope on his end of the row, and he quickly swung onto the ATV he'd parked on the other side of the fence. He fired it up and spun out on the dirt in his haste to get away from the rows.

Bluegrass Ranch had dozens of them, and Duke knew every square inch of each one. They boarded dozens of horses, and housed plenty of trainers' offices. They shared three to a space, usually in the row where their horses lived.

Lawrence kept the schedule for the training tracks, and since Trey had been using their track in the middle of the night, Lawrence had added that slot to his books. Trainers were taking the spot too, as they wanted the track all to their horse so it wouldn't get spooked, or they wanted to train without any other eyes watching what they were doing.

It had become a premium spot, but it also required that Lawrence be awake at midnight to make sure the track got used appropriately. He'd been mowing the past couple of nights anyway, and the brothers had actually decided to split the responsibilities with that late-night track slot.

Duke had avoided it so far, mostly because of the ranch management classes he was taking.

He hurried through his shower and slid into his seat in front of the screen only moments before his professor came on. He welcomed everyone, and Duke started shuffling through his binder for the notes he needed. He gave a quick smile and wave when it was his turn to say he was there, and he hated that he couldn't remember what they'd talked about last time.

Had he forgotten an assignment? Did he need to have something prepared?

Duke had never excelled at schoolwork, but he wanted

to be the best rancher he could be. Spur wouldn't be around forever, and though he and Olli had announced they were going to have a baby, it would be at least twenty-five years before anyone would be ready to take over Bluegrass Ranch.

Spur would be over seventy then, and he and Duke had already talked about Duke taking over for a season in between generations.

To do that, he needed the administrative training these classes were giving him. He didn't like them, but he found the notes for this particular class and looked up as his professor put his presentation on the screen.

CHAPTER 8

Lawrence pulled up to a perfectly normal brown-brick house in a nice, quite neighborhood. It had a closed two-car garage and a small porch with empty flower pots hanging from the corners.

He put his truck in park and watched the house, as if it would whisper secrets about its owner while he waited. No such thing happened, and Lawrence got himself out of the truck and down the sidewalk to the steps leading to the front door.

He went up them, his heartbeat sounding loudly in his ears. He wasn't sure why these nerves pounded so strongly through him. He'd been out with Mariah before, and he'd said all kinds of things to her he wouldn't have dreamed of saying previously.

Somehow, she'd still wanted to go out with him.

He knocked on the door before he saw a doorbell, and when he spied that, he pressed the button too. He promptly cursed himself for doing both, and he fell back a couple of steps while he waited.

Standing on the front stoop of a woman's home was one of the worst things in the world. No wonder Lawrence didn't date a whole lot, and he wondered why he'd minded meeting Mariah in that doughnut parking lot. At the moment, he'd have preferred that over standing here waiting for her to answer the door.

Then, all at once, she stood in front of him. "Evening, Lawrence," she said smartly, and Lawrence blinked to take her all in at once.

Mariah's hair had always called to him, and tonight she'd straightened it into silky, gorgeous strands. She wore quite a bit of makeup, but he liked the way the darker colors accentuated her dark blue eyes.

She wore one of her trademark prints, but only on the top. She'd paired the cotton blouse with a pair of skinny jeans that had his eyes tracing the curve of her hip and then her leg before he cleared his throat and yanked his eyes back to hers.

"Evenin'," he said, tipping his cowboy hat. "You look great tonight."

"You just said regular dinner attire."

"Yes," he said, clearing his throat. "Just a normal restaurant." He hadn't actually chosen one yet, but he kept that to himself. "Are you feeling adventurous?"

Mariah cocked one eyebrows at him as she stepped back inside her house and turned her attention to something just beside the door. When she came back out onto the porch, she slung her purse over her shoulder and pulled the door closed behind her. "Adventurous? In what way?"

"A culinary way," Lawrence said, his throat so dry. He wasn't the best at flirting, that was for sure. "We could go normal, to a steakhouse or even that Wild Wave Pizza. Have you had that?" He reached for her hand, sort of grabbing it a little too roughly.

Mariah smiled at him though, and Lawrence took a moment to settle their fingers together, sparks showering through his bloodstream. "Or we could go on a little adventure," he said.

"I'm all for adventure," she said, and she was far better at flirting than he was.

"Great." He smiled at her, and they went down the steps together. Lawrence breathed in the late summer air of almost September, enjoying the blueness of the Kentucky sky above them. "Did you grow up here?" he asked as they went down the sidewalk.

"In Louisville," she said. "For the first little bit. My family moved here for my last two years of high school." She glanced at him, her pretty pink lips curled into a smile. "Been here ever since."

"College?" he asked.

"I have a communications and marketing degree," she said. "I've been with The Gemini Group for about twelve years."

Lawrence thought he heard something in the words, but he wasn't entirely sure what. She flashed him another smile, though, and Lawrence returned it as he opened her door for her.

"This thing is huge," she said. "Good thing I didn't wear a skirt."

"I've got a little step-ladder for it," he teased. "Kind of like the one you used getting on that horse."

"That was embarrassing enough, thank you." She put her foot on the running board and pushed herself to standing. Then a quick bend, and she sat in the passenger seat. Lawrence closed the door, sealing the flowery, fruity scent of her perfume inside his truck with her.

"It's not the first time she's ridden in your car," he told himself as he went toward the tailgate. "She's fine. She knew about the size of your truck."

He got behind the wheel and said, "Okay, so for our first course on this choose-your-own-adventure dinner, I thought we'd go to Croutons for soup. Or is it too hot for soup?"

"They have the best clam chowder there," Mariah said with a light in her eye. "I'm all for Croutons for soup."

Lawrence finally felt himself relax as his first real smile crossed his face. "Croutons it is," he said.

The drive there happened quickly, and because restaurants had two-for-one specials on Tuesday nights just to get people to come in, Croutons wasn't busy. The soup was hot and delicious, and Lawrence enjoyed his bowl of gumbo while Mariah talked about the schemes she and June had devised over the years.

"So let me get this straight," he said, dusting his hands of saltine crumbs, his soup long gone. "You've got numbers all the way up to fifteen?"

"Skipping thirteen, of course," she said, her whole countenance aglow. "That's just bad luck."

"Of course," he said, grinning back at her. "And double-oh-seven is code for help with contracts."

"Yes." Mariah tucked her hair, and Lawrence found himself wanting to do it.

"Should we move on to our next course?" he asked.

"Definitely."

"So I was thinking we could hit Sally Mae's," he said. "They have a good assortment of dishes, from salads that are really meals to steak, if that's what you want."

"My favorite is their chicken pot pie," Mariah said as Lawrence tossed a twenty-dollar bill on the table. "It has whole pearl onions in it that are like pops of candy they're so sweet."

"I'll probably get the smothered meatloaf," he said. "They make the best red eye gravy in the whole state."

That got Mariah to laugh, and Lawrence's pride swelled in his chest. "The whole state?" She shook her head, that ultra-straight hair swinging with the movement. "I guess you'll have to let me try it."

Lawrence only nodded, quite pleased with how well tonight was going. Mariah seemed to be having a good time, and if he played everything just right, he'd get dessert at his favorite place and maybe a kiss goodnight.

No, he told himself sternly. He wasn't going to kiss Mariah tonight. If this was really to be their first date, he wouldn't. He'd never kissed a woman on the first date before, and he was sure tonight wouldn't be the exception.

Besides, he'd kissed her in the orchard. *No*, he told himself. *You agreed to start over. This is the first date.*

Over her chicken pot pie and his smothered meatloaf, she asked, "What was happening with Duke today?"

"My word," Lawrence said, shaking his head. "He's got this breeder he doesn't get along with, and she showed up unannounced today. It wasn't pretty." He detailed everything for Mariah, right down to, "I think he has a secret crush on her, in all honesty."

"Wow," Mariah said, her leftovers tucked into a box now. "He dates a lot, you said, so he should know better."

"Well, he dates more than me," Lawrence said, wishing he hadn't. "Which, uh, isn't that hard to do, actually."

"No?" Mariah teased. "You don't get out much?"

"No," he said. "Ready for dessert?"

"Who was your last girlfriend?" she asked instead, leaning her elbows on the table and looking at him with blazing interest in her eyes.

"Oh, uh." He stood and picked up his carton of meatloaf. He'd probably feed it to one of the dogs that lived on the ranch, because he wasn't a big leftover eater. Mariah had said she loved having leftovers, so maybe he should offer it to her instead.

"I was thinking dessert at Hobbiton," he said. "Have you been there? The woman who owns it makes all these tiny desserts. I can eat about six of the apple crisps in one sitting."

"I've never been," she said, standing too. "Dr. Biggers

had them bring in desserts for his secretary's birthday a few months ago, though. I had a mint brownie that did exceed most other mint desserts I've eaten."

"Mm."

"Don't think you've gotten off the hook about the girl-friend question," she said.

"There's not much to tell there," he said.

"Then get it over with quickly."

Lawrence played the gentleman and opened her door for her. Leaning into the truck as she pulled her seatbelt across her lap, he said, "The last woman I went out with was Terri Wilson, about fifteen months ago. There was just...nothing there." He reached up and stroked his fingers down the side of her face.

Pops and crackles exploded through the bones in his hand, moving right up into his arm. "Plenty here, though," he said, his eyes moving to lock onto hers.

"Plenty," she whispered, and Lawrence leaned toward her.

Don't kiss her, he coached himself. *Don't do it.* He'd felt something between them with the kiss from last week, and he could wait until he knew more about her. There had to be more than just physical attraction for a relationship to work.

He pressed his cheek to hers and whispered, "Hobbiton closes in twenty minutes, so we better get going."

* * *

An hour later, Lawrence whistled to himself as he walked through the darkness, a brown paper bag swinging from his fingers. It held at least a dozen desserts from Hobbiton, as they'd been there when the shop closed, and he could get the treats for half-price.

He'd have brought them home if they'd have been full price, because he loved everything the pastry chef there made.

He wasn't sure his feet touched the ground as he entered the homestead, and he didn't even mind that most of the lights in the house had been turned off. Only the dull light over the stove glowed into the kitchen, and Lawrence added a little light to the room when he opened the fridge to put away the desserts.

He'd just closed the door and sealed the light back inside when he heard someone opened the door he'd come through a minute ago.

"I'll tell them in my own way," a man said, and it only took Lawrence a moment to recognize Ian's voice. He was only fifteen months older than Lawrence, but he'd seen some hard times in his life that had taken him in a different direction than Lawrence could understand.

He did not want to eavesdrop on Ian. Lawrence quickly opened the silverware drawer and continued humming the song he'd been vocalizing on the way inside. His mind spun with questions, though, because Ian didn't live in this house. What was he doing here?

Footsteps came toward him, and Lawrence pulled open the fridge to get out the desserts as if he hadn't just put them inside. Ian appeared, his phone at his ear, and he said, "I'll call you back, okay?" before shoving his device in his back pocket.

"Brownie or pie?" Lawrence asked, holding up one of each in a delicate plastic container. "I took Mariah to Hobbiton tonight." He turned and put them on the countertop. "What are you doing here?"

"I just left something here," Ian said, not committing to taking a dessert. He scanned the dining room and living room and walked over to the hall that led to the front door that hardly got used. "Here it is." He went down the hall, causing Lawrence to frown.

Ian returned a few seconds later, nothing new in his hands. "Did you just get home?"

"Mm." Duke cracked open the lid on the peppermint brownie and dug his fork into it.

"How was the date?"

Lawrence looked up, trying to determine Ian's mood. His brother generally wore thunderclouds when he wasn't training horses, especially when it came to girlfriends and relationships. Lawrence supposed he would too, if he'd been married and found out his wife didn't love him but wanted his money.

"It was pretty good," Lawrence said, deciding Ian could handle the truth. "We're going out again on Friday."

Ian's jaw locked as he nodded. "Okay," he said, as if Lawrence needed his brother's permission to go out with Mariah.

"Who were you talking to?" Lawrence dropped his eyes

to his brownie so Ian wouldn't think he was attacking him. Out of any of the Chappells, Lawrence would be the least likely to press Ian into a corner, but he didn't need to take any chances.

"Conrad," Ian said, and that was clearly a lie.

Lawrence simply nodded, giving Ian the space he wanted. He'd want someone to do the same for him, and he took one more bite of brownie before boxing it up and putting it away. "Well, I'm headed to bed."

"'Night," Ian said, focused on his phone again.

Lawrence put his fork in the sink and went toward the stairs. When he reached them, he turned and looked back to Ian, whose face was illuminated by his phone as he typed furiously. He went up the steps, a prayer in his heart that Ian would find the peace and happiness he so clearly needed.

CHAPTER 9

Mariah lifted her phone the moment it trilled out. "Mariah Barker," she said into the receiver. So she was in a happy mood, despite the staff meeting that morning that hadn't gone well for her.

She didn't care. She didn't need to be on Dr. Biggers' good side at the moment, and no, she wasn't going to volunteer to take on any more clients.

"Miss Barker," a man drawled, and Mariah could tell he had a big personality.

Her smile only grew. "Yes, sir," she said. "What can I do for you?"

"It's Don Colburn from the Kentucky state tourism department."

"Oh." Mariah leaned forward and pulled open her desk drawer. "Did you...?" Had she missed a memo? Had Dr. Biggers assigned her a new client without telling her?

"I got your name from a file Mayor Densfield had. I guess you were helpin' the Chappell brothers with their racing event a month or two ago?"

Mariah looked up from her drawer. "Yes," she said slowly.

"Well, we had the brothers all committed to a billboard coming into Horse Country, but things have been set aside in the transition happening in our office. I'd like to get back to it and figure out where we are with it."

"Oh," Mariah said. "Well, a billboard wasn't part of the race..."

When Don didn't say anything, she added, "Can you fill me in on the details? Perhaps we should meet for lunch to go over everything." She didn't want to take on another client, especially one as high-profile as the State Office of Tourism.

At the same time, she couldn't turn down the opportunity.

"I can send over everything I've got," Don said. "Basically, the tourism office wanted to use real cowboys on a billboard and as marketing materials to get more people out to Horse Country. The Chappells are Kentucky-famous, and Bluegrass Ranch is one of the premier racehorse farms and training facilities in the Lexington area, and they'd agreed to be the face of the campaign. I've got the proofs of the pictures, but nothing else has been done."

"A photo wasn't chosen?" she asked.

"No, ma'am." Something scratched loudly on his end of the line. "We'll need print media, online items, full coordination with the Horse Country branch of tourism, the full nine yards. And your name was in the file as the woman who could take this campaign to the next level."

"Well, I appreciate that," she said. "Whether it's true or not."

"You do know the Chappells," he said, clearly leading her toward an answer.

"Yes," she admitted, thinking of the way Lawrence had pressed his cheek to hers last night. The soft, yet strong way he conversed made Mariah warm just thinking about him. The feel of his skin against hers when he held her hand. The scent of his skin...

Don said something else, and Mariah pulled herself out of last night's date. She'd had such a great time with Lawrence, and he'd asked her for another date on Friday night. He hadn't said what they'd do, but this morning, he'd texted already to say he'd gotten them tickets to the Wild-flower Festival.

Wear your walking boots, okay? he'd said.

Mariah had said she would, and she'd been to the Wild-flower Festival several times. She loved going to it, and she wondered how Lawrence had known when she hadn't told him.

"Yes," she said. "I'll look for the email, and I'll go over everything." She gave Don her email address, and she promised she'd be in touch just as soon as she had a plan of action for him. Then she said, "Do you have an active contract with us?"

"If we do, it'll be in the files," Don said.

"I'll look for it then," she said, moving her mouse over to the tab with her email. "If we don't have one there, I'll have to get that in place first, with all the fees agreed upon."

"Fair enough," Don said. "Let me know."

"Will do." She let Don hang up, and she checked her email. Nothing from him yet. Her heartbeat flopped around in her chest, because if she had to work with the Chappell brothers, would she be able to keep dating Lawrence?

"Of course," she whispered to herself. She wouldn't have a contract with the Chappells; the contract would be with the State Office of Tourism. Just because she was working with the Chappells as part of that didn't mean she couldn't be with Lawrence.

"Hey," June chirped. "Can you sneak away for lunch?"

Mariah tore her eyes from her computer. "Yes." She stood and opened her drawer to get out her purse. "Even if I couldn't, I would." She cast one more glance at her email, but even if Don's message had been there, she'd have walked away. She loved lunches with her friends at work, and she finally had a good story to tell them about the most perfect date she'd experienced last night.

* * *

"What do you mean, he's not going to be happy?" Mariah tilted her head and looked at Lawrence with questions pouring from her. "The file I got said everyone here at Bluegrass Ranch had consented to the billboard."

"Spur consented," Lawrence said as he jotted something down in his notebook. Mariah had found him in an office of sorts. It was really just a tiny room tacked onto the end of a row of stables, and two desks had been crammed into the small space. Apparently, the other desk belonged to Duke, and he dealt with all the breeding that took place here on the ranch.

Lawrence looked up. "But he's not happy about it. Spur isn't usually happy about anything that takes away from the core purpose of Bluegrass Ranch, and I'm pretty sure I've heard him say that it's not our job as cowboys to get more tourists to Horse Country." He shook his head, a small smile forming on his mouth, drawing Mariah's attention there. "In fact, Spur couldn't care less if there are more tourists in Horse Country. It's not like our ranch benefits from that."

"No?" Mariah challenged. "I'm pretty sure this ranch made quite the sum of money from all the people who came to the Summer Smash...right?"

Lawrence blinked, and Mariah had her answer. "I'm sure some of them were tourists, Lawrence. Don't you think?'

"I honestly don't know."

"If not, your family knows a whole heckuva lot of people." She leaned against Duke's desk and folded her arms.

"I mean, Mom does know a lot of people." Lawrence looked uncomfortable, and Mariah wanted to know what that was about. She wasn't quite sure how to phrase the question, because she didn't know what she should be asking. Lawrence didn't volunteer any more information, and Mariah drew in a deep breath.

After a glance at her phone, she said, "Okay, so we need to go over all the pictures from the shoot and pick one for the billboard. Then we need to pick photos for the print media, and I need to meet with the tourism branch here in Horse Country. Actually, I'm doing that on Friday. I'd love to have samples or something to show them."

"All right." Lawrence sighed as he stood up. "Let's see if we can find Spur, and I'll start prayin' that he's in a good mood." He picked up his phone and sent a text. His device buzzed not two seconds later, and he said, "Spur's at home. Olli's pregnant, and he said she's not feeling well today."

He met Mariah's eye. "That's probably a good thing. We won't be interrupting him in the middle of an important task."

"I like Olli," Mariah said with a smile.

Lawrence shook his head, but his smile graced his face too. He led her to his truck, and they made the short ride down to the highway, trundling down it a little ways, and then going up a straight, gravel road to the adjacent property.

"That's her perfumery right there," Lawrence said, indicating the building on his left as he passed it. A car sat out front, but otherwise, Mariah wouldn't have known it was where Olli made all of her scents. She'd been selected by a big company a year or two ago, and now her perfumes, colognes, and candles were in every state in the United States.

Mariah had watched her videos, and she wasn't ashamed to admit that she'd sprayed *Glass Slipper*, one of Olli's newest scents, in her hair for her date with Lawrence last night.

"And they live here," Mariah said as the house came into view. Rows and rows of flowers covered the ground between the house and the perfumery, the driveway carving a path right through them.

"Yes," Lawrence said. "She grows a lot of her flowers right here on her property. It's several acres, and it borders Bluegrass."

"So she literally fell in love with the cowboy next door."

Lawrence nodded and grinned. "Literally."

"How romantic," Mariah said as he came to a stop. As she and Lawrence got out of the truck, the front door of the house opened, and Spur Chappell came out onto the porch.

"Hey, Lawrence," he said, a smile crossing his face. Mariah counted that as positive, though when Spur's dark eyes flitted toward her, her stomach definitely sent out a flutter of nerves. "Mariah."

She didn't like the surprise in his voice, nor the way his gaze immediately swung back to Lawrence. "What's going on?"

"Mariah's been asked by the State Office of Tourism to finally get that billboard thing done." Lawrence reached his brother and shook his hand. Spur pulled him right into a hug, and it was clear that surprised Lawrence.

Mariah watched as Spur said something to Lawrence, clapped him on the back, and released him. They both faced Mariah, and Lawrence said, "Be nice, Spur."

"I'm nice," he said.

"Be my brand of nice," Lawrence said, grinning at his older brother.

"We really just need to pick the photos you guys like the best," Mariah said. "I'll really handle everything else."

"I thought this billboard thing was done," Spur said.

"Apparently, the person working on it quit at the tourism office," Mariah said. "They've got someone new in there, and he sent me everything he had. It wasn't much. There wasn't even a signed contract to use the photos, or any way to compensate you guys, or—"

"We don't need to be compensated," Spur said.

Mariah cocked her head, trying to see inside his. "Even if you don't *need* to be," she said slowly, employing her most professional voice. "You should be. You run a commercial racehorse operation at Bluegrass Ranch. The state of Kentucky wants to capitalize on your family name, your legacy, and your ranch. You should be compensated for that."

Spur exchanged a glance with Lawrence. "All right," he drawled. "You'll take care of that?"

"Yes, sir," she said. "Have you guys looked over the pictures that were taken last spring?"

"I did," Spur said. "Months ago. It was Cayden doing most of that."

Mariah looked at Lawrence, who simply looked back. "Should we meet with him?"

"I think you and Lawrence should handle it," Spur said with a big grin. "Cayden's got a ton on his plate with the Summer Smash still, and the upcoming yearling sale, and his wedding, and everything Ginny does at Sweet Rose."

"All right," Lawrence said dryly. "I can take a hint."

"Great," Spur said, clapping Lawrence on the back. They definitely had an interesting relationship. It seemed like everything to do with Bluegrass ran through Spur, but he was very good at delegating to the other brothers.

"I'm busy too, you know," Lawrence said.

"Of course you are," Spur said, his smile faltering. "I'm not saying you're not. But you and Mariah are seeing each other, right?"

Lawrence shifted his feet, and Mariah wasn't sure she liked the hesitancy in his stature. "Yes," he said, only a moment later than she'd like.

"So it'll be easy to talk business while you're out," Spur said. "Help her pick some pictures. Go over the plans. I trust you, Lawrence."

"Thank you, Spur," he said.

The crunching of gravel beneath tires met her ears, and Mariah turned to find Ginny Winters coming up the driveway.

"Praise the Lord," Spur said. "Ginny's here. Excuse me."

Lawrence fell to Mariah's side as Spur went to meet Ginny. Mariah wanted everyone to know she and Lawrence were seeing one another, and she took his hand in hers before Ginny and Spur returned.

Ginny Winters saw it; Mariah watched her eyes draw down to where their hands were connected. She smiled at Mariah and then Lawrence, who took a quick step forward and said, "Ginny, do you remember Mariah Barker? She worked with me and Cayden on the Summer Smash."

What a perfect gentleman, Mariah thought as she shook the heiress's hand, and the moment she and Spur stepped inside the house, Mariah squeezed Lawrence's hand.

CHAPTER 10

L awrence tossed the picture Mariah had given him
that morning onto the dining room table where
four of his brothers were eating lunch.

"What is that?" Cayden asked, reaching for the picture.

"We look good," Duke said before shoving in the rest of
his ham and cheese sandwich. The homestead smelled like
stewed tomatoes, as Ginny had made chili that morning.
Cayden, Duke, Ian, and Blaine all had a bowl of it in front of
them, and Ginny came to the table with two more bowls in
her hand.

"Chili, Lawrence?"

"Yes, ma'am," he said, taking the bowl. He dang near
dropped it as the heat seeped into his fingers, but he
managed to bobble it onto the tabletop without losing more
than a couple of drops.

"Sorry," she said with a smile. "It's hot." She indicated
the bagged cheese and sour cream in the middle of the table.

A pile of spoons sat there too. "Toppings." She took the seat next to Cayden and reached for the corn chips. She put a healthy handful on top of her chili, and then added a few dollops of sour cream.

"Is this the best picture there was?" Blaine said. "Didn't we pick the one with Spur smiling a little more?"

"Mariah said she doesn't want Spur to be smiling. It looked unnatural to her." Lawrence took the last seat at the table and reached for the bag of shredded cheese. "She liked the murderous look way better."

A beat of silence filled the house, and then Blaine burst out laughing, Lawrence hot on his heels. Even Ian chuckled, and that was saying something. Just the fact that Ian was here, eating with everyone—and without Conrad—said a lot.

Speak of the devil, Conrad's voice entered the house, and he and Trey joined everyone at the table. People shifted around, and Trey got out two folding chairs from the hall closet.

"There's sandwiches in the fridge," Blaine said amidst the noise, and Lawrence jumped to his feet.

"I'll get them," he said. "I want one. Who else wants one? Conrad? Trey?"

"Yes," they both said, and Lawrence went into the kitchen with Ginny right behind him. She dished up the chili while he pulled out the tray of sandwiches and put it on the counter.

"Where's Spur?" he asked her as he put sandwiches on paper plates for his brothers. They didn't have family luncheons in the middle of the week very often, but Ginny had sent a text about the chili and the sandwiches she'd be bringing over from an event Sweet Rose had put on yesterday for its shareholders.

"He's dealing with Samuels," Blaine said from the table, and it was a miracle Lawrence could hear him. With so many voices in the room, one had to yell to be heard. Lawrence didn't usually like meals like this, but today, for some reason, being with his family fed his soul.

"Olli's on her way," Ginny said. "She had to finish a batch of candles for shipment." She took two bowls of chili around the peninsula to the table and came back into the kitchen to get a roll of paper towels.

Lawrence delivered the sandwiches and tapped the picture in the middle of the table. "That's what we're thinking for the billboard on I-64 from Louisville. It's going to be *huge*. But we'll do some different ones in the brochures, online media, and other print media."

"He really does look like he could commit murder, doesn't he?" Cayden asked, picking up the eight-by-ten Mariah had printed. He shook his head.

"It looks very serious," Lawrence said. "And I think that's how we want to be portrayed. We're a serious operation. We know our horses here."

"They're not going to expect us to do tours, are they?" Conrad asked. "We're not Keeneland."

"No, no, nothing like that," Lawrence said. "We're just the public face for Horse Country. The ranch is getting a tidy sum of money because of it too, and you can thank

Mariah for that." He grinned at everyone, took his seat again, and dug into his chili.

The talk continued on about how their belt buckles were too big for anyone to take them seriously, and Spur and Olli joined the conversation after only a few minutes.

"Is that the one you chose?" Spur asked, and Cayden handed him the picture. He studied it, his eyebrows drawing down by the second. "I look like I'm about to light something on fire."

Everyone laughed, and Spur tossed the photo back onto the table. "I actually like that one." That only got a louder reaction, and Lawrence met Spur's eyes.

He'd whispered yesterday that Lawrence and Mariah sure did look good together, and Lawrence hadn't known how to respond. He loved his oldest brother, and he looked up to Spur in a lot of ways. He certainly didn't want to run Bluegrass Ranch, and he didn't want to have to approve everything everyone did.

The load Spur carried was one unique to him, and Lawrence supposed they each bore a burden like that.

"Hey, Beth wants to enter another horse in the Sweetheart Classic," Trey said, and Lawrence looked over to him. "Can we get the midnight spot starting just after Halloween?"

"I'll look," he said, picking up his sandwich. He took a bite and swiped on his phone while he chewed. If he could book Trey during that spot, no one would have to be up in the middle of the night to monitor the track.

"It's free starting the second week of November,"

Lawrence said. "I can put you on it through February."

"If you would," Trey said as he stood up. "Also, I have an announcement to make." He knocked a couple of times on the table and waited for everyone to settle down. "Beth and I are finalizing TJ's adoption the third week of October. We have a court date of October seventeenth, and we're going to have a big dinner at the farmhouse that night."

"That's great," Spur said, and several others chimed in, including Lawrence. He put it on his personal calendar, because Beth was a great cook, and Lawrence did love spending time at the farmhouse with Trey, Beth, and TJ.

Trey was one of the more easy-going brothers, though he did have some strong opinions and a definite Chappell personality if pressed into a corner. He was a great dad to TJ though, and the boy had gotten into everyone's heart.

None more than Mom's, though, and Lawrence reminded himself he needed to get over there and talk to his mother. He wasn't hiding his relationship with Mariah, and it would make Mom happy...

Soon, he told himself.

"How's Olli doing?" he asked Spur, because Lawrence couldn't wait to be an uncle to Spur and Olli's baby.

"I'm not done with my announcement," Trey said, shooting Lawrence a glare.

"Sorry," Lawrence said. "Go on."

"Beth and I are expecting a baby just after the Sweetheart Classic." He beamed out at the table. "She'll be mad I told you lot without her, but we've known for a while, and it felt like the right time."

Spur stood up and grabbed onto Trey. "That's great news, brother."

More congratulations went around, and Lawrence took his turn hugging Trey too. They finally all settled back to eating, and boy, could they eat. The ham and cheese sandwiches disappeared, and Ginny ended up ladling up a single Tupperware container for Cayden to take to Mom and Daddy.

They left to do that, and everyone else scattered to get back to their afternoon chores and tasks around the ranch. Lawrence cleaned up the kitchen while Duke went upstairs to attend one of his classes.

With that done, he headed out to his office in the family stable row, invoices to send and next week's schedule to finalize. After that, he'd send all the weekly reminders, and then he'd be done for the day.

Just those tasks would take a few hours, but Lawrence loved it when things lined up. He enjoyed getting back the texts of gratitude from those he sent reminders to, and he enjoyed balancing the books in the scheduling tab of the financial workbook Spur had shared with him.

Cayden did quite a lot with the financial side of the ranch too, but Lawrence didn't get into all the tabs for marketing and sales, boarding or breeding. He kept track of who used their track and when, and he took care of those fees.

As he approached the office he and Duke shared, he noticed the door sat slightly open. A frown pulled at his eyebrows, and his step slowed. He glanced left and right before opening the door, a familiar scent hanging in the air.

"Mariah," he said as she turned from the single window that sat opposite the door.

"There you are," she said. "I texted you a couple of times."

"You did?" Lawrence pulled his phone out of his pocket, his mind registering her distress a moment too late. He wasn't sure if he should look at his phone for the texts or ask her what was wrong. "I don't have them." He looked up at her. "What's going on? Are you okay?"

She didn't look okay, if the twisting hands and wide eyes were any indication. He entered the office and closed the door. Two steps later, he'd gathered Mariah into his arms.

She clung to him, and Lawrence didn't like the way she'd stayed silent. What could've possibly changed in the past five or six hours? He'd seen her that morning in her office, where he'd gotten the photo from her, as well as several others he'd go over with Cayden for the online and print media.

"Mariah," he said. "Tell me what's going on."

"Dr. Biggers found out about the State Office of Tourism and the Bluegrass Ranch billboard."

"Okay," he said, not getting the dots to line up.

"No, it's not okay," she said. "He said you Chappell brothers were turning out to be great clients."

Lawrence pulled in a breath then. "I'm not your client."

"He thinks you are."

"That's ridiculous," he said, stepping back. "Are you going to employ your dating rules?" He wanted to tell her the rule she had about not dating her clients was ridiculous. Lots of people met at work, dated at work, and enjoyed lasting relationships despite working together.

"He basically said he was glad I'd never started anything with you," she said, wringing her hands together again.

"What did you say?"

"I was so surprised, I didn't say anything."

Lawrence pressed out a frustrated sigh. "All right. Well. What are you going to do?" They'd literally just gotten back together. Not only that, but she was the one who'd driven out to the orchard to pick peaches, and Lawrence didn't think that had happened by accident. Not for a single second. She'd wanted to see him, and he knew she'd felt the spark between them just as strongly as he had.

"What would you do?" she asked.

Lawrence took a moment to gather his courage together. He'd said some hard things to Mariah in the past. He could again.

"Honestly, Mariah? I'd tell your boss that he doesn't get to dictate who you date. That I'm not your client, and even if I was, you'd still go out with me, because you like me, and there's something between us."

His throat hurt, and he needed a cool drink. He forged ahead anyway. "Tell me you don't feel this thing between us."

Mariah softened and swallowed. "Of course I feel it," she said quietly. She closed the small distance between them and cradled his face in her hands. "I feel it."

"Then what are you going to do?"

CHAPTER 11

Mariah couldn't bear the anguish in Lawrence's face. She hated that she was the one who'd put it there. Of course she was going to choose him. She wasn't going to let Dr. Biggers dictate any more of her life, especially when it came to who she called her boyfriend.

"I'm going to tell Doctor Biggers that he doesn't get to dictate who I date. That you're not my client, and even if you were, I'd still go out with you." She tried to smile, and it wobbled only a little on her lips.

Lawrence reached up and put his hands over hers, and Mariah giggled. "Will he fire you?"

"Honestly, I don't care if he does," Mariah said. "I don't really like my job anyway."

"No?" Lawrence took both of her hands in his and curled their fingers together. "You sure are good at it."

"I'm thinking of opening my own firm," she said. "I

don't know about the marketing side of it. I do like some aspects of the marketing. It's event planning I really like."

"Then do that," Lawrence said, and he made it sound so easy. Like everyone could simply quit their jobs and do whatever they wanted. As if mortgages paid themselves and office space came for free.

"I have bills to pay," Mariah said, swallowing. She released his hands, because she didn't want the knowledge of her past to seep into him by osmosis. She returned to the window. "A lot of bills." She didn't mean to say the words with so much dismay, but they came out that way nonetheless.

"Mariah," Lawrence said, half questioning her and half just stating her name. He joined her in front of the window, but he didn't touch her.

"I..." She wanted to be with him, and she did trust him. No, she didn't want to tell him about her past, but she realistically couldn't keep it a secret forever. Not if she wanted a real, long-lasting relationship that could weather tough storms, the way Dani had.

Start small, she told herself. She only had to tell him one story right now. There'd be time for more later.

"I was married in my twenties," she said to the glass in front of her. The very real warmth of Lawrence beside her fed her bravery, and she drew in a breath filled with the scent of him. He smelled like sunshine and leather, horses and home. She sure did like it.

"It only lasted a couple of years," she said. "He was...it

was a mistake to get married, and it cost me a lot in a lot of ways."

That was beyond true, but she also knew it was vague. She wasn't sure how to explain in more concrete terms right now.

"I'm still paying for some of those costs," she said. "In actual dollars. I need a job, and I don't have the funding to start my own business."

Lawrence very carefully slipped his fingers between hers, each motion taking a long second to complete. "I'm so sorry," he said. "I didn't know."

"I know you didn't." She tried to smile now, but it fell off her face before it really appeared. She drew in a deep breath and let it out again. "I can tell you more another time." She finally dared to turn and look at him, and he wore the sweetest look of compassion on his face.

"Of course," he said. "Whenever you're ready."

"You don't even want to know his name?"

"Sure," he said. "Tell me his name."

"Robert Prince," she said. "His last name is very misleading, by the way." She scoffed and shook her head. "The man was no prince." Mariah smiled then, glad when Lawrence did too. At the same time, she knew she covered over hard things with a joke when she should let them hurt. She played them off as funny when they were anything but funny.

"What are you doing this afternoon?" she asked. "Can you play hooky?"

"Uh, let's see." He turned toward his desk. "I don't

think I can. It's the end of the month, and I have invoices to get out and reminder texts to send for next week."

"Oof, you're no fun." She put one hand against his chest, but Lawrence didn't change his mind. "Maybe we can go to dinner tonight too?"

"Tell you what. You can hang out here and watch me work if you don't want to go back to the office. Or you can ride a horse or two?" He lifted his eyebrows in a playful way. "And we can order pizza and eat it on the roof of the race-track if you want. The sunset from up there is incredible."

"You've got yourself a date," she said. "But I have some shopping to do this afternoon, and that'll be way more fun than watching you send texts."

He chuckled, and Mariah was glad the mood between them had lightened. She tipped up and pressed a kiss to his cheek, saying, "Okay, I'll be back in a few hours with pizza."

"Sounds good," Lawrence said as she turned and headed for the door. Mariah opened it and stepped outside, realizing that the tiny office was air conditioned. The smile dropped from her face, though, because Mariah was well-aware of what she'd just done.

She'd told Lawrence a very tiny snippet of her past. A past she might not have dealt with in the healthiest of ways, though she had seen a therapist for a couple of months after her divorce. The thought of entering a courtroom still made her hands shake, and the thought of telling anyone that wrapped her stomach in knots.

She definitely needed to move past those things if she was going to have a real relationship with a man, and she wanted one with Lawrence Chappell. As she got behind the wheel of her car, she said, "You better figure out if you're even ready for a man like him, Mya. Because I guarantee he's not going to wait around forever while you straighten out your life."

She would. She'd figure things out, one step at a time, just like she had when she'd needed to file the protective order against her husband. Like she had when she'd hired a lawyer to help her with that, and with the subsequent divorce.

"It's more than that, and you know it," she said as she reached the highway and turned to go back toward town. She did like Lawrence. He was the first man who made her want to straighten out her life.

But she'd seen relationship after relationship fail when hard times came. She wasn't even sure she believed people could stay together through thick and thin. Her mother had left. Her husband had not kept his vows.

"Dani and Doug are doing it," she told herself. "People do it."

Now, she just had to start believing that *she* could have a relationship where both she and her husband wanted to be there, and that they would both work to have the kind of love Mariah had literally only seen in the movies.

"Pass that grape jelly, bug," Mariah's dad said. "And keep talking about your billboard."

Mariah reached for the jar of grape jelly on the table beside her, passing it to Alicia, who handed it to their dad. "It's not my billboard, Daddy."

"Right, right," Daddy said as he spooned far too much jelly on his biscuit. She preferred hers with sausage gravy and grits, which she currently had on a plate in front of her.

Dani had offered to have Mariah give her news first today, and she needed to wrap it up, as they'd already been served. Alicia surely had something to talk about today too.

"That's it," she said. "It's a big new client, and it'll be fun to work with the cowboys at Bluegrass Ranch again." She looked at Dani, clearly telling her sister it was her turn to talk.

"Great," Daddy said, smiling at her. Mariah loved her father, because he was the perfect example of someone who never gave up. Ever. When things had gotten incredibly hard after Mom had left, he didn't quit. He learned how to do Alicia's hair, and he went to the maturation programs with his girls. His sister had come several times over the years, and Mariah loved her Aunt Sally with everything she had.

"Dani?" he asked.

"So we met with Isaac, our adoption counselor," she said. "No official news yet." She glanced around the table quickly before spooning up another piece of melon. "But we're meeting the birth mother this week, and Isaac said she wants to make a decision quickly. The baby is due in about six weeks."

"That's amazing news," Alicia said, the words gushing out of her mouth. She reached over and gave Dani a side-hug, and Mariah just smiled widely at her and scooped up a bite of biscuits and gravy.

"I'm so excited for you, Dani," Daddy said, laughing as he said the words. "I'll start praying for you and Doug—and the birth mother too."

"Isaac seemed really positive," Dani said, glancing down at her omelette. "Doug and I are trying to be hopeful and positive too, without getting our hopes up too high."

Mariah knew her sister, and Dani's hopes hovered somewhere in outer space about now. "How's everything at the nursery?" she asked, just so Dani would know Mariah understood she didn't want to speculate everything to death.

"Good," Dani said. "Our fall bulb sale just started, and we're getting in our seasonal stuff for Halloween. Oh." She turned to Alicia. "If you want the scarecrows, they're coming on Wednesday, and they'll sell out by evening."

"I'll come in the morning," the youngest Barker said. She glanced around the table. "Is that it for everyone?"

"I have something small," Daddy said. "I'll go last." He gestured with his fork for Alicia to go next.

Before she could speak, the waitress approached with their next round of drinks. "Here you go. How is everything here?"

"Great," Mariah said.

"Can I get one more side of bacon?" Daddy asked. "And maybe another biscuit?"

Mariah grinned and shook her head while Dani said, "More bacon, Daddy? Really?"

"Sure thing, sugar," the waitress said, smiling at him before walking away.

"I can eat more bacon," Daddy said. "I just had my physical and all of my numbers are good." He dug into his scrambled eggs again. "Go on, Leesh."

"I've been seeing Malcolm for a while," she said, and Mariah's heart simultaneously perked up and fell to the bottom of her sandals. Alicia glanced around the table, and it felt very purposeful that she didn't meet Mariah's eyes for longer than half a breath. "We've started talking about getting married."

"Wow," Dani said, ever the diplomatic one. "You've been dating for six months."

"That's a while for me," Alicia said.

It would've been for Mariah too, given her dating history the past several years, since the divorce especially.

"Do you love him?" Daddy asked.

"You know what?" Alicia asked, a slow, beautiful smile filling her face. "I think I do."

It sure looked like she did. Mariah had met Malcolm a handful of times, and he was a nice guy. He was articulate and funny, and he had the blond hair that Alicia particularly liked.

Mariah herself preferred dark hair and dark eyes and the whole general sense of mystery that came with those.

Just like Lawrence, she thought. She didn't say anything about him, though Dani knew she'd started seeing him again. She and her sister had some silent understandings when it came to sharing things with the family, and Mariah knew Dani would never say anything about Lawrence unless Mariah did.

"That's wonderful then," Daddy said, smiling.

"I want to be married in the spring," Alicia said. "So it's not going to happen super fast, Daddy."

"Good," he said with a grin. "Because I need some time getting used to my baby getting married."

"I'm thirty-four, Daddy." Alicia giggled and shook her head. "Tell us your thing."

Daddy took a minute to finish his eggs and wipe his face. He took a long drink of his orange juice and surveyed the three of them. "I'm going to put in my retirement papers, with an end date of May thirty-first."

"Finally," Dani said.

"That's fantastic," Mariah said.

"Good for you, Daddy," Alicia said.

"It's time," he said, holding Dani's gaze the longest. "I'm almost seventy, and I have a good nest egg built up."

"Good," Mariah said. "What will you do in retirement?" Her father had worked for thirty years in the education system before retiring from that. Then, for the past twelve years, he'd been working in the consulting business, working with businesses of all sizes as they upgraded their computer systems. He'd worked with a lot of people over the years, and that was how she'd been at Tamara Lennox's wedding to Blaine Chappell.

That was when her real love affair with Lawrence Chappell had started, and Mariah ducked her head as she thought about the sexy, sensitive cowboy she probably wouldn't see again until Wednesday.

The Wildflower Festival had closed on Friday, due to a burst pipe, and their tickets had been rescheduled for Wednesday evening.

Mariah suddenly couldn't wait.

CHAPTER 12

When Lawrence pulled up to Mariah's house on Wednesday afternoon, he found her sitting on the top step, her phone pressed to her ear. She held up one finger to him, indicating she needed another minute, and then she got to her feet and went back inside the house.

Lawrence got out of the truck and turned toward the sound of a couple of dogs barking. One was clearly small, with a high-pitched yap that drove nails into Lawrence's nerves. The other was bigger, with a deeper, throatier voice. They sounded very close, and when he approached the steps, he determined at least one of the dogs was in Mariah's back yard.

He frowned, because he hadn't known she owned a dog. He still faced the side of the house when she came out, her footsteps slapping the concrete steps as she came down.

"Hey," she said breathlessly. "Sorry, I had to talk to my sister for a sec."

"Do you have a dog?" he asked, tilting his head.

"It's Dani's," she said, glancing back toward the house. She faced him again, and he drank in the beauty of her face. She smiled at him, and Lawrence automatically returned the gesture. "She's here right now," Mariah added. "Because her husband is working graveyards at the hospital right now, and she needs somewhere to go in the afternoons so he can sleep."

"Oh, gotcha." Lawrence reached for her hand, dropping his eyes to the movement of his arm. He watched himself weave his fingers through hers, and he enjoyed the crackling energy that came from her touch. "You ready for the festival? We don't have to go."

"No, I want to," she said, but her voice pitched up. She also didn't move a muscle. "I'm wondering..."

"What?" he asked.

"Is it too soon for you to meet my sister?" she asked. "She owns a nursery on the west side of Dreamsville, and she loves flowers. Obviously."

Lawrence blinked, though he wasn't too terribly surprised. Mariah was very involved in her sisters' lives, and they were involved in hers. She'd talked about them plenty of times, and Lawrence had met Alicia briefly once.

"I'd love to meet her," Lawrence said. "And she can come with us tonight if she wants."

"I told her you'd say that." Mariah tugged him forward, and they went up the steps to the porch instead of down the sidewalk to his truck. She led him toward the front door, which had a big, beautiful wreath on it.

The scent of fresh flowers met his nose, and Lawrence did like that. It made the evening still feel like summer, though September had begun, and the weather had been unpredictable the past few days.

Mariah led him inside, where another woman stood in the kitchen. Dani had honey blonde hair and she obviously didn't share Mariah's proclivity for prints and patterns as she wore a plain black tank top with a pair of jeans. She looked toward the front door as Lawrence passed through it, and a smile sprang to her face.

"He said you can come," Mariah said. "Come meet Lawrence."

Dani wiped her hands on a dish towel and started toward them. A big, black dog came before her, and Lawrence released Mariah's hand to greet the animal. "Hey, there," he said. "Was that you barking outside?"

"He has a love-hate relationship with the neighbor's dog," Mariah said. "He can't help himself."

Lawrence grinned at the curly-haired dog, who was obviously grinning back at him. He looked up and into the blue eyes of Dani, who extended her hand. "I'm Dani Welkins, Mariah's sister."

"Lawrence Chappell," he said, shaking her hand. "You really can come with us to the festival if you'd like. The tickets allow a group of four."

"I'll call Doug," she said. "My husband. Maybe we can double?" She looked from Lawrence to Mariah.

"Sure," he said, and he honestly didn't mind if he walked around the festival with Mariah's sister and her husband. He had been thinking about kissing Mariah that evening, but that possibility faded before his eyes.

There's plenty of time, he told himself. They still had loads to learn about one another, and Lawrence hoped the attraction between them would only grow, blossom, and bloom.

Dani put her phone to her ear and stepped away. Mariah grinned at him and put both hands on his chest, smoothing down his shirt. "Thanks for letting them come."

"Of course," he said. "You could've texted me about it too."

"She mentioned it about ten minutes ago," Mariah said. "When Doug called to say he was up and didn't have to work tonight after all."

"Ah." Lawrence nodded. "Do you still want to get dinner there? We could go somewhere first. The festival is lit, and it's open until ten." The thought of staying up that late had him yawning already, but he stifled it and waited for Mariah to answer.

"I'd love to go to House of Hash," she said. "I've been craving their BLT and salted watermelon."

Lawrence's mouth watered at the same time his stomach cramped. "House of Hash will feed you for a week," he said with a chuckle.

"Are we going to House of Hash?" Dani asked, pulling the phone down from her mouth. "Doug says he can meet us there in twenty minutes."

Mariah's face glowed as she looked from Dani to Lawrence. "Doug loves House of Hash."

"Let's hit House of Hash then." Lawrence looped his arm through Mariah's, and they went back outside. Dani came running out after them once Lawrence had already helped Mariah into the passenger seat. He opened the door behind the driver's seat for Dani, and she flashed him a smile.

She was a couple of inches shorter than Mariah, and her face a little fuller. They certainly looked like they belonged to the same family, much the same way Lawrence definitely belonged to all of his brothers, though they were all a little bit different.

He glanced at Mariah, admiring the bright pink, purple, and blue flowers on her blouse before he buckled in. "Ready?" he asked, glancing in the rearview mirror. His gaze easily went back to Mariah, because when she was around, he couldn't keep his eyes off of her. She wore jeans tonight too, as the weather had been cloudy and windy all day today.

"Ready," Mariah and Dani said at the same time, and Lawrence enjoyed the harmony of their voices. They giggled together too, and Lawrence backed out of the driveway.

"Mariah says you own a nursery," Lawrence said to Dani. "How did you start that?"

"I worked there right after high school," Dani said. "We'd just moved here, and I wasn't sure what I wanted to do in college. So I didn't go."

Lawrence nodded, and Mariah reached across the console and took his hand. He glanced at her. "Dani is brilliant with plants," she said. "She worked her way up, and when the owner wanted to sell five years ago, she and Doug bought it."

"That's great," he said. "And your husband works in the hospital?"

"He's an emergency room nurse," Dani said. "He does three-week schedules. Day, swing, then graveyard."

"And they have Phantom," Mariah said. "That labradoodle I'm assuming you left to lie on my couch?" She twisted and looked at her sister.

"He'd just been outside. He'll be fine."

"I think I left my socks out," Mariah said, glancing at Lawrence as she faced forward again. "That dog *loves* socks."

"If that's one of his worst faults," Dani said. "I'll take it."

"Dani made the wreath on my front door," she said. "She's started doing some online orders of her floral designs."

"Okay, this isn't going to be a brag session on me," Dani said from the back seat.

Lawrence liked the pride and love in Mariah's voice, because it told him how important her sister was to her. He smiled to himself, navigating them toward the restaurant as Mariah argued with her sister.

"Well, then I could say some things about you," Dani said.

"No," Mariah said instantly, and maybe with too much force. Enough to draw Lawrence's attention to her.

"What would you say?" he asked, meeting Dani's eyes in the rearview mirror.

"Dani," Mariah warned.

Lawrence chuckled as he turned into the parking lot at House of Hash.

"I better not say anything," Dani said, turning toward her window. "I sometimes eat what Mariah makes for dinner." That got them both laughing, and Lawrence did like the sound of it. He'd grown up with only brothers, and he liked the dynamic between the two sisters.

"There's Doug," Dani said. "See the red truck?"

"Yep." Lawrence kept going straight and found a spot only a few away from Dani's husband. She got out of the vehicle the moment it stopped, but Lawrence took a moment to reach over to the glove compartment and open it to get out his wallet.

"Thanks for letting her tag along," Mariah said. "They met with this birth mother today, and Dani didn't think it went very well."

Lawrence met Mariah's eyes, seeing the sadness there. "I'm sorry. Is this something I say anything about?"

"No," Mariah said. "But it means a lot to her—and to me—that she can come with us tonight. She's not good alone, and Doug...he's great. He is. But it's different for Dani."

"I'm sure it is," Lawrence murmured. He glanced out his window and then looked at Mariah again. "Give me a minute, and I'll come open your door."

"Okay."

He hurried around the truck and opened the door for

her, stepping into that space again. "Do you want kids, Mariah?"

Her pretty blue eyes widened, but she nodded. "Yes," she said slowly.

"You didn't have any from your previous marriage, right?"

She shook her head, her eyes returning to normal and her lips pressing together into a slim line.

"I come from all boys," he said. "And you come from all girls." He backed up and extended his hand toward her, hoping to make the moment much lighter than it currently felt. "I guess that gives us a fifty-fifty chance."

She burst out laughing, put her hand in his, and joined him on the ground. "I think it's always a fifty-fifty chance, Lawrence."

He grinned at her and slung his arm around her waist. "And probably too early for us to be talking about kids, right? I mean, this is our third date. I'm so bad at this dating thing." He chuckled, glad when she snuggled into his side and kept giggling too.

They approached Dani and Doug, who stood talking, their hands joined. Dani turned toward Lawrence and Mariah and smiled. "Doug, this is Mariah's boyfriend, Lawrence Chappell. Lawrence, this is my husband, Doug."

"Great to meet you," Lawrence said, removing his arm from Mariah's waist and shaking Doug's. He had medium brown hair and medium hazel eyes. He seemed average in every way, though he stood almost as tall as Lawrence. He tried to imagine him coming into his curtained-off area in the emergency room, and he did have kindness and wisdom in his eyes that Lawrence would appreciate in a stressful situation.

"And you," Doug said. "Thanks for letting us come along tonight."

"Sure." Lawrence looked toward the front door of House of Hash. "Shall we? I think this place fills up, even on weekdays."

The evening was filled with conversation and laughter, and Lawrence sure did like it. It was somehow easier to talk to Mariah with another couple around, especially one she was so comfortable with. Lawrence got a good vibe from both Dani and Doug, and he didn't mind that the pressure to carry the conversation didn't land on him.

He went to the flower displays Mariah led him to, and he read the signs if she wanted him to. He held her hand, and smelled the scent of her hair and clothes, and thoroughly enjoyed the presence of her at his side.

When he dropped her off, Dani had gone with her husband, but they were right behind Lawrence and Mariah. They needed to pick up their dog, and Mariah claimed she would not babysit the beast overnight, because Phantom liked to go out really early in the morning to take care of his business.

"I don't have to be to work until ten," Mariah said, glancing at him in the truck. They sat there, the light from her garage illuminating them.

"I'll walk you to the door," he said, his heart pounding in his chest. He wasn't going to kiss her, not with Dani and

Doug incoming. He helped Mariah from the truck, thinking of the next time he could see her.

"When do you want to get together again?" he asked on the way up the sidewalk.

"Are you mowing this weekend?"

"Tomorrow night," he said. "I could take a break at lunch, come to town, and then take a nap after that."

"Lunch tomorrow?" She paused at the bottom of the steps and dug her phone out of her purse. "I can do that. I'm free from eleven to two." She glanced up. "Early or late lunch?"

"You pick." He didn't really care, and Mariah had once planned all of their dates so completely that he'd worn what she wanted him to. Since their talk, though, she hadn't done that, and he really appreciated that.

"Let's go at twelve-thirty," she said. "Then I can make a few phone calls in the morning that are out west."

"Okay," he said, leaning down before any headlights or additional cars joined them at her place. "See you then." He swept his lips along her cheek, hearing her sharp intake of breath. She grabbed his collar as he retreated from her, holding him in her personal space.

They breathed in together, and then out, headlights washing over them as her sister pulled into the driveway.

"Tomorrow," Mariah whispered, and she released Lawrence's collar and went up the steps while he was still trying to get his balance. He found it and turned toward his truck.

"Sorry," Dani murmured as she went by, but he just

raised his hand as if to say, *It's fine. Wasn't going to kiss her anyway.*

Back in his truck, and all the way back to the ranch, though, all Lawrence could think about was kissing Mariah Barker again.

CHAPTER 13

Mariah tapped on her phone and pulled up the email she'd gotten from Wanda Hillborough at the Horse Country tourism office. "She thinks we need to do trifold brochures like this."

She handed the phone to Lawrence, who'd asked how things were going with the campaign for the State Office of Tourism. Mariah had only had the account for a week, but they weren't messing around this time. The hardest part—getting the photos taken—had already been done, and now it was just a matter of picking layouts, stories, and papers to get fliers and brochures printed.

Horse Country had a beautiful website that they maintained on a daily basis, and once Mariah had connected with Wanda, things had been moving quickly.

"Trifold?" Lawrence asked, studying the phone. "Why?"

"Yours would only be part of the brochure," she said. "See how there's the stuff about farm tours for where

Secretariat is buried? There's a racing schedule. And then there's the picture of you guys."

"Right on the middle section," he said. "It's the first thing you see when you open it." He looked up. "Why? We don't do tours or anything at Bluegrass. Spur was *very* clear on that."

"They've got a short film they've been making about the racehorse industry here in the Lexington area," Mariah said, pulling her napkin-wrapped silverware toward her and unwrapping it. "So they're using your family's picture to talk about that. It's at the visitor center, and they're trying to get more people to stop there for all their Horse Country Tourism needs." She smiled at him. "It's a great place. Very clean. Quaint. People who know more about horses and Lexington and the surrounding area than I'll ever know in my whole life."

She picked up the single-sheet menus the hostess had put on their table and handed Lawrence one. She loved Rapid Response for lunch, because they made fantastic composed salads, as well as the tallest roast beef sandwiches she'd ever seen.

She was hardly hungry after the tower of bacon she'd eaten last night, but she'd already skipped breakfast. She should be fine.

There were no waiters at Rapid Response. Runners brought food out from the kitchen at the back of the restaurant, and Mariah pulled the ordering table-top kiosk toward her. "I know what I want. So have a look and tell me what you want, and I'll put it in."

"Oh, uh." He scanned the menu. "I've never been here."

"You Chappells don't eat out a lot, do you?"

"Duke and Conrad do," he said. "They go on a lot of dates." He flicked his eyes up, and Mariah noticed for the second time that day that he didn't make true eye-contact. "I don't get out much, remember?"

"Take your time," she said, tapping on the screen. Her mind whirred, one loud part of it telling her not to make a big deal out of his behavior. He'd been happy to see her at her office, and he'd hugged her hello in front of Jane. The conversation here had been easy and light, and he'd let her pick the time and place for lunch.

They'd talked about her campaigns on the way here, and maybe his mind was preoccupied on the brochure or something going on at Bluegrass. She tapped to put in her balsamic wedge, which came with candied walnuts, avocado, bacon, dried cranberries, tomatoes, olives, and ranch dressing along with a balsamic glaze.

She put in that she wanted the wheat bread with it, and she considered changing it out for a half portion so she could get a half sandwich too. In the end, she decided to stay with just the salad, and she tapped to order a tall glass of strawberry lemonade while she waited for Lawrence to choose.

"I'll have a Rueben," he said.

"Single or double?" Mariah tapped on the sandwich header and found the Rueben.

"Double me up," he said with a grin, and Mariah smiled too as she tapped it in.

"Drink?"

"I order it all now?"

"All now, sir."

"Get me a Diet Coke."

"You got it." She glanced up at him, and he met her eyes this time. The moment lengthened, and something coursed through Mariah. She was extremely glad she hadn't asked him if there was something wrong, because there obviously wasn't.

She'd at least learned that from her first marriage. It never served anyone well when assumptions were made or conclusions jumped to. A little bit of silence, and a little bit of space, and Lawrence was fine.

He was probably fine to begin with. She didn't need to go asking questions all the time, simply because she had insecurities and doubts. Looking into Lawrence's eyes, there were no doubts.

No insecurities, especially when Lawrence reached across the table and took both of her hands in his. "You look great in blue. Makes your eyes light up." He ducked his head, concealing his face with his cowboy hat, but not before Mariah caught a glimpse of the smile riding his mouth.

"Thanks," she said. "What are you working on this week?"

"Next month's schedule," he said. "I'm helping Conrad with a couple of our horses right now. Cayden asked me to make a master list of the yearlings for our November sale." He waved his hand. "That kind of thing."

"And mowing."

"The harvest is in full swing," he said. "Trey is busy

filling the barns, and yes, I have to take a turn mowing. I only drew one day this week though." He gave her a brilliant smile, and Mariah wanted to reach out and touch that strong jaw with that glorious grin within. So she did.

He leaned into the touch, and then straightened as a runner brought their drinks. Lawrence reached for the straws she left on the table and handed one to Mariah. "Tell me about your dream vacation."

Mariah giggled, part of it mixed with a scoff. "My dream vacation?"

"Yeah," he said. "If you had the money to travel the world, where's the first place you'd go?"

She searched his face, trying to latch onto that one place that would be like a dream. "I...don't know."

"I do," he said with a devilish little grin.

"Do tell." She settled her face in her hands and couldn't take her eyes from him.

"I'd love to go to a really big city. Somewhere with a lot of buildings and a lot of history."

"Europe," she said.

"Italy," he said. "I want to ride on those gondolas in Venice, and see the architecture there. All of it."

"It's a long flight to Italy, you know." She sure did like teasing him, especially when he took it so well.

"Yeah," he said. "You get one of those flights that goes overnight, and you sleep."

"How many airplanes have you been on?" she asked.

"Just a couple," he admitted. "Do you fly a lot?"

"When I was younger, I did," she said. "The first couple

of years at the firm, I worked with clients out of Charlotte and Boston. I flew a few times a month."

"Charlotte can't be that far."

"It's not," she said. "Boston isn't a picnic, though, mostly because there don't seem to be any direct flights out of Louisville. To anywhere but Atlanta, at least."

"Hmm." He looked up again as their lunch arrived. "Holy cow," he said. "That's a huge sandwich."

"You said to double you up," Mariah said, eyeing the massive piles of corned beef on his rye bread.

"I had no idea it would be an entire pound," he said. "This is probably *two* pounds of corned beef."

"And you thought House of Hash had big portions," Mariah said, her mouth watering as the runner put her salad in front of her. She picked up her fork and watched as Lawrence said thanks and looked at his sandwich like it was a monster and not food.

"I'm going to have to take up jogging," he said, but he picked up his sandwich with both hands, ready to dive right in. He did, which caused Mariah to laugh as he clamped his mouth around the massively tall sandwich.

"Wow," she said. "You've never been more attractive than you are right now."

With his mouth full, Lawrence couldn't answer, but his eyes shone with joy.

Mariah wanted to go in with both fists too, but she mixed her salad around, getting the iceberg lettuce coated with the balsamic and ranch dressings before forking up her first bite. A party started in her mouth from the creamy dressing and the sweet walnuts. The crunch of the salty bacon and the fatty avocado made her so happy, and she could only smile at Lawrence with pure joy in her countenance too.

"So," he said after he'd finally swallowed. "Did my trip to Italy inspire you?"

"I've always wanted to go on a cruise," she said. "You know, with all the food I want, any time I want it. Exotic locations. White sand beaches."

"Don't have a lot of that here in Kentucky."

"No, sir, we do not."

"Plenty of amazing green fields," he said. "I like those too."

"You'd have to," she said. "To do what you guys do all day."

"It's a good life," he said, a little defensively.

"I didn't mean to say it wasn't," she said quickly, glancing at him. She put together another bite with several of the components of her salad. "Sorry if it sounded like that."

"Did you, um, read the copy on the brochure?" he asked.

"It's not final copy," she said. "In fact, I'm meeting with Wanda next week to go over it and make sure it's right." She glanced at the brochure. "It's just a placeholder right now."

"It's actually pretty right," he said, nudging the folded paper toward her. "Read it again." He took a smaller bite of his sandwich while she picked up the brochure.

She scanned the single paragraph above and below the

picture of the eight cowboy brothers, this one of them smiling out at the camera. "One of the biggest and best horse racing operations in the Lexington area." She looked up. "Annual revenue in the millions."

Lawrence lifted one shoulder as if to say, *What can you do?*

"Lawrence Chappell," she said. "Are you a millionaire?"

"It's rude to ask someone how much they make," Lawrence said, clearly teasing her. "Isn't it?"

"I didn't ask you how much you made," she said. "I asked if you had a lot of zeros in your bank account. Or is all of that left to Spur?"

"Spur runs the ranch," he said. "But we all got an equal share of my daddy's inheritance." Lawrence cleared his throat and wiped his lips with his napkins. "Listen, I don't want this to be a big deal, but I did want to tell you."

"Tell me, then."

"The inheritance had a lot of zeros," he said, picking up the bag of kettle potato chips that came with his sandwich. "More than six."

"I'm sorry," Mariah said, leaning away from the table and her food. "You sort of mumbled that last part. Could you repeat it?"

"More than six," he said, hitting the X-sound quite hard.

Mariah blinked at him, not sure what else to say.

"I draw an annual salary from the ranch," he said. "But I don't need it. I've been managing my investments this week too. Me and Ian get together every few months and manage the portfolio for the ranch, as well as for ourselves—and any

PROMOTING THE COWBOY BILLIONAIRE

of the brothers who'd rather have someone else do stuff like that."

"So you're a financial whiz," she said. "You said you didn't have a degree."

"I don't," he said. "I've taken classes in investing and financial management. They used to offer stuff like that at the community center."

Mariah took another bite of her salad, glancing to the table next to theirs. The women there were engaged in their own conversation, but Mariah still felt like she needed to lean closer to Lawrence to keep their conversation going.

"My boyfriend is a really handsome, really rich cowboy. Is that what you're saying?"

"I don't know about the handsome part," he said, his face taking on a ruddy quality. "But yes, I wanted to talk about the money. It's not an issue, is it?"

"Why would it be an issue?"

"Uh, well." He cleared his throat. "A couple of my brothers have had trouble with women once they've found out how—about the money."

"What kind of trouble?"

Lawrence shifted in his seat and took another big bite of his sandwich. Mariah herself had employed a similar tactic on a date when she didn't want to talk, so she recognized the move. He finally finished eating and said, "I don't want to tell all their stories. Let's just say trouble. I've seen enough of them date, get married, divorced, and then remarried—or not—to know that I need to talk about the financial stuff with the women I'm serious about."

"Oh, so we're serious."

Lawrence's smile slid right off his face. "For me, this is serious."

"Me too," she said quickly, though her stomach quaked at the thought. "I..." There was still so much she needed to tell him. She reminded herself she had time, because Lawrence hadn't even really kissed her yet.

He'd once said on the third or fourth date, and maybe she'd let him. She'd definitely let him, because the mere memory of the kiss he'd instigated in the orchard a couple of weeks ago was enough to make her body flush.

"You what?" he asked, popping a few chips.

"Nothing," she said. "Let's do a hypothetical." She pushed her salad around her plate. "If we get serious enough to get married, let's say. Would I be signing a prenuptial agreement?"

He ducked his head, all the answer she needed. He said, "Yes, probably," anyway.

She poked another bite of salad and put it in her mouth, trying to figure out how she felt about such a prospect. If she had "more than six" zeros in her bank account, she might want to protect what she had.

"I trust you," he said, as if he could read her mind and knew about the doubts flying through her head. "It's just... I've seen what money can do to people, and while I don't think...what I mean is, I think it'll just be better if...I'm messing this up pretty badly." His face flushed red, and he actually pulled at his collar. "Sorry."

"It's okay," she said. "I think I can see where you're coming from."

"Ian's first wife didn't really love him," he blurted out. "She only married him for the money, and she got quite a lot of his too. He's a huge proponent of prenuptial agreements, and I don't know." Lawrence fiddled with his silverware, which he didn't need for his lunch. "That's all."

"Wow," Mariah said, staring at Lawrence. "That's crazy."

"The world has a lot of good people in it," he said. "But it has some bad ones too." He blinked rapidly. "Not that I think you're a bad person. Oh my word. I'm never talking again."

Mariah laughed, the sound starting small and growing. "It's okay, Lawrence," she said between giggles. "I understand." She wasn't sure if she did completely or not, but she would if she had a bit more time to think it through.

He let a few minutes of silence go by as they ate, and when they were ready to leave, he said, "Do you want to go horseback riding on Saturday?"

"I think I humiliated myself plenty the first time," she said, linking her fingers through his.

"It gets easier every time you do it," he said.

She glanced at him, a little unsure if he was teasing her or not. "Okay," she said. "But if I come out to Bluegrass again for horseback riding, you have to do something I want to do."

"What do you think the Wildflower Festival was?" he asked.

"I mean an activity," she said. "Like yoga or something."

"Do you do yoga?"

"No," she said, pulling back a laugh. "But something like that."

"What would it be?" he asked, leading her around to the passenger side of his truck.

"Roller blading or something."

He grinned at her and took off his cowboy hat, reseating it on his head. "Do you own rollerblades?"

"Not at the current moment." She giggled as she tiptoed her fingers up the front of his shirt.

"So you'll be deciding the activity I have to do at a later date."

"That's right," she said. She took his collar in her fingers, drawing him closer to her. Was that too obvious? Could she kiss him, or should she wait until he made the first move?

His hand slid along her waist, and he leaned in further without any more encouragement from her. His other hand came up behind her head, sliding down to the back of her neck. "Thanks for making time for lunch."

"Anytime," she murmured.

He drew in a slow breath, and Mariah's brain misfired. She barely had time to inhale before his lips touched hers, and she experienced the second-best kiss of her entire life, right there in the parking lot.

CHAPTER 14

Duke yelled and raised both his hands as he moved toward the rearing horse. Conrad fell backward, and a panicked whinny filled the air. Duke's heart fired wildly in his chest, but he'd been knocked to the ground plenty of times. Not always by a horse either.

"Whoa! Ho there!" He waved his arms above his head and dodged as the horse landed on his front feet and darted forward. Duke lunged for the rope Conrad had secured around the animal's neck, his fingers burning.

He managed to grip the end of the rope and yank hard. "Whoa. Whoa."

Conrad got up in a flash, didn't bother to dust himself off, and ran toward Duke. He reached up higher on the rope and pulled too, adding his voice to the commands to stop. The horse tossed his head, and Conrad spoke in a softer voice.

He was the horse whisperer of the family, and the dark

gray stallion he'd been working with for only two days started to calm. "There you go, Horace," Conrad said, moving closer to the horse. He put his other hand on the animal's neck, which seemed to calm it further.

"Got him?" Duke asked.

"I think so," Conrad said over his shoulder. He'd lost his cowboy hat when he'd fallen, and his breathing still came in great gulps. "Can you stay for a bit just in case?"

"Sure," Duke said, releasing the rope. He walked over to where Conrad's light brown hat lay on the ground and picked it up. He returned it to his brother, who used one hand to settle it on his head. Then Duke climbed the fence in the small paddock Conrad used to start breaking horses, and sat on the top rung to watch.

Conrad was very good with horses, that much was certain. He'd definitely inherited Daddy's calm demeanor and natural tendency to communicate with horses on a wavelength they understood. Duke could do the same thing to a lesser degree, and he'd tried to learn the skill to keep up with Conrad.

It had taken him almost a decade to realize that the skills Conrad possessed couldn't be learned. They were innate, and some people were simply better than others at specific tasks. Duke had a more analytic mind, and he didn't mind sitting part of the day behind a desk. He loved the notebooks he'd kept over the years, and he had the perfect system down to monitor and document the breeding side of Bluegrass Ranch.

They made a lot of money from the horses they sold

every year, and a large part of that came from the work Duke did. He knew he was vital to the well-being of Bluegrass Ranch, but he operated behind the scenes most of the time, while Conrad and Ian took most of the public glory.

Spur received a fair bit of public credit too, though he hated it. He'd much rather it go to someone else, and Duke had learned over the years that his oldest brother just loved the ranch, horses, dogs, and working. No one loved working more than Spur, and a wave of exhaustion hit Duke.

He liked being out in the sunshine too. He loved wide blue Kentucky sky on a pristine summer day. He loved horses and the way they could calm his spirit. He loved the way they moved, and he loved the loyal way they enjoyed running around a track. Duke had never been happier than when he was in the saddle, out in a wild part of the ranch.

Conrad kept the gray horse still for several long minutes. Long enough that the horse cocked his back leg. Only then did Conrad start to walk with Horace, keeping him near the middle of the paddock. The closer the horse got to a rail, the more nervous it became until it learned that the rail wasn't going to attack him.

Duke enjoyed the wavering sunshine as clouds moved through the sky until Conrad signaled to him that he didn't need to stay. Not a moment later, an alarm went off on his phone, and Duke pulled it from his back pocket.

"I've got a meeting," he called to his brother, and he jumped down from the fence. He hurried through the ten-minute walk to the small office he shared with Lawrence, glad his brother wasn't there. Duke didn't need privacy for his meeting, but he liked it.

He quickly set up his phone on the stand he'd carved for video meetings like this, and he tapped to make the call to David Stansfield. He owned one of the biggest stud farms in the Lexington area, and he liked to schedule his entire breeding season in a three-day event. Duke had signed up for a thirty-minute slot the moment David's secretary had sent out the schedule, and there would be no cancelations and no rescheduling.

He typed in his name and the name of his ranch, and then waited for someone to connect the call. He was let in, but David wasn't there yet. Duke hated being on this side of the equation, and he much preferred it when breeders came to him, wanting to bring their studs to Bluegrass. The ranch owned nine previous Derby winners, a couple with only a year or two left in their breeding careers.

Most people thought the money made in horse racing came from winning the big races, but Duke knew differently. More money came every year from the breeding rights the ranch owned, and Duke tried to keep horses at Bluegrass that would continue to bring in money through reproduction.

"Afternoon, Duke," David said, his smile pleasant. He was only two minutes late, and Duke reached up to touch the brim of his cowboy hat.

"Afternoon, Dave."

"Let's see," David said, glancing down. "You've got Everybody's Hero in the lineup if you want him." He looked up at the screen. "If you can put him with one of your Derby winners, I'll take fifty grand off the stud fee."

"What dates?" Duke asked, flipping open his notebook. His Derby-winning mares took up the front of his current notebook, and he knew exactly when they might be ready for a stud to visit.

David outlined the three available options for Everybody's Hero, and Duke found a place for him with Sunflowers and Sins. "She's really personable," Duke said. "I don't think there will be any problems."

David nodded and scratched out a note. "I've got a risk, if you're willing." He glanced up, his eyebrows raised. "He's poised to win the yearling race at Belmont, and he's been named one of the top five horses to watch for next year's racing season. I'm offering Cloudy With a Chance for real cheap, but your foal might be worth a ton more if he wins."

"I can take a risk," Duke said, flipping a couple of pages. "We've got a three-year old heading to the Derby this year, and they might be the perfect storm of risk."

They worked through that deal, and Duke then asked, "What about Beastly Boy? Does he have openings? Or I've got Warhammer who has slots if you've got mares."

"Beastly Boy is full," David said. "I'm taking a waitlist for him."

Duke tried not to let his disappointment show, but he'd been trying to get Beastly Boy to Bluegrass for a couple of years now. The horse wouldn't be a stud forever, and every year made him less and less valuable.

"Put me on the waitlist," Duke said. "But we're almost

full too, so even if he does come up, I might not be able to take him."

"I understand."

"What have you got for Warhammer? I have Stakeout Springs and Runs for Money with space."

"Uh, let's see." Duke turned more pages and found the schedule. They went back and forth, throwing out possibilities and prices. Duke's head started to pound, and he hated this round and round with big breeders. He just wanted to make a phone call and talk for a few seconds. Everything felt so hard—and definitely more complicated—this year.

Finally, David said, "I'm sorry, Duke, but maybe it won't work out this year." He glanced off-screen. "I have another call."

"Of course," Duke said. He gave David his best smile and thanked him for his time. The call ended, and Duke sighed as he sat back in his chair. "That was kind of bust, honestly." He slid the notebook to the side so he could see his oversized desk calendar.

He kept track of scheduled appointments here, and he transferred them to his computer once he got back to the homestead and his bedroom. He penned in the two horses he was able to schedule for covering season, and he stood as his stomach growled.

Hungry, slightly annoyed, and with class in only thirty minutes, Duke needed to get back to the homestead and check to make sure he was ready for his presentation today. The familiar tiredness moved through him, but he pressed against it. He wouldn't be tired like this forever. His fifteen-week ranch management course would be over before he knew it, and he really was learning a lot.

He exhaled heavily as he grabbed his phone and headed for the exit. Right as he reached for the door, it flew inward, smacking him right in the face.

"Ow," he cried, stumbling backward as he dropped his phone and both hands flew toward his nose. He tasted the tinny tang of blood on his tongue, and the warm stickiness of it met his fingers.

"What in the world?" he said, plenty of disgust in his voice. He looked up through the pain radiating through his face, his eyes watering, and he expected to see Lawrence.

Instead, he saw a gorgeous brunette who caused him heartburn with a single thought. "Lisa?" he asked. "What are you doing here?"

CHAPTER 15

Lisa Harvey scowled at the sight of blood seeping between Duke Chappell's fingers. She wiped that look off her face as his eyes finally seemed to focus on her. "I'm sorry," she managed to say past the lump in her throat and the pounding of her heart. "I didn't know you were there."

"Obviously." He wasn't going to give her a pass, though she wasn't sure why she expected him to. The last time they'd been together on this ranch, he'd been so angry with her—for probably a good reason. She'd regretted that interaction since, and she'd been trying to find a way to apologize to him—and everyone else she'd dealt with on that very awful day.

He glanced around for something, and Lisa assumed tissues. "Are there any paper towels out here?"

"A dispenser by the sink about halfway down the row," he said, his voice muffled and nasally.

"I'll get you some," she said, ducking out of his office quickly. She hurried to the sink and pumped the paper towel dispenser. She wetted the wad of towels, squeezed them out, and turned to find Duke had followed her.

"I'm sorry," she said again, thrusting the wet paper towels toward him.

"It's fine." He took the paper towels and began wiping his face. He turned away from her a moment later, and she let him have the privacy he wanted. A few moments later, he asked again, "What do you want?" and not in the nicest of voices either.

"I wanted to stop by and see if..." Lisa exhaled and then drew in another breath. "I wanted to apologize, Duke."

That got him to turn toward her, and she couldn't hold his gaze. "What?"

She turned toward the sink again and pumped out more paper towels. After ripping them off, she got them wet again. She squeezed the water out and faced him. "Can I?" She indicated his face. "You've missed some spots."

His eyes narrowed, and it took him several seconds to nod. "Okay."

She reached up and gently wiped his right cheek, moving slowly and gently toward his nose. "I don't think it's broken."

"I don't think so either," he said, his voice much softer. "Why are you apologizing to me?"

As close as she now stood, she couldn't really meet his eyes. She glanced up toward the dark depths of them anyway, noting that hers were definitely a deeper brown than his. He was still handsome and touched with danger, and Lisa sure did like that in a man.

Focus, she told herself. She hadn't come here to get a date. Not the romantic kind, anyway.

"Because I feel bad about the way we ended things last time," she said, wiping a clean part of his face now. "You are a real client, Duke. I shouldn't have said you weren't."

"I haven't called Bruce again."

"I appreciate that."

He hesitated, and Lisa finally stopped stroking his face. She forced herself to pull her hand away and back up a couple of steps.

He cleared his throat and stared at her. "Thanks for apologizing. You could've just texted."

"I was in the area."

Duke cocked his head, almost like he could hear the lie in her words. No one was ever in the area of Bluegrass Ranch. It sat out on the northwest side of Dreamsville, and it was definitely one of the farthest ranches from the main epicenter of Lexington. They didn't do tours or allow the public on their ranch—except for the one race they'd done a few months ago and their sales events.

"Okay," he finally said. "I apologize too. I didn't realize you'd taken over all of the scheduling."

There was so much he didn't realize about how things worked at the Harvey farm now. Lisa herself wasn't even sure of that, and the next breath she took in shook in her lungs. She opened her mouth to say something, but nothing came out. She didn't know what to say. She'd spent so long in denial about her father's health condition, and the rest of her time was spent fighting with her brothers, Bruce and Kelly.

"Daddy's sick," she blurted out, her eyes widening in the next moment. A breeze kicked up then, and Lisa turned her face into it, trying to get more oxygen into her lungs. Then maybe her brain would start working, and she'd stop telling Duke—a man she barely knew—all of her family's dirty laundry.

"I'm so sorry," he said softly, and Lisa had no idea the man could use such a tone of compassion and kindness. His touch landed on her arm, and while the autumn afternoon was still warm, Lisa shivered. She flinched, and Duke quickly removed his hand from her skin.

"What's going on with him?" he asked. "I mean, you don't have to say. I've known your dad for years, though. He's a good man."

"He's been in the hospital the past couple of weeks," Lisa said, folding her arms and keeping her focus out on the ranch, away from Duke. "He originally went in for a routine physical, but his white blood cell count is elevated."

"Cancer," Duke said, and she nodded. She'd said the C-word in her own quiet moments, but she didn't like telling people her dad might have cancer.

"They're still doing a lot of tests," she said. "But he's not feeling well. He's lost some of his mobility, but of course, he's been out in the stables and row houses every blasted day anyway." The worry ate at Lisa's patience, and she could snap at anyone, for anything. She knew that all too well when it came to Duke.

"It was a bad day the other day. Last week. Whenever I argued with you." She cut a look at him out of the corner of her eyes. "I wasn't in a good place, and I shouldn't have snapped." She nodded like she'd come to say what she needed to, and now that it was done, she would be okay.

"I don't even have an excuse," he said. "Maybe I'm just a monster."

"You're not a monster," she said. "You were frustrated."

He sighed and moved over to the fence that separated the row house from the patch of grass running in front of it. "Yeah. I suppose I was." He leaned down into the fence, his voice quiet and contemplative.

Lisa joined him, because it sure did feel nice to stand next to another human being who wasn't mad at her, who wasn't trying to push her away, or who wasn't trying to tell her she had no place on the family farm where she'd worked for the past twenty years.

"You'll let me know if I can do something for him?" Duke asked, tipping his chin down in her direction. "Or your family? I can send out dinner or help with your scheduling. I'm really quite good at it, and I'm real organized."

Lisa looked up and into his eyes, the moment seizing and stopping when she did. Duke's throat worked as he swallowed, and Lisa let herself get lost in his eyes. "I think we're okay right now," she managed to say, her voice slightly robotic.

"I can shovel stalls and drive big trucks with trailers

attached," he said, his own voice rough around the edges. "Just so you know. Don't hesitate to ask me. Wayne's been a good friend to me here. Blaine knows him real well too, and once I tell him, you won't be able to stop him from doing something."

A smile touched Duke's mouth, and Lisa wondered what it would be like if her mouth could touch his.

She blinked, utterly shocked by the train of thoughts currently moving through her head. "Thank you," she said, tearing her gaze from his. Could he feel that current running between them? Or was she just so mixed up emotionally right now that she could do something potentially crazy?

"You don't need to tell Blaine," she said. "Daddy's kind of private. I had to strong-arm him to even text his brother and let him know." She let a smile cross her face, though her father's insistence that he was "fine" wore on Lisa's nerves as much as anything.

"If it comes up, I'll tell him," Duke said. "Otherwise, I'll just hold it to myself."

"I'd appreciate that." Lisa took a deep breath, as she was holding so much deep inside her. If she stood here for much longer, talking to this kind man, she'd tell him everything about Bruce and Kelly, how her place in the Harvey family had never been very secure, and she knew her step-brothers were both trying to get her out of the family business.

She knew that was why she was clinging so tightly to making all of the appointments for the Harvey studs. She'd sent countless emails and texts to all their clients, asking them to please book through her. She needed to show Bruce especially that she was important to the business, that she knew what she was doing, and that he and Kelly wouldn't survive without her.

"I stopped by to see if you were still interested in King Arthur," she said.

Duke turned fully toward her, and Lisa couldn't ignore him when he gazed at her with those powerful eyes. "Really?"

She smiled and ducked her head. A lock of her hair fell forward, and she tucked it back behind her ear. "Yeah, he's not booked out yet. Just another, uh, bad moment for me." Heat filled her face, and she glanced toward the office door. "If you have a minute to look at your schedule, I'll pull up what we've got on my phone."

"Sure," he said, grinning at her. He had beautiful, straight, white teeth and full lips that once again had her mind derailing with thoughts about kissing. Kissing *Duke Chappell*.

Thankfully, he moved away from her, and Lisa paused a moment to take a deep breath before she followed him. Shutting herself in a tiny office with the tall, broad-shouldered, charismatic cowboy didn't seem like a good idea. Not if she wanted to maintain her focus and get back to the family stud farm, where she needed to check on Daddy and then clean out stable G.

CHAPTER 16

L awrence chuckled as Mariah started to giggle, breaking the kiss they'd been sharing. "I should get back to work," she whispered, her fingers still knotted in the collar of his jacket. She didn't back up and give him any breathing room, and she was a whiz at making up excuses for why she and Lawrence needed to sneak down the hall from her office and get in a few stolen kisses.

"Go then," he whispered. "Thanks for carving out an hour for lunch." The ranch sat a healthy distance from her office, and Lawrence had been making the drive to see her for their midweek lunches. He took her to dinner sometimes, and she came horseback riding at the ranch on the weekends.

She had yet to take him along to any yoga classes or romantic comedies. She kept teasing him about this thing she was going to make him do as payment for all the horseback riding. She seemed to like it, as she'd been to Bluegrass to ride several times now. She could get on and off her horse easily these days, and he'd caught her whispering secrets to Reid the last time they rode.

She kissed him again, and Lawrence sure did like the feel of her lips against his. He liked the shape of her in his arms. He liked the scent of her as it filled his nose. He could take the fruity, clean scent with him when he left, and the memory of the way she sighed was enough to fuel him until he could see her again.

Mariah broke the kiss and leaned her forehead against his. "So you'll go to that Halloween party with me?"

"What are we going to be again?" Lawrence really didn't enjoy dressing up for Halloween. He normally didn't have a reason to, as there was still plenty of work to do around the ranch and the only thing the Chappells did was have a chili dinner at their parents' house.

Mom had already texted the family string about the Halloween dinner, which would be complete with corn-bread, chili, pecan pie, hot apple cider, and fresh pumpkin doughnuts. Lawrence had invited Mariah to the family dinner, as four of his brothers would have their wives and fiancées there.

Lawrence and Mariah had been dating long enough for him to invite her, but he hadn't told his mother yet. He would...soon.

"And it's not on Halloween, right?" he asked. "Remember, you're coming out to my parents'?"

"It's the night before," she said. "I thought we could go as Keith Urban and Nicole Kidman," she said, "Then you can still be a cowboy, and you won't want to break-up with me." She grinned up at him, and Lawrence smiled down at her.

"Maybe this could be that thing you keep threatening me with," he teased.

"Oh, no, Mister," she said. "I'm saving that for something really good. Like...a restaurant that only serves salad."

Lawrence laughed, and Mariah's smile sure was beautiful as she disentangled her arms from around him. "Okay, cowboy," she said. "I'll see you tomorrow night? Dinner at my place?"

"Yep," he said. "Text me if you need me to bring anything."

"I've already got my grocery order in," she said. "See you then." With that, she turned and walked back toward her office. Lawrence watched her go, giving himself a couple of moments before he left.

He made the drive back out to Bluegrass Ranch, but instead of going past the homestead and out to the row house where he worked, he made the turn before even getting to the house. He drove down the dirt lane and around the ranch toward where Spur and Olli lived.

Soon enough, his parents' house came into view, and Lawrence didn't have a couple more minutes to gather his thoughts, because his mother was out in her flowerbeds, cleaning them up for the winter.

She looked up at the sound of his truck approaching, and Lawrence cursed himself for getting the vehicle with the big, throaty engine. Mom dusted her hands against one another as he pulled in the driveway, and Lawrence waved to her, putting a smile on his face.

His pulse thumped against his breastbone as he got out of his truck. Mom walked toward him, her smile wide and genuine. "Lawrence," she called. "What brings you by?"

"Oh, nothing," he said, but he didn't just drop by this house for nothing. Some of his other brothers had made peace with their mother, and Lawrence needed to take advantage of this opportunity. "Actually, I wanted to talk to you."

His mother couldn't be more than a hundred and twenty pounds, and she had a smear of dirt across her forehead. She wore gardening gloves and a pair of dirty jeans, along with a T-shirt that had a logo so faded Lawrence couldn't even tell what it was anymore. She ran in the mornings, and she'd raised eight tall, opinionated boys while Daddy worked the horse farm day and night.

She had plenty of authority, and she'd ruled their house with an iron fist. Lawrence hadn't been afraid of her, but he hadn't wanted to disobey her. He hadn't been like Conrad and Duke, who seemed to think all family rules had only been made to be broken. Spur gave Mom and Daddy quite a bit of grief for a couple of years there, and Blaine was no saint.

Now that Lawrence thought about it, Mom had dealt with a lot, but that was what families did.

"Should we go inside?" Mom said. "I can get out some banana bread."

"Sure," Lawrence said. He followed Mom into the

garage, where she left behind her gloves and then went up the few steps to the house entrance. Lawrence did love this house, as it had big, open spaces. Daddy had designed it so he and Mom could live on a single level as they grew older, and they'd made sure to have a large, nearly industrial kitchen so all the boys could come for family dinners.

Mom busied herself with getting out banana bread and making coffee. While Lawrence buttered a piece of bread, he said, "Mom, I'm going to bring someone to the Halloween dinner."

She sucked in a breath a moment before the shattering of ceramic filled the kitchen. Lawrence flinched and spun around to find she'd dropped a coffee mug and broken it. She stared at him with such wide eyes that annoyance sang right through him.

He rolled his eyes and bent to pick up the larger shards of ceramic. "This is why I haven't come to talk to you about her," he said. "You act like me going out with someone is the most shocking event ever to happen in Kentucky."

"I do not," she said.

"Mom," he said. "You literally just did." He straightened and pulled out the garbage can, dropping the broken pieces into it.

"I didn't mean to," she said. "I just...even when you do date someone, Lawrence, you don't bring them to the ranch to meet the family."

"Maybe we just never made it to that stage," he said.

"And this woman—what's her name?"

"Mariah."

"You and Mariah...you are to that stage?" She handed him a dustpan and hand broom.

"Halloween is another month away," he said, bending to start sweeping up the broken pieces.

"I'll get the tiny shards," she said. She pulled off a couple of paper towels and got them wet. He traded places with her and let her finish cleaning up. "So how long have you been seeing Mariah?"

"About six weeks," he said, going with when she'd shown up at the orchard. "A little over the summer that wasn't very...serious." He hadn't lied. He and Mariah hadn't been very serious in the couple of months over the summer where he'd gone to all of her parties. Mom didn't need to know about the break-up and weeks without Mariah.

"Remember, Halloween is another month away," he said. "But things are going well, and I asked her to come with me. It's not a problem, is it?"

"Of course not," Mom said. "There's plenty of room for anyone who wants to come." Her smile grew and grew, though the homestead could house more people than Mom's place. She simply loved entertaining, and she didn't mind cramming a lot of big cowboys into a small space. "I can't wait to meet her."

"Mom, you're not going to go crazy with this," Lawrence said, his chest tightening again. "That's another reason I came over." He had no idea how to talk about this. "Even if I wasn't dating Mariah, you know I wouldn't want you to set me up with anyone, right?"

"I know," she said. "I stopped when you asked me to."

"Sort of," he said. "You pestered me with at least three more potential dates."

Mom opened her mouth, her eyes searching his. "I'm sorry, Lawrence." She put one hand over her heart. "I will not set you up with anyone ever again. And I will be on my absolute best behavior on Halloween when Mariah is here. I swear."

She looked so sincere and so earnest, and Lawrence couldn't stay mad at her. He stepped forward and took her into a hug. "Thanks, Mom."

"Please forgive me," she whispered. "I've done some stupid things over the years, but never anything to hurt you intentionally."

"I know that, Mom."

She sniffled, and guilt cut through Lawrence. "Don't cry, Mom. I'm not upset with you."

"Right now," she said. "But you have been."

"Maybe a little," he said.

"I will be so good when I meet her."

"Please don't make it a big deal." Maybe he could get Duke or Conrad—or both of them—to bring dates to the dinner party too. "Please."

"I won't, I won't." She stepped back and continued getting out mugs for the coffee. "Tell me about her. Where did you meet her? What is she like? Do you have any pictures of the two of you?"

Lawrence returned to his banana bread and butter to give himself a couple of moments to think. He took his bread around the island and sat down. "Yeah, I've got a picture of her." He tapped on his phone and opened his gallery. He and Mariah had taken some selfies together a few nights ago on a wagon ride they'd taken at Sweet Rose Whiskey's Fall Festival.

He found a good one, his and Mariah's faces pressed close together, both of them smiling. They looked really happy, and Lawrence smiled just looking at the picture before he passed his device to his mother.

"Where's Daddy?" he asked as she peered down at the phone.

"Lawrence, she's gorgeous." His mother looked up, once again with wide, surprised eyes.

"I can get women who aren't trolls to go out with me," he said, reaching for his phone. "I know I'm not Duke or Conrad, but I'm not a bad catch."

"You're a brilliant catch," Mom said, passing back his device. "I didn't mean to imply differently."

"You didn't say where Daddy was."

"He's out on the ranch," Mom said. "He promised me he's not riding, but I'm pretty sure he is. Have you seen him saddle up out there?"

Lawrence looked blankly at his mother, not sure how to lie to her about this. "I don't know, Mom. You'll have to ask him." He ducked his head and hid his face from Mom with his cowboy hat.

"I knew he was," Mom said, sighing as she got up. She poured herself a cup of coffee and opened the fridge. She got out a plastic restaurant container with chocolate cake in it.

"I'm eating this to prepare for a little chat I'm going to have with your father."

"I think that's my cue to leave," Lawrence said, stuffing the last of his bread in his mouth.

"Lawrence," she said, cracking open the lid on the cake. "Listen...don't stay away so long, okay?"

"Okay, Mom," he said, all kinds of awkwardness moving through him. He turned back to her and saw the hope in her eyes. She had apologized, and he had high hopes that she would be on her best behavior at the Halloween shindig.

He went around the island to her and drew her into another hug. "I love you, Mom."

"Love you too, son."

Lawrence left through the front door and out in his truck, he quickly texted his dad to let him know that Mom was eating chocolate cake in preparation for "a little chat."

Uh oh, Daddy said. *She knows about the riding, doesn't she?*

I couldn't lie about it, Lawrence said.

I don't expect you to, Daddy said. *You were out to see Mom today?*

Yeah, Lawrence responded. *I told her about my girl-friend and that I'm bringing her to dinner on Halloween.*

That's great, Lawrence, Daddy said. *I'm sure that meant a lot to your mother.*

Lawrence knew it meant a lot to Daddy that his sons were trying to make things right with Mom. Things weren't perfect between them yet, but Lawrence had just completed a hard conversation with her, and coupled with the ones he'd had with Mariah, Lawrence felt like he wasn't quite as soft as he'd once been.

As he pulled out of his parents' driveway, he smiled to himself. He was happier than he'd been in a long time, and he sure did like Mariah. Things were going well between them, and he couldn't wait to see what the next month would bring.

CHAPTER 17

Mariah waved to Lawrence as he passed her SUV, the sight of him in that big, black truck, wearing that big, black cowboy hat, accelerating her pulse. She liked that he still stoked her fire every time she saw him, and she tucked her wallet-purse under her arm so she could open the lift gate.

She got the back open, and she pulled the box with his costume to the edge of the car. Dressing him up as a sexy cowboy wasn't going to be that hard, and she didn't like carrying around props all night long. If she could get him in the V-neck T-shirt, that would be enough for people to know who he was, no guitar needed.

"What's all this?" he drawled, his footsteps slowing as he neared.

She turned toward him as a gust of October wind kicked up. He immediately reached up to press his cowboy hat to his head, and Mariah shivered as the breeze brought a chill with it.

"Your costume," she said.

"You said I could be a country music star."

"Keith Urban has a certain aesthetic," she said, opening the flaps on the box. "So you can wear jeans and your cowboy boots. I would prefer no hat, but I don't think you leave the house without a cowboy hat." She looked at him, her eyebrows raised.

Lawrence simply shook his head, his smile of the devastating sort. "He's a country music star. I can wear a cowboy hat." He stepped closer to the back of the SUV and peered into the box. "What is this?"

He pulled out the V-neck and shook it out. The light blue shirt had a darker blue swirling pattern across it, and she'd been able to see her hand through the fabric when she'd held it up.

"I can't wear this," he said.

"That's what he wears," Mariah said, taking the shirt from him. "I got your size and everything."

"This is not big enough for me," he said, settling his weight on his back foot.

"You said extra large," she said, glancing at the tag in the collar of the shirt.

"In a men's size," he said. "That is a shirt for ladies."

Mariah laughed and shook out the shirt. She held it up to his broad shoulders, and she thought he probably had a fair point. "You'll have to try it on," she said among the giggles.

"If Conrad or Ian sees me in this, I'll never hear the end of it."

"They won't be at the party." She put the shirt back in the box. "If you don't wear the shirt, you'll just look like a regular cowboy." She reached up but hesitated before removing his hat. "May I?"

She'd seen him without his hat on, obviously. He kissed her better without the brim getting in the way, and his hair was definitely long enough to part down the middle and "Urban up."

Lawrence ducked away from her. "What are you going to do?"

"It's Halloween," she said, almost whining. "My favorite holiday ever. Can you stand to wear a T-shirt and *not* wear a cowboy hat for two hours?"

"Come on. Your company party will be way longer than two hours." He did take off his hat and run his hand through his hair.

"Your hair is definitely long enough to turn into Keith Urban," she said. "We can mess it up a little, part it in the right place... With the V-neck, everyone will know who you are. Your other option is to carry around a blow-up guitar for the whole night."

The look of horror on Lawrence's face should've been captured on film, and Mariah couldn't help laughing again. She stepped over to him and started running her fingers through his hair, pushing some of it this way, and the rest of it that way.

She about got it split down the middle, and if she had a

spray bottle and a comb, maybe a little bit of gel, she could achieve some serious Keith Urban hair. "What do you think? The shirt and the hair?"

"What are you going to wear?"

"I'm having Jane do my hair, complete with a replica of the headband she wore to the American Music Awards a few years ago. I'm going to wear my makeup the same way, and I've got this really awesome gold dress."

His eyebrows went up, and a light switched on in his eyes. "Yeah? A gold dress?"

He smoothed his hair back and reset his hat on his head. "Okay," he said. "I'll take the V-neck home and try it on." He nodded toward the art gallery. "Can we go in? It's starting to rain."

"Yep. Let's go." Mariah closed the back of her SUV and linked her arm through his. "Have you been to this gallery?"

"Do I look like the type of man who goes to art galleries in his spare time?"

She giggled again, some of the magic she always felt on their dates seeping into the air between them. "You don't even have spare time."

"Hey, I took a half-hour nap yesterday." He slid her a look out of the side of his eyes. "Right there at my desk."

She grinned at him. "Yeah? Did you hit your head when you conked out?"

"That was last week."

They entered the gallery together, as the outer doors had been propped open. He stepped in front of her to get the next set of glass doors, and Mariah entered the heated space ahead of him.

She took a deep breath, because she loved the smell of art galleries. She loved the bright lights positioned just-so on the paintings. She loved the cleanliness of the lines, and she loved how furniture didn't clog the space. Humans used entirely too much furniture, in Mariah's opinion.

She turned back to Lawrence as he slipped his hand into hers, and he glanced around as if he were trying to break out of prison without getting caught. He'd confessed he didn't get out to "refined" places like this, and Mariah had told him she wouldn't take more than two steps away from him all night.

"Ready?" she asked.

"Yes," he said. "We're just looking?"

"Yes," she said, smiling up at him. "Susan has a couple of pieces here somewhere. When I see her, I'll introduce you." She led him into the bigger space, where more people mingled. On a thin side table, trays of hors d'oeuvres and champagne waited, but Mariah wasn't going to drink tonight.

"I've seen a couple of these pieces before," Mariah said. "They belong to the owner of the gallery."

"So you've been here before?"

"Oh, several times," she said. "I used to date this guy named Kevin Douglas, and he was the most talented sculptor. He knew a lot of artists, and we came to a lot of exhibits." She stepped up to a particularly beautiful painting of aspen trees in the fall. "I love these yellow leaves."

"They're great," Lawrence said.

"Yeah, Kevin knew a lot of interesting people," she said. "He'd take me to the neatest little clubs and these tiny restaurants." She wandered to the next painting, this one of a pair of wild horses running as fast as they could. "Once, we went to this bistro with only four tables. We had to wait for a while, but it was okay, because in the middle of the place, they had an elevated floor, and every twenty minutes, a new musician would get up and perform."

"Wow," he said.

Mariah glanced at him, but he didn't look away from the painting. Something shook in her stomach, and Mariah didn't know what to do about it.

"I like this one," he said.

"Yeah, they're horses."

He grunted and immediately turned away from the painting. She'd definitely said something wrong, but she didn't know what. She went with him to the next painting, but this one was abstract. She didn't know what to say about it, and Lawrence wasn't going to say anything.

They stood there awkwardly for a couple of seconds, and then they both moved at the same time. By the third painting, Mariah felt ready to snap. "What did I say?" she asked.

"I like more than horses," he said, his voice tight. "I know about more than just horses."

"I...know," she said. "I didn't say you didn't."

Lawrence released her hand and walked away, saying, "I'm sorry I'm not very interesting."

"Hey," she said, practically lunging after him. "I didn't say you weren't interesting."

"But I'm not," he said. "I don't have any cool clubs or tiny little restaurants to take you to." He didn't stop at the next painting, and Mariah thought this date would be over in five minutes at the pace with which he moved. The art gallery wasn't that big, and she caught sight of Susan in the corner, talking to two men.

"So what?" she asked, trying to keep her voice down. "Have I ever complained about that?"

"You just did."

"I did *not*," she said, grabbing onto his arm. He paused and turned toward her, but she didn't know what else to say. "You're interesting."

"Am I? What's so interesting about me?"

Mariah searched his face, but the river of darkness running across his face told her she better get this answer right. Unfortunately, she didn't know what to say to reassure him that of course she found him interesting.

"Mariah, hello."

She turned toward Susan, half-relieved and half-annoyed at the interruption. "Susan, hi." She could hear the falsities in her own voice, but she leaned in to hug her friend. "We're almost to your things."

"I've sold them both," Susan said, the excitement in her eyes obvious. "But stop by. And did you see who I was talking to?" She stepped next to Mariah and pointed to the corner, where the two men she'd been talking to still stood. "Kevin Douglas is here. Did you see his pottery?"

Mariah's heart stalled completely, and she could only stare as she recognized Kevin's medium brown hair and very square jaw.

"I'm just going to talk to Carrie real quick," Susan said. "I'll be right over." She grinned and walked away, and Mariah felt like someone had turned all of her bones to wood. They didn't quite move right, and they for sure couldn't hold her weight.

"I need to go," Lawrence said, and he didn't waste a moment before heading toward the same doors they'd entered through.

With him gone, her sight-line to Kevin and his friend was unobstructed. Kevin caught her eye and lifted his hand to wave, his face lighting up.

Go, she told herself. *You go right now. Go after Lawrence!*

She tore her eyes from Kevin and told herself she could call Susan and apologize later. Right now, she had to figure out how to fix what she'd inadvertently broken with Lawrence.

CHAPTER 18

Foolishness raced through Lawrence, driving every stride to be longer than the one before it. No wonder he didn't come to art galleries.

He liked steak and sandwiches. Was that so wrong? He didn't plan very interesting dates, but no one had ever complained before.

"Yes, they have," he grumbled to himself as he entered the light, misting rain outside. "That's why they break up with you or won't go out with you again." He reached into his pocket and pulled out his keys. He didn't need them to unlock his truck, but he felt a little bit like stabbing something, and the keys would accomplish that.

"Lawrence," Mariah called behind him. A fair bit of panic accompanied his name, but he didn't slow down or stop. He'd humiliated himself enough for one night. For a lifetime.

He knew he wasn't interesting. He knew he didn't have

a whole lot to offer someone, especially a pretty, interesting woman like Mariah. She interacted with a lot of different people, and she liked live music and funky places to eat. She must be so bored with him, and that final thought drove him to move even faster.

It was a real testament to her that she caught him before he made it to his truck. She panted as she darted in front of him, holding up both hands. "Please, will you wait?"

Lawrence came to a full stop, using all of his energy to glare at her. He didn't know what to say, which was about his normal—a fact he hated with all the power of the sun. The rain increased, getting his shoulders and cowboy hat wetter with every passing second.

Mariah wiped her hair back and looked up at him. "I didn't mean to imply that an ex-boyfriend is more interesting than you," she said, her chest still heaving. "He's not. We're not together for a reason, obviously."

"Oh, yeah? Why aren't you still with him? His art wasn't good enough? He didn't know enough local artists?"

"No," she said, clearly flustered. "Lawrence, I like *you*."

"You didn't even know me when you were dating him."

She heaved a great big sigh, and Lawrence felt her frustration boiling down inside his gut. He felt the same way, and all of those negative feelings were aimed at himself.

"I didn't mean to imply that you'd like the painting of horses because you only know horses."

Lawrence pressed his teeth together, because he realized his behavior was fairly childish. "This is not your issue," he said, indicating they should keep walking. "It's mine. I'm working on it."

"What issue is that?" she asked, going with him.

"I don't really want to talk about it."

"I'm starving," Mariah said as they approached his truck. "You said we could go to dinner after the gallery."

"The thought of taking you to a chain restaurant has my stomach in knots," he said. "I can't do it."

"Lawrence." She stepped closer to him and put both hands on his chest. He could only feel the pressure of her touch through his jacket, and he did start to calm with her nearness. "This is what couples do. They help each other with their issues."

"What could I possibly help you with?"

"Remember how you told me I was bossy and over-bearing?"

"I did not," Lawrence said instantly. He fell back a step, and she dropped her hands. "When did I say that?"

"When you told me you didn't want to wear what I was bossing you to wear." She looked at him with wide eyes. "I *was* bossy and overbearing. I've been working on it."

The Halloween costume did remind him of the way Mariah had once told him what shirt to wear, and how she'd bought him a new pair of cowboy boots because his were too dirty. But it was Halloween, and she loved the holiday and she'd gone to the trouble to get him the costume so he didn't have to think about it.

He'd try on the shirt, and he could wear it for a few hours.

"So tell me what you're working on," she said, closing the space between him again as the rain picked up. "I don't want to trigger you again."

"I feel like an idiot that I got triggered," he muttered, ducking his head.

She slid her fingers between his, both hands into both of his. "Lawrence, you can tell me. You can trust me."

He looked up and into her eyes. The parking lot was lit with orange street lamps, and they stood almost directly underneath one. The glow of it on her hair made her bright blonde hair almost pink, and Lawrence found her absolutely stunning in the rain.

"I know I'm boring," he said. "I am. I'm dull and uninteresting and I've never been able to keep the attention of a woman for very long."

"We've been dating for a while now," she said. "And I'm really happy with you. I like going horseback riding, and I've enjoyed all of our dates." She smiled at him, but it didn't make Lawrence feel any better.

If anything, her reassurances made him feel weaker.

"I don't want you to pity me," he said.

"I don't," she said.

"I don't need to be reassured," he said. "I am who I am, Mariah. Yeah, I live a simple life on the horse ranch, but I like what I do." He bit back what popped into his head, because he didn't want to admit he was comfortable at Bluegrass Ranch.

He *was* comfortable there, and maybe it was time he

broke out of his comfort zone. The problem was he didn't know how.

He'd work on it.

"What about Security Zone for dinner?" he asked, wrapping his arms around her. "They have that bowling alley, and maybe tonight won't be a total loss."

"Okay," she said. "Will you bring me back here to get my car, or should I drive myself over?"

"I'll bring you back," he said. As he reached to open her door for her, he kept her close. "I'm sorry I ruined the art gallery."

"You didn't," she said. "Though I think you should've met Kevin."

"Yeah? Why?"

"Then you'd know how much better than him you are."

* * *

Lawrence shimmied into the V-neck T-shirt, hating the silky feel of it against his skin. He took it off again and started to dig through his laundry for his white tank top. He'd worn that yesterday at Mariah's work party, and she hadn't said anything.

They were just going to dinner at his parents' that night, and no one would come trick-or-treating out at the ranch. Lawrence wanted everything to go well, and he'd told everyone in the family he was bringing Mariah.

They'd all promised to be on their best behavior, but Lawrence had seen the Chappells at their best and their worst, and sometimes it was hard to tell the difference between the two. Several of his brothers had met her before, but that didn't stop the nerves from cascading through him with the force of a swiftly-moving current.

"I hate this shirt," he grumbled as he pulled it over his head again. When this night ended, he'd burn it, that was for certain. No one should ever have to wear a see-through V-neck, especially a man.

Lawrence had looked up Keith Urban, and while he knew his music and admired his talent, the man was definitely not a cowboy. Lawrence had felt like a giant just looking at pictures of him, and it was no wonder Mariah had had to size up this flimsy V-neck to a double-XL.

He told himself he could wear the T-shirt to avoid carrying the inflatable, cartoon guitar, and he pulled his boots on and went downstairs. Mariah's laughter floated toward him from the kitchen, and he found her there with Ginny and Olli. The three of them laughed about something, and Lawrence paused to watch how effortlessly she fit in with Spur's wife and Cayden's fiancée.

She really did, because Mariah could talk to anyone. She was articulate, and she knew how to get people to talk about themselves. She caught his eye and lifted her eyebrows, her gaze sliding down the length of his body. She nodded her approval, and a rush of heat moved through Lawrence's body.

"Oh, my goodness," Olli said, coming out of the kitchen and approaching Lawrence. "You're right. A simple V-neck, and he's Keith Urban."

"I've got to do the hair," Mariah said, reaching for the spray bottle and comb she'd brought.

"I hate the hair," Lawrence said.

"It's part of the fun of Halloween," Olli said with a grin.

"Oh? Is that why you're literally wearing a denim skirt and a blouse?" Lawrence asked her. "What are you supposed to be?"

"I'm not in my costume yet," she said. "This is all I have that still fits, Mister." She pierced him with an icy glare, and Lawrence raised both hands in surrender.

Ginny wore a red turtleneck, but he'd seen her shimmy into the lobster costume once tonight already.

"Where's Cayden?"

"He's putting on his chef's hat," Ginny said. "He said it's the only thing he'll wear." She went into the living room and retrieved her lobster body off the couch while Mariah pressed on Lawrence's shoulder to get him to sit down.

He did, a bit begrudgingly, and let her spray his hair, work the sticky gel through it, and then comb it into the most ridiculous hairstyle in the world. What man parted his hair right down the middle?

Lawrence's wasn't anywhere near as long as Keith Urban's, but he had let it grow out a little the past few months. He hadn't meant to; he'd just been busy around the ranch, busy dating Mariah, and busy trying to make things right between him and Mom.

The party tonight would go a long way with that, if everything went well. He almost blurted out that they didn't need to go tonight, but he caught the words before they left his mouth. He'd told Mariah that several times, and each time, she assured him she wanted to meet his parents and all the brothers, and she "couldn't wait" for the party.

Without her, Lawrence might honestly attend for dinner and then make an excuse to leave.

Cayden came down the hall, saying, "I don't want anyone to make a single comment."

Ginny gave a little squeal and hopped on over to the end of the hall. "Come on out, baby."

"I hate Halloween," he grumbled, and Lawrence could relate to that really well.

Cayden appeared next to Ginny, and she squealed again. "You wore the jacket. Thank you, love." She tipped up and kissed him, as if dressing up like a lobster and a chef wasn't awkward enough.

Cayden wore his jeans and cowboy boots too, but he'd put a white chef's jacket over his normal polo. He wore a tall, white chef's hat instead of his normal cowboy attire, and his face definitely held more of a flush than normal.

Men like Cayden weren't cut out for Halloween. Lawrence was surprised Ginny liked it so much, but she said she'd spent so much of her life dressing up in fancy ball-gowns and playing a part it was like every day was Halloween.

Now, she got to choose what she wanted to wear, and she'd literally gone with the least serious thing she could find.

Cayden glared at Lawrence, who glared right back while Mariah kept pushing his hair left and right, trying to get it just perfect. She finally deemed it good enough, and Lawrence got to his feet.

"All right," he said, blowing out his breath. "Let's go get this done."

"Why do you sound like you're about to die?" Mariah asked, swatting at his chest. "It's *your* family party."

"That's exactly why," Lawrence said as Cayden said, "You just said why."

"Stop it," Ginny said. "Your family is great." She met Mariah's eye and shook her head. She joined Mariah in her gold ball gown, and Olli led them all down the hall and out into the garage.

Lawrence watched them go before meeting Cayden's eyes. "What are the chances we can just stay here?"

"Zero," Cayden said, patting him on the shoulder. "It'll be okay, Lawrence. Conrad and Ian will want to be in the spotlight, and Mom has all the heaters going on the decks. Just take your doughnuts out there and enjoy your time with Mariah."

Lawrence nodded, but he knew he couldn't go into a family party with a plan. The chaos that existed when all the Chappells got together was unpredictable, and he'd just have to roll with whatever came his way.

CHAPTER 19

M ariah smoothed her hair back and readjusted her headband as Lawrence pulled up to a two-story house that looked well-taken care of.

"Nervous?" Lawrence asked.

"To meet both of your parents, all seven of your brothers, and all invited significant others?" Mariah looked at him, and he seemed to just now realize the gravity of the situation before them. "Yeah, I'm a little nervous."

Lawrence grinned at her and nodded. "You're not the only one."

"We probably can't sit out here," she said. "I've already seen the curtains flutter twice."

"My mom might be a little anxious to meet you," he said. "The last time I came out here, she kept asking me questions about you."

"What kind of questions?"

"What does she do for a living? Is her family still here? Did she grow up here? How long have you been seeing her? Do you like her? Are you going to get married?"

"Wow," Mariah said. "She asked all of that?"

"All of it," Lawrence said. "And more. My mother is the Queen of Questions." He glanced from her to the house and back. "I should've warned you about that specifically."

"I've met mothers before," she said, smiling at him. "I think I can do it."

"I think you can too." He opened his door and got out of the truck, glancing toward the house.

Mariah watched it too, and the front door opened. One of the Chappell brothers came out onto the porch. He didn't look super happy with whatever was happening inside the house, and Mariah's nerves tripled.

He went down the steps and around the side of the house in quick steps, and Lawrence watched his brother for an extra moment before he came to open her door. He looked somewhat troubled too, and none of these cowboys seemed to know how to relax at a party.

Her door opened, and she slid out of the truck, flashing Lawrence a smile. "Who was that?" she asked, nodding in the direction his brother had gone.

"Conrad," he said, glancing over his shoulder in the direction Conrad had gone. "He didn't look happy."

Maybe it was because he was currently dressed like a mailman, if mailmen wore cowboy hats.

"Does he get along with your mother?" Mariah asked.

"I thought so," Lawrence said. "I mean, well enough. Most of us keep the peace with her, and some of us have started to figure things out."

"What do you two need to figure out?" she asked as they started toward the house.

"Uh, Mom liked to set me up on blind dates." Lawrence slowed his step. "Implying that I couldn't get my own date. Then she'd want me to come over and tell her everything that happened on every date. It was exhausting."

"Sounds like it."

"She even tried to get me to go out with someone named Nancy right after we started dating."

Mariah giggled, the ice in her chest finally cracking up enough for her to start to feel more normal. Lawrence led her up the steps and reached for her hand before he reached for the door handle. Just like she'd promised not to leave his side at the art gallery, he'd told her he wouldn't let his mother steal her too far from him.

She'd met Ginny and Olli at the homestead, and they were surprisingly easy to talk to. She knew them both from her work on the Summer Smash, particularly Ginny, but she was much more relaxed when not working on a project.

Plus, Ginny understood what Halloween was supposed to be—fun.

One step inside the house, and Mariah knew Lawrence's mother knew how to throw a good party too. Creepy music played through the house, but it wasn't too loud to make conversing too hard.

Several people milled about in the kitchen, and she and
Lawrence had started to join them when the door opened
behind them. Another couple came in, and Mariah turned
to see Tam and Blaine. Relief hit her, and she released the
breath she hadn't known was trapped down inside her lungs.

"Tam, hi," she said, stepping over to the other blonde.

"Mariah." They embraced, but Tam wasn't the super
touchy-feely type, and the hug didn't last long. She indicated
Blaine. "You remember Blaine."

"Of course. Hello."

Blaine finally looked away from Lawrence and at
Mariah. A smile bloomed on his face, and he shook Mariah's
hand too. "I didn't know you and Lawrence were dating."

"Yes," Lawrence said quickly. "I put it on the brothers
thread, and you even responded."

"He hasn't been sleeping much lately," Tam said, linking
her arm through Blaine's. "Don't listen to anything he says."
She gave him a meaningful look, and they clearly continued
their conversation without saying a word.

Mariah didn't like that, though she had started to be able
to know what Lawrence was thinking just by meeting his
eyes.

They went into the kitchen, which spanned across the
back of the house. Windows ran along the wall, with a break
for some cabinetry.

"There you are," a woman said, and Mariah turned
toward Lawrence's mother. She was barely five feet if she was
an inch, but she clearly didn't take any attitude from anyone.

She had a powerful spirit, and her smile matched one Mariah had seen on her son's face plenty of times.

"Hey, Mom," he said, squeezing Mariah's hand at the same time. "This is Mariah Barker. Mariah, my mother, Julie."

"So nice to meet you, dear," Julie said, reaching to shake Mariah's hand.

"You too," Mariah said. "Lawrence obviously gets his smile from you."

Her eyes lit up even more. "I've always said that too. Most of the boys look so much like Jefferson. He's got the long, straight nose and those long eyelashes. But his clones have a crooked smile. Mine is straight." She glanced into the kitchen as a couple of people burst into laughter.

"Lawrence, Cayden, and Ian look more like me," Julie said. "A little lighter, with those straight smiles."

"I can see that now," Mariah said. "Of course, I don't know which one is Ian, but I did meet Cayden at the homestead."

"Ian's the one in the white cowboy hat," Lawrence said. "Over by the door. He's standing next to Spur. My oldest brother."

Mariah spotted the two men he'd referenced. Neither of them was smiling at the moment, but now she kind of wanted to see the Chappell men all lined up and smiling so she could analyze who looked like Julie and who looked like Jefferson.

Then she remembered she literally had dozens of photos

with that exact thing. "Have you seen the photo that will be on the billboard?" she asked Julie.

"No," she said. "Do you have it?"

"On my phone," Mariah said, extending her hand toward Lawrence. There was no way she could carry her phone in her gold dress, and Lawrence had carried it at last night's party and he'd agreed to do so again today.

"When is the billboard going up?" Julie asked.

"Any day now," Mariah said. "We're waiting on the truck we need to dig a hole deep enough to hold the pole."

"You're going to let us know, right?" Lawrence asked. "I meant to ask you about it, because Cayden wanted to do a big thing."

"What kind of big thing?"

"Oh, a family gathering or something." Lawrence lifted his hand, and Cayden came over. "She said the billboard is going up any day now."

"How much notice will we get?" Cayden asked Mariah.

"About a week," Mariah said.

"That's enough time to get everyone there when it happens and then organize a meal after." He looked at his mother. "Right, Mom?"

"Absolutely," she said, seemingly gleeful. "Oh, Jefferson, come meet Lawrence's Mariah."

"Mom," he said. "It's just Mariah." He cut a look at her. "She's not mine. I don't own her."

Mariah smiled at him and laced her arm through his. She leaned into his bicep, and she sure felt like she was claiming him. He leaned his head down, creating a small, intimate space for the two of them amidst chaos.

An older gentleman came over, along with another brother, and Julie indicated her. "This is Mariah Barker. She and Lawrence are dating."

"My daddy, Jefferson," Lawrence said. "And my brother Duke."

"Nice to meet you both," Mariah said, wondering if she'd be able to keep all the names straight. She shook their hands, reciting the names. *Jefferson, Duke, Julie.*

Lawrence. Her eyes darted over to the back door. *Ian. Spur. Blaine. Tam.*

Ginny. Cayden.

Olli.

And the brother who'd left already... Conrad.

She counted quickly in her head. Seven brothers. His parents. The women were much easier to keep track of, but Mariah's mind felt like it was about to explode. She couldn't pinpoint who wasn't there, though she felt like she should know.

The front door opened, and a little boy ran through it.

Of course. Trey—the last brother to arrive. His wife Beth, and his stepson, TJ.

"Gramma, Gramma," TJ yelled as he ran toward them. "Look at my costume." He wore a Batman costume with the fake muscles, a long, billowy cape flying out behind him.

"Oh, my," Julie said, giggling as she scooped the little boy right into her arms. "Who's this superhero in my house?"

He lifted his mask and grinned at her. "It's me, Gramma."

"Oh, TJ," she said, hugging him tight. "Look at you. How was school?"

"His teacher deserves a medal," Beth said as she arrived in the kitchen. She set down two loaves of fresh bread and gave Julie a quick hug.

"Okay, everyone's here," Julie said, setting TJ back on the ground. "Let's eat. Everyone come into the kitchen." She stepped away from Mariah, her voice growing louder with every word she spoke. "Over here, everyone. Jefferson."

The man thinned his lips and whistled, the sound nearly deafening for how close he stood to her.

"Dad," Lawrence complained. "We're in the house."

"Mom wants everyone in the kitchen. Spur, find Conrad, would you?"

Spur nodded and started tapping on his phone. A few seconds later, the mailman—Conrad—came in the back door and barely took one step inside the kitchen before taking up a position against the wall.

Mariah faded out of the way with Lawrence, and she was glad to do it. He had a lot of siblings, and with the guests they'd brought, there really were a lot of people in the house.

"You okay?" Lawrence asked, his lips very close to her ear.

She shivered and nodded.

"We can get our food and go eat on the deck," he said just before his mother did.

"There are heaters out there," Julie added. "So feel free

to stay in here or go outside. We'll be doing the doughnut on a rope and bobbing for apples in forty-five minutes."

Mariah's eyebrows went up at the traditional, old-school autumn games. Not to mention Julie's commitment to a schedule. Most people would just say they'd do the party games after they ate dinner.

She watched the dark-haired powerhouse flit around the kitchen, getting out jams and plastic cups. Then everyone seemed to know exactly when she was ready to say grace, and anyone wearing a hat of any kind took it off and bowed their heads.

Jefferson said the prayer, thanking the Lord for their family and that they could all be there that Halloween. "We're so grateful for the additions to our family as well, and please help those that aren't quite used to a meal with nine men to forgive us and find a way to enjoy themselves."

"Amen," someone said, and a whole slew of male voices chorused it back.

She'd barely opened her eyes before the crowd surged forward to get plates and start getting food from the long line of dishes on the counter. Lawrence wasn't one leading the charge, and that was just fine with Mariah.

She normally enjoyed parties, and once she and Lawrence got their food and went out to the deck, the noise level decreased, and she found that the table out there had two spots left. The other four had been taken by Spur and Olli and Blaine and Tam.

"Is this okay?" Lawrence asked under his breath.

"Totally fine," Mariah said, though she could've stayed

inside and been okay too. But she suspected Lawrence was more comfortable out here, and she wanted to be with him, so she sat down at the table where no one was talking and glanced around. The awkwardness descended from the darkening sky, and Mariah breathed it in, and then said, "So, Olli, tell me about the latest scent you're working on."

CHAPTER 20

Blaine didn't mind when others carried the conversation. He knew how to talk when he wanted to, and he didn't need to be the standout cowboy in the family. Conrad, Ian, and Duke seemed to need to be in the spotlight, and that was just fine with Blaine.

He and Tam had come outside during dinner, because the noise level inside was almost unbearable for him. For any human being, in all honesty. He almost hadn't been able to get Tam to come, and while he could've made the announcement about why and where she was without her, he didn't want to.

Everyone would've understood, but then he would have to stand there alone to accept their congratulations.

Tam was already struggling with her pregnancy, and Blaine wanted her to see how excited his family would be for them. They'd told her parents and one of her sisters, and they'd shown a great level of enthusiasm as well. Tam still cried every morning when she was sick, and she'd actually lost weight in the past six weeks since they'd found out she was pregnant.

He glanced at her as she said something to Mariah about the saddle she was making right now. She didn't want to give up her craft to be a mother, and they'd had a lot of conversations about what life would be like come next summer.

Blaine was thrilled to be a father, and he knew the moment Tam saw their baby, her worries, doubts, and fears that she would not be a good mother would vanish. She claimed not to be feminine enough to raise a girl, and she'd sobbed and sobbed at the possibility of having a daughter.

For a week or so there, Blaine thought she might need to see a therapist, but she'd worked through the feelings, and she mostly just got frustrated with her symptoms. She had about three weeks left in her first trimester, and all the websites—as well as their doctor—had said she should start to feel better soon.

Blaine knew she wouldn't be better in her mind though, and he wondered if he should mention seeing someone again. She'd be a great mother, because she was Tamara, and he knew who she was deep in her core.

No, she didn't do frilly hair or wear a lot of makeup. He'd assured her over and over that those things didn't make a good mother.

She claimed she wasn't nurturing, and he argued that she nurtured him just fine. They had two dogs she adored. A baby would be no different.

The fact was, Tam was not very good at change, and introducing a tiny human into their lives would be a huge change.

He met her eye and smiled, glad when she already wore one. They spent most of their social time with her sister, Stacy, and Stacy's boyfriend, or Spur and Olli. Blaine had always had a great friendship with Spur, and the two couples went to dinner or stayed home if Olli had the gumption to cook for them.

Spur was as Spur as ever, though some of his rougher edges had been worn down by Olli. In Blaine's opinion, that was a good thing, and he couldn't wait to watch his older brother become a father first. Maybe then Blaine would know what to do.

Olli started to get up from the table, and Spur turned toward her and leapt to help her. "You okay, hon?"

"Just fine," she said, sort of pulling her elbow away from his hand. "I'm just going to get that apple pie and bring it out here." She gave everyone a sweeping smile in only the way Olli could, and she headed for the house, Spur staying on his feet and watching.

"You seem tense," Blaine said as the frown deepened on his brother's face.

That broke the spell on Spur, and he sat back down. His chair scraped on the deck, causing Blaine to twitch. He said nothing, because if given enough silence, Spur would start to talk.

"How long have y'all been married?" Mariah asked, and Blaine turned his attention to her. She didn't seem to understand the concept of silence, and she'd kept the conversation going by asking all the women at the table question after question. Normally, Blaine didn't mind that, but there was something going on with Spur and Olli.

"Spur and Olli got married last August," Lawrence finally said when no one else answered. "Tam and Blaine just got married at the end of May." He nodded at Blaine, who blinked his way back to the conversation.

"I was at that wedding," Mariah said with a friendly smile.

Beside him, Tam tensed. Blaine slid his hand from his lap to hers and pressed his palm against her thigh. She wanted kids, but whenever she somehow got reminded of how early into their marriage that was going to happen, she started to spiral.

"What about Trey and Beth?" Mariah asked.

"They got married at the end of last year," Spur said.

"Oh, I thought you went to something for them this summer," Mariah said, glancing at Lawrence.

"Theirs is a complicated situation," Lawrence said. "I'll explain it later." He practically mumbled by the end of the sentence.

Mariah started to ask something else when Spur jumped to his feet and darted toward the door. "Olli," he chastised, and Blaine met Tam's eye as he turned to see what was going on.

"I'm fine," Olli said, but she relinquished her hold on the apple pie she'd managed to procure. "You're being over-protective."

"Am I?" Spur asked, glaring as he came back to the table. He practically threw the pie, and it skidded toward Lawrence, who actually flinched and leaned away, as if he'd be covered with apples, cinnamon, and sugar by the end of the night.

"Okay, what's going on?" Blaine demanded, looking from Spur to Olli.

"Nothing," Olli said.

"You almost killed Lawrence with an apple pie," Blaine said. "What's he smothering you about now?"

A triumphant smile lit Olli's face, and she spun toward Spur. "See? Your own brother—"

"Has no idea what's goin' on," Spur growled, cutting a look at Blaine. He looked back to Olli. "I'm going to tell them."

"You dig your own grave," Olli said.

Spur drew in a deep breath, his broad shoulders lifting higher and higher. He held the air in his lungs for a moment, and then pushed it all out. Every second of silence that passed increased the tension, but Mariah didn't jump in with another question, thankfully.

"Olli's fallen a few times in the past couple of weeks," Spur said. "I'm allowed to be concerned and want to be extra helpful for my pregnant wife who keeps falling down."

Falling down didn't sound good. The body didn't just fall down for no reason. Blaine's eyes flew to Olli, needing to hear her reasons for falling.

The door behind them opened again, letting out a rousing round of laughter. "See? They are out here.

Hoarding the apple pie too." Ginny and Cayden approached the table, both of them smiling. "Oh, we interrupted something." She scanned everyone sitting outside, her eyes finally going to Olli. "What's going on?"

"Your best friend has fallen a couple of times," Spur said, getting to his feet. "And she thinks *I'm* the one who needs to see a doctor." He glared at his wife. "I'm going to get the ice cream." He practically stomped away.

Ginny and Cayden pulled over a couple more chairs, and everyone shifted to make room for them. "You're falling down?" Ginny asked.

"Just twice," Olli said, her voice pitched high. "I'm fine. The first time, the toe of my flip flop just caught on the step. It was nothing I haven't done before." She rested her hands on her seven-months-pregnant belly. "I'm a little top-heavy right now. Front-heavy. Off-balance. He thinks there's something wrong with me, and I told him there is—I have his huge cowboy baby growing inside me."

She glared at the back door, and Blaine could only blink at her.

Someone started to laugh, the sound low and slow at first. Lawrence's chuckle broke the tension on the deck, and before he knew it, Blaine was laughing too. "Huge cowboy baby," he said, glancing at Tam. She'd reached across the table and taken one of Olli's hands in hers. Olli smiled around at everyone, though she did still look a little upset.

"Why'd you fall the second time?" Ginny asked, slicing into the pie as if they were talking about how it might snow next week.

"Because I'm a slob, and I left my shoes on the floor," Olli said, sniffling. "I have to go to the bathroom about every twenty minutes, and my bladder doesn't care if it's day or night. So I got up to use the bathroom in the middle of the night, and I tripped on my shoes. That's all." She looked at Ginny, and they had a long moment of unspoken conversation. "I swear."

"Have you talked to the doctor about it?" Tam asked.

"No," Olli said. "I don't go for another couple of weeks, and I'm *fine*." She glared at the back door and then sighed, the fight leaving her expression. "But now I can't take two steps without him leaping up as if someone's set his belt on fire."

"What about the baby?" Mariah asked. "Do you feel like...I'm sorry, I don't know if you're having a boy or a girl."

"They don't know either," Lawrence said.

"Oh, okay." Mariah flashed him a grateful smile. "Do you feel like the baby is okay?'

"Yes," Olli said firmly. "I can feel him moving and he's just as ornery as his father. I'm fine. We're fine. He's overreacting."

"It's kind of what Spur is good at," Blaine said quietly. "Especially when it comes to you, Olls."

Olli met his eye, hope entering hers. "Could you talk to him?"

"Absolutely not," Blaine said quickly.

"Come on," Olli said. "He listens to you better than anyone." Her voice had turned into a whine by the end of the sentence. "I can always tell when he's talked with you, because he's so calm."

Blaine appreciated that, but no. He wasn't going to talk to Spur about being concerned about his pregnant wife. He shook his head, and thankfully, Spur called, "I'm coming back out, so y'all can stop talkin' about me." He returned to the table with a fistful of bowls, spoons, and a five-gallon container of vanilla ice cream. "Mom says there's no cake."

No one said anything, not even Mariah. Blaine surveyed the group, and he figured he might as well start revealing his and Tam's news with these brothers right here. Mom would forgive him for not telling her first—he hoped.

"I have some news," Blaine said, clearing his throat. Tam's hand came down on his like a vice, but they'd already agreed he'd tell his family about her pregnancy at this Halloween dinner. He met her eye, searching her face for the sign that he should abort.

She smiled and nodded, and Blaine leaned over and pressed a kiss to her temple. "The Lord has blessed Tam and I with a baby," he said, a smile forming on his face in a slow, joyous way. "She's due at the beginning of June."

A beat of silence draped the deck and everyone on it, and then Olli squealed, her tone only matched by Ginny's high-pitched voice saying, "Oh, that's *so* wonderful, Tam."

CHAPTER 21

Ginny Winters mixed the mustard, mayo, and pickle juice together in a separate bowl from the potato salad. Traditionally, she started and ended summer with one of her favorite foods, but the warmer months had given way to a near-winter in Kentucky.

She needed the potato salad, though, because she only had seven weeks until her wedding, and another one of Cayden's brothers was going to have a baby. That would be all three of them currently married, and Ginny felt more failure moving through her now than she ever had before.

She couldn't provide Cayden with a baby, and they hadn't told anyone but Spur and Olli. When Blaine had announced that he and Tam were expecting a baby next summer, Ginny's first reaction had been excitement. She did want to be the most amazing aunt to the Chappell babies, just like she'd tried to be for her brothers' children.

The longing deep inside her to be a mother wouldn't go

away. She could soothe it with food, or staying busy, or even with therapy and meditation. It never truly went away though, and Ginny pressed her eyes closed and sent a silent prayer to heaven that she could find a way to cope with this.

It certainly wouldn't be the last time someone in Cayden's family announced a pregnancy at a family party. She couldn't eat two pieces of pie and take home three caramel apples every time someone talked about babies.

The heat in her house blew, keeping out the chill that had come this week. She still lived in the farmhouse north of town that she'd rented over the summer, and she needed some time to figure out what to do with the house she owned on Virginia Avenue.

She'd made things right with her mother, and she still worked at Sweet Rose, albeit only about half as much as she once had. She'd hired an event coordinator just after the Summer Smash, and Carla was handling all of the events at Sweet Rose this holiday season.

All Ginny had to do was prepare for her wedding.

She wanted to marry Cayden as soon as possible, but the truth was, she was a Winters. The only Winters female, and the heir to the entire fortune and empire. If she and Cayden snuck away and got married in a private ceremony some-where, the media would seize upon the story. If she and Cayden took their time and made every step of the wedding available to the press, they'd take everything special to her and cheapen it.

Ginny was trying for a wedding somewhere in the middle. She needed to give her media contacts *something* so they'd leave her alone, but she really just wanted to elope. Mother would never forgive her if she did such a thing, and Ginny could admit that was why the idea held some of its merit.

She mixed together the potato salad and tasted a bite. "Needs salt," she said, tossing in a healthy pinch. Another stir, another taste, and Ginny deemed it her best batch yet. She covered the bowl with aluminum foil and put it in the fridge.

The binders she'd been using to plan the wedding waited for her on the kitchen table, and Ginny sighed as she walked toward them. She might as well get today's tasks over with. Then she could take the dogs out for a stroll in the countryside and try to rid herself of the melancholy feelings about her inability to get pregnant.

She sat down and flipped open one of the binders. Today, she needed to order the centerpieces for the wedding dinner. She wanted as many flowers as she could get, and she'd narrowed her choices to three only yesterday.

She studied them all again, her mind wandering to other topics. Perhaps she should look at what it would take to adopt a baby in the state of Kentucky. She and Cayden both had plenty of money. Maybe she should look at international adoptions.

Her mind raced forward, and she thought of children in the foster care system, and children whose parents might be in jail or otherwise in trouble. Perhaps she should open her home to them. To all of them.

Ginny never had small ideas, and this one grew and grew

and grew until she realized she was jotting down notes about starting a foundation through Sweet Rose to fund activity centers for underprivileged kids of all ages.

She thought of the house on Virginia Avenue. No one lived in it, and the building was easily big enough for a dozen children. She could hire a caretaker, and she could house kids. Try to give them an upper hand in a life that had dealt them bad cards.

She sighed and looked down at the binder with the photos of the flower arrangements. Minnie, Sarge, and Uncle Joe all napped at her feet, and they all perked up when she stood. "Come on," she said to the three dogs. "Let's go for a walk."

Maybe the answers she needed would come to her under the open sky. She put on her shoes and jacket, made sure she had her gloves, and opened the back door. Sarge charged outside, leading the way with a few barks. Minnie and Uncle Joe followed a little slower, and Ginny left the house last.

She walked and walked, letting the time go by and allowing her mind to wander where it wanted as well. She was no closer to any answers by the time she returned to the house, but she took one look at the flower arrangements in the binder and made her decision.

Her stomach grumbled and she pulled out the now-chilled potato salad to enjoy. As she ate, she texted the florist her choices for the centerpieces. She'd just finished feeding cubes of potato to the dogs and herself when the doorbell rang.

The dogs flew into a frenzy, their nails skidding on the

hardwood floors in the farmhouse as they raced toward the front door. They were all bark and no bite, but Ginny could admit they could sound ferocious.

"Enough," she said, following them. "Go in the office. Go." She waited until all three of them had trotted into the nearby office. Minnie and Sarge would stay there, but Uncle Joe would make a break for it the moment Ginny opened the door.

She twisted the knob anyway, not sure what to expect on the other side of the door. Cayden didn't need to ring the bell, and no one else ever came to the house.

A man stood there with a huge flower arrangement in his hands. "Virginia Winters?" he asked, his eyebrows raised and almost under the ball cap he wore.

"Yes, sir," she said.

"These are for you." He grinned at the mass of roses in his hands, and Ginny took a deep, heady breath of them as she took them from him.

"Wow," she said. "They're beautiful." The arrangement had deep, red roses, pale white ones, and light pink blooms.

"There's a card pinned in there," he said. "Have a great day."

"You too." She stepped back and called for Uncle Joe to get back in the house. The little dog stood at the top of the steps and watched the delivery man go, ever the guard dog. He finally turned and trotted back inside, and Ginny closed the door behind him.

"These are so beautiful," she said, returning to the kitchen. They'd be from Cayden, and he'd have written the most perfect words inside the card. He always seemed to know how she was feeling, and he knew the exact antidote to give her when she needed one.

She set the heavy vase on the countertop and started digging through the greenery and leaves for the card. She found it, and sure enough, her name had been scrawled in Cayden's cowboy handwriting on the outside of the envelope.

Ginny didn't need to open it. She pressed the small card to her pulse and breathed in the scent of the gorgeous flowers. She didn't want the huge wedding, with literally everyone in Dreamsville invited. She hated that she'd had to write a press release announcing her own engagement and the date she and Cayden would be married.

She knew her family was a big deal in Kentucky, and Cayden's was too. Combined, the two of them would be hosting a wedding celebration for a thousand people, and the only thing Ginny had insisted upon was no press at the actual event. To appease them, she'd given them little details and insider looks at the preparation of the wedding, and a new article about the event came out every week.

The weight of the world settled back onto her shoulders the moment she opened her eyes. Did Cayden feel like this too? Would he run away with her tonight, get married, and keep it a secret until the announced big day?

She picked up her phone and dialed him.

"Hey, sweetheart," he drawled, seemingly distracted. "I'm assuming you got the flowers."

"Yes," she said, her emotions spiraling and lodging right

inside her throat. "They're wonderful, Cay. Thank you so much."

"Hey, you're not crying, are you?"

Almost, Ginny wanted to tell him. She sighed as she went into the living room and collapsed on the couch. All three dogs converged on her, settling against her thigh and hip and each other. "No," she finally said. "But Cayden, I want to run away. I want us to just get in the car and drive. We'll stop at the first church we see, and we'll go find the pastor and ask him to marry us. Right there. Wherever we are."

"Ginny," he said softly. Nothing else. Not *we can't do that,* or *I wish we could, sweetheart.*

"Your mother would get over it," she said.

"Yours wouldn't."

"What if we get married tonight in secret? No one in Las Vegas would care. Or even know us. Then, we pretend like we're not married. We'll keep planning the wedding, and we'll have the wedding as planned. No one would know."

"You want to get married twice?"

"It wouldn't really be twice," she said. "We would know we're married at the second wedding, and we could tell the pastor to just make it sound like a vow renewal. Like what Beth and Trey did."

"Then your mother would know," he said.

Ginny blew out a frustrated sigh. "I know. I'm just...I don't want to wait. I just want this done."

"I know that," he said, but he didn't offer any other solutions. "Sweetheart, I'll marry you tonight if you want. You know I will. But one thing I won't do is pretend we're not married. If we're sayin' I-do, you'll not be living out in that house a half an hour away from me."

Ginny's face heated, because of course he'd want her right at his side. She *wanted* to be there, sleeping in the same bed as him, and waking up next to him, and wearing his T-shirts while she made coffee in the house they shared together.

She stared out the window, unsurprised when the rain started to beat against the glass. "We can't get married tonight," she finally whispered.

"I know we can't."

"Will you come as soon as you can?" she asked, hating the pleading tone in her voice. Cayden Chappell just made everything so much easier to swallow. She could breathe when she was with him, and she loved him like she'd never loved anyone before. "Even just bring what you're working on and sit with me."

"I'll be there in an hour," he promised, and Ginny nodded to her faint reflection in the glass. "I love you, Ginny."

"Love you too, Cay."

The call ended, and Ginny leaned over to lay down. The dogs adjusted themselves around her, and she stroked Minnie absently while she closed her eyes and tried to sort through her tangled thoughts. "Dear Lord," she whispered. "Please take some of my burden from me."

She didn't have to specify what that burden was. God knew, and Ginny was so glad he did. Her mind quieted, which was a huge blessing and an answer to her prayer, and Ginny managed to sleep until Cayden arrived.

She opened her eyes when he pressed his lips to her cheek, easily turning her head enough to catch his mouth with hers. "Mm." She loved kissing her fiancé, and he let her carry on for several moments.

Then she sat up and he took the spot where she'd been laying. She leaned against him, and he stroked her hair, no words necessary. "It's getting dark," he said a few minutes later, but neither of them moved to turn on a light.

"Cayden?" she finally asked.

"Mm?"

"What do you think about adoption?"

He tensed for a single moment next to her, then Ginny felt it drain from him. "I think we should look at it," he said, his voice stuck somewhere in his throat. "I know you want a baby, Ginny. You'll be such an excellent mother." He pressed his lips to the top of her head. "I want a family with you."

"We have the dogs," she said tearfully.

"Dogs are not babies," he murmured. "I'm so sorry Blaine and Tam's news upset you."

"I hate that it upsets me," she said. "I should be happy for them. What kind of terrible person isn't happy for a couple who love each other and are starting a family?"

"First, you're not a terrible person," he whispered. "You're human, and human emotions are complicated." He stroked her hair, and Ginny calmed with each touch. "Second, you're happy for them. It's there. It's just buried under your own longing. That's okay, sweetheart. You're happy for Olli, right?"

"Yes," Ginny whispered.

"It just took you some time to get there," Cayden said. "No one—except you—expects anything different."

Ginny nodded and kept her eyes closed. He really did know the perfect thing to say to her, and she knew he'd been put in her life to make up for the weaknesses she possessed. "I want a baby," she said.

"Let's start learning what it takes to adopt one then," Cayden said, and he leaned down to kiss her again.

CHAPTER 22

Lawrence tucked in his shirt and straightened his belt buckle, all while Mother Nature tried to steal his cowboy hat and chill him to the bone. "I can't believe today is the day this stupid billboard is going in."

The sky was practically foaming with black clouds, and it would be a miracle if they could get a picture out here at all. The light felt like soup, and Lawrence glanced toward the highway as yet another pickup truck slowed to make the turn. This one belonged to Trey and Beth, and Lawrence could see both of them in the front seat.

Mariah and the Tourism Office had wanted to do a little ceremony the day the billboard went up. The problem was, the pole-digging company had been behind schedule, and previous bad weather had prevented them from getting the job done sooner. Only a week remained until Thanksgiving now, and the southeastern quarter of the country was preparing for a huge winter storm that had already rolled across the Rocky Mountains and the Midwest.

Everyone in Kentucky had been warned about this storm for a week now, and Lawrence pressed his eyes closed and offered up a prayer. "Dear Lord, we just need fifteen minutes. Please hold back the snow for fifteen more minutes."

The noise from the highway roared through his ears, amplified without his sense of sight. He finally felt the pieces of himself stitch together, and he opened his eyes and turned away from his truck.

After slamming the door, he made his way toward the group that had gathered. Almost everyone in the Chappell family was there, along with Mariah, two men and a woman from the Tourism Office, and the machine operator who'd dig the hole.

The crane truck had arrived ten minutes ago, and the billboard was on its way.

"The driver just radioed," Mariah told him when he stepped to her side. She carried a clipboard and wore the cutest little beanie he'd ever seen. Her blonde hair spilled out the bottom of it and was in direct contrast with her tight-fitting black coat. She wore jeans and a pair of black boots, and she looked absolutely amazing.

He couldn't believe he'd been able to get and keep her attention for over six months now. Every time he thought of it, he experienced a stupor of wonder.

"They're ten minutes out," she said. "We're going to have the eight of you line up just like you are in the picture."

She turned her clipboard and showed it to the crowd. "Exactly the same. We'll get some shots with the hole being dug, which will only take about fifteen minutes. Then, the pole will go in, and we'd love some candids of that. So mill around, talk to each other, all of that."

She returned the clipboard to her chest. "Then, when the billboard goes in, we'll get some pictures and video with all of us. The Tourism officers and the eight of you. A family picture, including Julie and Jefferson and any spouses or significant others." Mariah spoke with a professional tone, and it was clear she'd thought this through and planned everything out. "Then just the brothers with the officers. Then just the billboard once it's in. Okay?"

People nodded and gave murmurs of assent.

"Great," Mariah said. "This is Scott, and he's the photographer." She indicated another man wearing a winter hat. "Do what he says, and let's get the hole dug and some of these pictures out of the way." She nodded, and that acted like the word "go."

People flew into action, and Lawrence found himself getting separated from her and lined up with his brothers. As the sixth brother, he didn't stand near the front. Spur and Cayden took up the two middle positions, with brothers fanning out beside them. Lawrence stood on Spur's side, with Trey between him and his oldest brother. Duke stood on Lawrence's other side, and they all turned a bit sideways and squished in closer together for the photographer.

He yelled out to them, "Smile," or "Okay, now each of

you on the left side put your left hand on your brother's back. Right side, right hand."

He revolved around them, taking pictures while the deafening sound of the drill carved a hole in the earth only twenty feet behind them.

The sound of a police siren bleeped through the air, taking everyone's attention from the happenings out in the field on the side of the highway. The red and blue police lights actually flashed in the darkness, though it was mid-morning.

"They closed the highway," Blaine said.

"Incredible," Trey added. "Look at the size of that pole."

"Let's huddle up," Daddy said. "I want to have a quick prayer." He glanced at Mariah. "Do we have a second?"

"You have about forty-five," she said. "Not one second more." She turned and started toward the officers, who'd gone to greet the policemen who'd escorted the pole to this location.

"Come on, boys," Daddy said. "Momma, you get in here too." They all shuffled and adjusted until everyone in the Chappell family stood in a circle. Beth, TJ, Olli, Tam, and Ginny had joined them, and Lawrence saw a place for Mariah in the circle too. She'd stand right next to him, and he realized she'd somehow become a permanent part of his life when he hadn't been looking.

Did that mean he loved her?

His eyes flew to where she stood with the cops, shaking their hands. If he didn't love her yet, he sure was close.

"Dear Lord," Daddy said. "What an amazing blessing we're witnessing. Please bless us all to get along with one another today and always. Bless our hearts to be forgiving. Bless the weather that it'll hold off for just a few more minutes. Amen."

Daddy had never been one to go on and on in a prayer, and he always stuck in something that caused Lawrence to think. This time, it was the plea that they'd get along and be forgiving. He glanced at Mom, who wore wide eyes and all smiles as she looked around at the people in her circle. She reached up and brushed at her eyes, and that only sent Lawrence's emotions into a tailspin too.

"All right," Mariah barked. "The pole is going in. Scott is filming now, as we're going to make a video of the erecting of this billboard. We don't want you in one big group, so can y'all split into some smaller ones? Couples, small groups, even singles is fine."

The circle broke, and Lawrence only wanted to stand next to Mariah. She was so busy, though, that he turned toward Duke and Spur.

"This is actually pretty amazing," Spur said. "I had no idea how they put these things up."

Lawrence simply nodded as he watched the crane truck maneuver the pole closer and closer to its target. When it finally made it, three men stepped forward to get the pole lined up with the hole. Down inside it went, and they made quick work of cementing it in place.

When Lawrence caught sight of the camera coming his way, he turned to Duke. "How are your classes going?"

"Good," he said, smiling at Lawrence. "I guess we're supposed to be talking casually."

"Yep," Lawrence said, giving his brother a grin too. "Has Cayden said anything to you about what he and Ginny are planning to do once they get married?"

A quick frown crossed Duke's face. "No. What do you mean?"

"Do you think they're going to want us living in the homestead with them?"

"I don't know." Duke's face turned blank, and he glanced at the camera, flinched, and put a smile back on his mouth. "What about you and Mariah? Are you getting serious? You've been seeing her for a while."

"Not long enough to get married and move out."

"No?" Duke asked. "I don't think Spur and Olli dated for as long as you've been with her."

"No one is Spur," Lawrence said, glancing over to his eldest brother, who was listening in on this conversation.

"Hey, I know what I want." Spur grinned and kissed Olli's cheek. He hadn't let go of Olli's hand for a single second, and Lawrence didn't blame him. He'd be concerned if his pregnant wife fell too, no matter what she said.

His mind immediately moved to what it would look like and feel like to have Mariah be his pregnant wife. They'd be married, and she'd be carrying his baby. He felt like a hole had been blown wide open in his heart and brain, but as the pieces slowly came back together, the scenario made sense.

It *made sense.*

She turned toward him, and his smile was instant. As she

approached, warmth filled him from head to toe. He lifted his arm, and she stepped right under it, moving straight into his side as if she belonged there with him.

Of course she did. In that moment, Lawrence realized he was in love with Mariah Barker, and he couldn't stop the unending smile as it filled his face and then his whole soul.

"Here's the billboard," someone called, and they all whipped their attention back to the highway. A huge eighteen-wheeler inched along behind another pair of police vehicles, the flat bed of it filled with the long, rectangular shape of the billboard. It was covered with brown tarps, and Lawrence's heart tapped out an irregular rhythm.

"That's us on there," he said to Duke and Spur.

"I can't believe it," Spur said. "It's kind of exciting. I was expecting to hate this, but I don't."

"You expect to hate everything," Olli teased, and he chuckled with her. As far as Lawrence knew, she hadn't fallen down again, and with only five more weeks until she delivered her baby, she looked uncomfortable and like moving was pretty hard to do.

The semi parked on the side of the highway, and the police officers got one lane of traffic moving by. The noise of it had reduced considerably, but the wind picked up with a vengeance.

"They need to hurry," Mariah grumbled, looking up into the sky. "I'm holding back the weather by sheer will."

"You and me both," Lawrence said, glancing at her. Her nerves wouldn't allow her to smile, and thankfully, the men working on the billboard got it uncovered and hooked up to the crane in only minutes.

Mariah stepped away from him "All right, Chappells. Family picture. Scott."

The photographer started calling out the shots he wanted, and people moved in and out of the frame according to his instructions.

Lawrence only got to stand next to Mariah once, but he'd squeezed her hand tightly, and she'd squeezed back.

The billboard went up quickly, and Lawrence fell back several paces to gaze up at it. He really liked it, and he couldn't stop smiling.

Just then, thunder broke the sky and rolled through the clouds. The wind warned them to seek shelter, and seek it now.

"All right," Mariah yelled. "I'm calling that a wrap. Let's load up before we get stuck out here."

Lawrence made a beeline for her, because she was riding with him. She'd need to have a few conversations, but she'd need to do it quickly.

"We're having lunch at our house," Mom said as he passed, and he nodded. He knew. He got all the family texts like everyone else. Just because he didn't incessantly add memes or the mundane events of his life didn't mean he didn't read the string of messages.

He reached Mariah and took her clipboard. "I'll bring the truck closer."

"I just have to talk to Wanda for two seconds," she said, darting toward the other woman. Lawrence watched her go, marveling at her for who she was. Smart, articulate, educated, gorgeous. She was funny and personable, and she put up with Lawrence and his silence. The horseback riding. The loud family dinners.

If he could get her to say yes to marrying him, he should definitely take advantage of that. He wasn't going to ask today or anything; he wasn't insane. He definitely thought it was time to start talking about their relationship and where she thought it currently sat.

He wasn't great at conversations like that, especially initiating them. He reminded himself that he'd been brutally honest with Mariah in the past, and if there was anyone he should be able to talk to about anything, it was her.

He would bring it up. Maybe not today, as she ran through the first snowflakes toward his truck after a stressful event, but soon.

Soon, he promised himself.

CHAPTER 23

Mariah stuck out like a sore thumb the moment she walked into The Dance Barn. Every person there seemed to be wearing only denim, and Mariah most definitely had missed the memo.

She was supposed to meet Lawrence for dinner and dancing, which were two of her favorite things. He'd called ten minutes ago—while she sat in her SUV in the parking lot —to say there had been an emergency at the ranch, and he'd be late.

"No problem," she'd said. "I'll just go see how long the wait is and get a drink." She'd be fine. She'd waited for plenty of dates in the past.

Not at a place like this, though.

"Just one, honey?" a woman asked, her voice with twice the sweetness of sugar. She plucked a menu from seemingly thin air while Mariah tried to focus on her face. Behind her, the strobing lights made such a feat that much more difficult.

"I'm meeting someone," she said, scanning the floor.

"Oh, go ahead and look." The woman gave her a bright smile and dashed away before Mariah could say a single word.

"I'm the first one here," she said to empty air. Frowning, she turned away from the dance floor, where everyone—including the women—wore a cowboy hat. Panic struck her as Mariah realized this place might have a dress code.

Yeah, she thought. *Denim and cowboy hats.*

That did not make a dress code in Mariah's book, and she giggled to herself that a place named The Dance Barn would even *have* a dress code. It wasn't the country club by a long shot.

To her right stretched the bar, and there were plenty of seats there. Mariah went that way, leaving the flashing, seizure-inducing lights behind. She slid onto a stool, the silky fabric of her flowery dress making the slide easy.

"What'll you have?" the bartender asked. She wore a nose ring and her hair the color of midnight—clearly from a bottle. Mariah sometimes wished she could be more adventurous, and then she remembered she didn't work in a bar. She couldn't even imagine showing up for a meeting with a CEO or the head of the marketing department at some of the companies she worked with wearing a nose ring.

They come out, she thought as her brain misfired.

"She looks like the type to take a mocktail," a man said, and Mariah whipped her attention to him. The handsome cowboy straddled the barstool and sat down, smiling at the woman. "Evenin', Roxy. I'll take my usual." He cut a look at Mariah out of the corner of his eye. "She'll want the mango smoothie."

"You got it." Roxy moved away, unsurprised by this stranger's appearance.

"I don't—" Mariah started, but Roxy had already gone. She glared at the man next to her. "I don't want the mango smoothie."

"Sure you do," he said.

"What is it?"

"It's this fruity, frozen drink. No alcohol. Tastes like paradise." He grinned as he said the last word, waving his right hand in the air as if conjuring up Hawaii right in front of his face.

"I was just going to get a club soda," she said.

"Yours takes a second, hon," Roxy said, returning. She set a tumbler of clear, bubbly liquid in front of the man. "You behave tonight, Steven." She grinned at him, shot a look at Mariah, and left again.

"Steven," he said, turning slightly to offer her his right hand.

She took it and shook it. "Nice to meet you."

"Ouch," he said with a chuckle. "I don't get a name in return?"

He was smooth and charming—and he knew it. He was the type of man Mariah would absolutely give her name and number to, flirt with shamelessly until her drink was gone, and then hope he'd call or text the next day.

If she were the type who hung out in places like The Dance Barn, which she wasn't.

Nerves ran through her, and she glanced around the dance hall and restaurant to her right. She turned back to Steven and said, "I'm Mariah."

"Pleasure to make your acquaintance." He lifted his drink to her and then took a sip. It wasn't alcohol, and he hardly drew any liquid into his mouth at all. He then made a smacking noise with his lips like he'd just taken the drink that would save his life.

His dark blue eyes glinted at her from beneath that cowboy hat, and Mariah's walls dissolved. She thought of Lawrence, and she quickly pulled out her phone to see if he'd sent an ETA.

He hadn't, and Mariah turned her phone over but kept it out.

"Meeting someone?" Steven asked.

"Yes," Mariah said, looking up at Roxy as she returned with a wavy glass filled with bright orange slush. Her mouth watered, because she did adore a good tropical smoothie, and while she'd never admit it out loud, Steven had pegged her with near-perfect accuracy.

Yeah, she thought. *Because he hangs out in bars on the weekends.*

He did have "a usual" and knew the bartender by name.

Or maybe every night.

"Thank you," she said to Roxy, and she picked up the straw the bartender had put on the counter. Unwrapping it, she forced herself to keep her attention on her own doings.

"Where are you from, Mariah?" Steven asked.

"Right here," she said, refusing to ask him a question about himself. She wasn't interested in this man. He'd simply sat down beside her.

"I once knew a woman named Mariah," he said, clearly not getting the hint that she didn't want to talk to him. "Most people know her, really. You probably do."

"There are thousands of Mariah's in the world," she said dryly. "I doubt I know this one."

"Sure you do," he said, grinning. "It's Mariah Carey."

That did get Mariah to turn toward him and gape. "Really?"

"Really." He laughed again and took another sip of his mystery drink. "I worked in LA for years. Music producer." He lifted one shoulder in a shrug as if everyone in the world had such a glamorous job. "I grew up in Louisville, and I missed it out here. So I moved to Nashville. Lotsa *amazing* talent in Nashville." He gave her a closed-mouth smile and stirred his drink.

"That's fantastic," she said.

He nodded. "What do you do?"

"I'm a marketing executive," she said.

"That's one of those terms that no one knows what it means."

"So is music producer," she shot back. "What does that even mean? You wave a wand and produce music?"

He burst out laughing and Mariah grinned at him. She tossed her hair over her shoulder and stuck her straw in her slushy drink. One sip, and she wanted to devour the whole thing. It helped that her stomach was empty, and she told herself to go slow. The last thing she needed was a frozen throat or brain freeze to set in.

Steven started to talk about what he did in the sound booth to produce music, and Mariah could listen to him for hours. He had a nice, rich voice with plenty of that Kentucky twang she liked, and she imagined him to have plenty of interesting stories to tell.

Before she knew it, she'd finished her drink, and he'd finished his story. "Well," he said with a groan as he got up. "I always like to leave the ladies on a high." He gave her a devastating smile and tossed some cash on the bar. "Have a good one, Mariah." He shoved his wallet in his back pocket.

"You too," she said with a genuine smile. He had made waiting more bearable, and a hint of nerves assaulted her again. Where in the world was Lawrence? She turned to survey the rest of the barn, but if he'd been seated at one of the booths on the far side, she'd never see him.

She turned back to her empty glass and pointed to his while he shrugged into his jacket. "What were you drinking?"

"Club soda," he said.

Mariah whipped her attention back to that symmetrical face.

Steven grinned at her, and even that rose to precisely the same height on each side of his face. "Can I get your number?" he asked. "I think you and I would get along real nice."

Surprise hit her right between the eyes. "Oh, I—"

"I'm so sorry I'm so late." Lawrence rushed onto the scene, his face showing a mixture of annoyance and relief. Mariah hastened to stand, but her foot caught on the rest of the barstool, and she stumbled.

Both Lawrence and Steven reached to steady her, each of them touching her on the arm now as she found her footing. Silence draped them, and along with that came only awkwardness.

"There you are," she finally said, breaking through the ice. She giggled awkwardly and stepped haphazardly into her boyfriend. "I'm sure you're going to have a great story for why you're so late."

She slid her fingers through his and faced Steven. He didn't look surprised or upset at all. "This is who I was waiting for," she said, pasting a smile onto her lips. "Steven, my boyfriend, Lawrence Chappell. Lawrence, this is Steven."

He wasn't anything to her, so she didn't tack on a qualifier.

"Thanks for keeping her company," Lawrence said with a smile. He shook Steven's hand and then slid his along the small of Mariah's back. Fireworks popped through her system, only intensifying when he leaned his head down and created a small, intimate space for them to talk. "Should we get a table, baby? You're hungry, right?"

"Yes," she said. "Let's go eat." She didn't even look at Steven as she turned to gather her purse. She went with Lawrence back to the hostess pad.

"You really didn't know him?" Lawrence asked, glancing back to the bar while they waited.

"No," she said. "He just sat down beside me." She watched him retake his seat and ask for another drink. "Interesting guy, though."

Beside her, Lawrence sucked in a breath, and Mariah realized what she'd said. "I mean…"

"Two?" the hostess chirped, and if she recognized Mariah from a half-hour ago, she didn't act like it.

"Yes," she said when Lawrence remained mute. "And can we get a booth as far from the dance floor as possible?"

The woman blinked at her, nodded, and said, "Right this way."

CHAPTER 24

The music at The Dance Barn was loud, but not loud enough to erase Mariah's words from his mind. *Interesting guy, though.*

Interesting.

Interesting.

Interesting.

The word vibrated through his ears and down into his throat. It screamed through his stomach and zoomed right back to the top of his head, shouting, shouting, *shouting*.

"Thanks," she said as the woman put their menus on the table and left. She slid into the booth, and somehow, Lawrence's body did the same.

The music was definitely quieter back here, and he watched while Mariah settled herself across from him. She wouldn't look directly at him, and he disliked that with a passion.

"You know, if you want to give that *interesting guy* your

number, you can." Lawrence leaned back in the booth and folded his arms.

Mariah stilled completely, finally bringing her eyes to his as they widened. "I don't want to give him my number."

"I heard him ask for it." Lawrence wished he had something to drink, so he'd have something to keep his hands busy. "You two must've had a very *interesting* conversation."

"Lawrence," she said, and his name held plenty of warning.

"What?" he asked. "What did you two talk about?"

"Nothing," she said. "His job."

If she'd wanted to drive the stake deeper into his heart, she'd just done it. His whole chest stung, and he found himself nodding and unable to stop.

"So let's just drop it," she said. "Tell me why you were late."

There was no way he could tell her he'd been delayed leaving Bluegrass Ranch because a beam in the barn had splintered. A load-bearing beam, and the whole barn was going to come down if they didn't get it shored up and fixed instantly. Every able-bodied human being had been recruited to start moving equipment and hay bales out of the barn, while more people had to actually stand under the beam and hold it up with two-by-fours while a new beam was purchased and brought to the ranch.

Lawrence had been one of those, and he'd stood down on the end, most of the somewhat urgent activity flowing around him. He'd hardly spoken to anyone and holding up a barn with an inadequate piece of wood had taken concentration and both hands. He hadn't been able to do much more than call Mariah the first time and then pray for a miracle that he'd actually make it to The Dance Barn tonight.

He'd still be standing there hugging that two-by-four if Duke hadn't finished his class and come to help in the barn. He'd taken Lawrence's spot so Lawrence could rush through a shower and a shave and race to meet his girlfriend.

"Lawrence," Mariah said again, this time reaching across the table with both hands. She'd done that before, and he'd willingly given her his hands to hold. Tonight, though, he kept his arms clamped across his chest.

She sighed. "I didn't give him my number."

"Only because I showed up."

"Exactly," she said. "You showed up. *You're* my boyfriend."

"Would you have told him that?"

"Of course," she said. "Believe it or not, I know how to handle myself with men."

"That's not hard to believe, Mariah."

She pulled in a breath and pulled back her hands. Shock covered her features, and regret lanced through Lawrence.

What a terrible thing to say, he told himself. *Apologize.* The last word sounded in his head in his mother's voice.

"I'm sorry," he said, dropping his eyes to the tabletop. "Really. That was mean."

Mariah took a long breath, the air hissing through her teeth. He looked up, and their eyes met. "I did introduce you as my boyfriend," she said. "If you'll recall correctly. I'm not interested in Steven."

"You said he was interesting."

"He was," she said. "Why is that a crime?"

"Because," Lawrence said, his heart starting to pound in a horrible beat. "Because, Mariah. I'm *not* interesting, and I can't compete with men like him."

"You don't need to compete with men like him," she said. "There is no competition here, Lawrence."

"Yes, there is," he said. "There always is when it comes to you."

"What does that mean?"

Lawrence searched her face, trying to find adequate words to explain. They'd had a version of this conversation before, and he'd thought she'd understood. At the same time, it wasn't her job to constantly reassure him that he was interesting enough for her.

"Mariah, think about your life with me. Think about a future with me. Just think about it."

"I have thought about it," she said.

That was news to Lawrence, as the billboard erection was only two days ago, and he hadn't had the guts or opportunity to bring up the topic of their future yet.

"What do you see?" he asked. "Anything interesting?" He shook his head. "No. There's just the ranch, and it's the same stupid, boring work that never changes."

She searched his face too, clearly surprised by what he'd said.

"You deserve someone interesting," he said, not sure where he was going with this, only knowing that it needed to be said. "You're interesting. You're gorgeous, and you're smart. You're capable of anything, and you can talk to anyone, anywhere, anytime. You kept me company during a wedding, just like you kept that guy company while you waited for me. But that doesn't mean you should be with me and not him."

"Lawrence, I don't even know what you're saying."

"I'm saying that what you've imagined for your future isn't going to happen with me."

"You have no idea what I've imagined for my future."

"I know you, Mariah." His mind wailed at him to stop talking. He needed to end this conversation now and pick up a menu. His stomach pinched, begging him to do that.

The waitress appeared and tossed two cardboard coasters on the table. "Can I get you guys something to drink?"

"Just water for me," Mariah said, her fingers scrambling over the slick menus in the middle of the table.

The waitress looked at Lawrence, who didn't know what to say. Was he really going to sit there and eat? Pretend he hadn't just told Mariah that she deserved someone far better than him?

The only thing worse would be to continue the evening as if he hadn't said anything at all.

"He'll take a Diet Coke," Mariah said, and that got the woman to walk away. Mariah glared at him. "What is wrong with you?"

Lawrence had planned on talking to her about diamond rings and marriage tonight. He'd been equally as excited to get to her as he was frustrated that he'd been delayed. Then he'd seen her sitting at the bar with that other cowboy. He'd paused, because she could easily be with that man and not him.

"I met with the finance team at—" she started.

"We have to finish talking about this," he interrupted. "Tell me what you see in your future with me."

Annoyance flashed across her face, and Lawrence told himself to take the demanding tone out of his voice. He didn't want to glaze over hard topics, though. He didn't want her to dictate everything for him in his life.

"I don't know, Lawrence," she said quietly. "A great life, with horseback riding and lazy summer evenings lying in a field somewhere." A soft smile touched her face, and she focused on unwrapping the silverware from the paper napkin it had been bound in.

"I don't even have a house for us to live in," he said.

"Then you'll build one," she said.

"The ranch is way too far for you to commute every day. I could make the drive from town out to the ranch."

"I only rent my house," Mariah said. "I don't want to live there forever."

"So what are you imagining?"

She sighed, cocking her head to the side in such a way that it appeared like she was rolling her eyes. Frustration shot through Lawrence, and he suddenly had no patience for this conversation.

"You wanna know what I see?" he asked. "I see myself living in a single bedroom in the homestead while all my brothers find wives and have families. I'm the quiet, dependable one, and that equates to overlooked and boring. I show up and I do my job every single day. No one thinks about me. No one worries over me. If I happen to be around in an emergency, they'll take my help, but I'm not the first person anyone calls."

His chest heaved, and he needed to get out of this place. Now.

"If you and I were to make it all the way to the altar, I see myself constantly worried that I'm not who you really want. I'd ask you all the time if you were happy out on the ranch, or if you wanted to move somewhere else, or what I could do to make life better for you."

"Wanting me to be happy is a good thing," she said. "It's okay for couples to want to do things for their partner to make them happy."

"That's just it," he said, seizing onto her words. "I *do* want you to be happy, Mariah. I desperately want that. I know you've been looking for that ever since your first marriage ended so badly."

He paused and forced his mind to move a little slower. "The truth is, Mya, is that I don't think *I* could ever make you happy."

"That's just not true," she said. "I'm happy with you."

"I also don't think someone should have to sacrifice too much of themselves in order to be with another person. To me, it feels like that's what you'd be doing. Sacrificing what *you* really like, and what *you* really want, to make me happy."

"I've done that in a relationship before," she said, her voice tight and snappy as she leaned forward. "I spent two years giving and giving and trying to make my husband happy. He was abusive and controlling, and it took a lot from me to finally work up the nerve to leave."

Anger rolled across her face, and she sat back in the booth again. "Maybe you're right. Maybe I don't want to sacrifice so much of myself to make someone else happy."

"At least you're being honest now."

"I've always been honest with you," she said. "Don't make it sound like I haven't."

"I've never heard that bit about your husband," he said.

"I spent thousands of dollars on him," she said, the words practically tumbling from her mouth. "Trying to make him happy. He was still mean and cruel, and I had to file a protective order against him when I filed for divorce."

Lawrence had no response for that, and his heart beat in a strange, new way now.

"That cost me a lot too, by the way. Lawyers are very expensive." She reached for a menu with a shaking hand. "When I think of a future with you, Lawrence, there's no drama. There's no berating words. There's no tension when I walk into the house after a long day at work. There's peace, and there's comfort, and that's good enough for me."

"I want to be more than just *good enough*. Who settles for good enough?" He shook his head and started to slide out of the booth. "You deserve better than *good enough*."

He took out his wallet and pulled out some bills. "Have dinner on me, but I need to get back to the ranch."

"Lawrence."

"I just..." He paused and looked out at the dance floor. Nothing about tonight had gone the way he'd thought it would. "I'm fine," he said. "I just need some space to think for a minute." He looked at her, hoping this wouldn't be the last time he could call her his girlfriend and have it be true, though it probably was. "Please, stay. Eat. I'll talk to you later."

With that, he put the money on the table and walked away, passing his waitress as she took water and Diet Coke toward their table.

No one said anything to him as he left The Dance Barn. Mariah didn't race up beside him and grab onto his arm, asking him to stop for a minute and talk to her.

Once behind the wheel of his truck, he glared at the dance hall. "That's because you've said enough," he muttered. "She doesn't need to hear anything else."

He drove away from the restaurant, and when he should've turned right to head out into the northern wilds where the ranch sat, he swung the truck left instead.

"Good enough," he scoffed. "Was that supposed to be a compliment?" He shook his head and pressed on the accelerator as the highway opened up before him. It didn't matter that he was headed in the wrong direction.

He needed to get away, and any direction that wasn't going to take him back to Bluegrass Ranch would do right now.

CHAPTER 25

Duke reached for the plastic container of food on his passenger seat and looked at the sprawling ranch house he'd parked in front of. A few other cars and trucks sat there too, and he supposed that was normal for Thanksgiving Day.

The pie he'd brought wasn't necessary, but Duke had learned from his mother that he couldn't show up at someone's house without something in his hands. More often than not, that was food, and Mom did make some delicious pies.

Duke made the quick trip from his truck to the front door, and he rang the doorbell. It sang through the whole house, including the solid wood door in front of him. He fell back a couple of steps, the container with individual spots for each type of pie suddenly too small.

"Coming," someone yelled a few moments later, and Duke moved to the right a little bit. The door opened, and

Bruce stood there. He was only a couple of inches taller than Duke, but he still felt like the older man towered over here.

"Hey, Duke." Bruce curled his fingers around the top of the door and leaned into it. His smile came a little slow, and Duke's pulse bounced in his throat.

"Hey, Bruce." He put a smile on his face. "I called your dad and said I was bringing him some of my mother's desserts." He lifted the container, though Bruce couldn't see what was inside. "He said it was okay to stop by for a minute."

"Sure," Bruce said, backing up. "C'mon in."

Duke stepped into the house, his senses on high alert for some reason. He swept the hall in front of him, but there was no one there. A study sat to his left, and the hall extended back into the house. He followed Bruce and emerged into a huge living room, which bled into a dining room and the kitchen.

Several people milled about back here, and they all turned to look at Duke when he entered. He automatically looked for Lisa, but he didn't see her.

"Duke," Wayne Harvey said from the recliner in the living room. The light from the window beside him painted him in weak, winter sunshine, and he definitely looked much older than when Duke had seen him earlier this year.

He put both hands on the armrests of the chair and attempted to push himself up. He couldn't quite do it, and another man said, "Daddy, don't get up. He'll come to you."

Kelly looked over his shoulder to Duke again. He

gestured for him to come forward, and Duke did, that plastic smile still on his face.

The couple of women in the kitchen went back to their conversation, and Duke relaxed a little bit as he took a seat on the loveseat next to Wayne's recliner. "Momma sent over five types of pie," he said, cracking the seal on the lid of the container. "She's got her famous apple pie. Pecan, of course."

Duke relaxed even more, though the tension in the house remained high.

"I love your mother's pecan pie," Wayne said in his gravelly voice. He smiled at Duke too, and it reached all the way to his eyes. He looked utterly exhausted, though, and Duke saw the man in a brand-new way.

He was certainly ill, and Duke's heart squeezed for Lisa. Why Lisa specifically and not all of Wayne's children confused Duke. He should've been concerned for Wayne himself, and yet Duke's thoughts tumbled around Lisa for some reason.

"I'll get you a fork, Daddy," Kelly said, and he got up and made his way into the kitchen.

"She makes this chocolate mousse pie," Duke continued, pointing to the whipped cream with crushed Oreos on top. "Key lime was her fruity pie this year, though she's made lemon meringue and coconut cream in the past."

He looked up as Kelly returned with the fork. Wayne made no move to reach for it, so Duke did. With the metal in his hand, his mouth watered as if he'd get to eat the individual pie squares.

"And last, the traditional pumpkin pie." He extended the container toward Wayne, who took it with both hands. He accepted the fork too and peered at the five pies Duke had brought.

"Which would you eat first?" he asked.

"Oh, definitely the chocolate," Duke said with a grin. He settled back into the loveseat and put his ankle on his knee.

Wayne went for the chocolate mousse pie, and the thick custard added more saliva to Duke's mouth. Wayne moaned as he ate the pie, his eyes closing in bliss. Duke chuckled, and Wayne smiled after he'd swallowed.

"Thank you, Duke."

"Of course," he said. He sighed and glanced across the space to where Kelly had sat again. Wayne had three children, and his two sons came from his first wife. They were both at least a decade older than Duke, but he'd always gotten along just fine with them. He had brothers a decade older than him, so it wasn't like he never spoke to a man in his forties.

"How's the ranch?" he asked Kelly, who seemed to grimace with the question. The action crossed his face in less than a moment, and Duke barely saw it.

Lisa, Wayne's third child, came from his second wife, and she was a couple of years older than Duke.

"Good," Kelly said. "Humming along real nice."

"Yeah?" Duke cut a glance at Wayne, who simply put another bite of pie in his mouth. "Lisa seems to be scheduling all the studs real well."

Kelly jumped to his feet, glared at Duke, and said,

"Excuse me. I need to check on the coffee." He strode away, leaving Duke as surprised as he was confused.

"What did I say?" he murmured to Wayne.

"Oh, the boys don't like talkin' about the ranch," Wayne said. "Or Lisa, for that matter."

"No?" Duke asked, leaning forward again, hoping to keep the conversation private. "Why's that?"

"Look at me, son," Wayne said, gesturing with his fork to his body. "I've lost forty pounds in four months. I'm sick. They've had to take over everything, which annoys and frustrates me. I'm no picnic to deal with." He smiled, and Duke's heart did start to bleed for the man.

"I'm sorry," he said. "I just found out you were ill. Lisa mentioned it."

"She's a good girl," Wayne said, poking his fork into the pumpkin pie next. A sigh leaked from his mouth. "But Kelly and Bruce think she's meddling in the farm business, though they've been running that clothing company for a while now. They're not here much, and Lisa is. But they aren't listening to me."

"It's as much hers as theirs, right?" Duke thought of his family arrangement. He and his brothers all owned Bluegrass Ranch, with Spur having twenty percent more than the others simply so someone would have the legal right to make business decisions. But Daddy had spelled it out clearly in the transfer papers—every son was equal on the ranch. Every son had a voice. Every son got the same amount of money.

"My will dates back to before her birth," Wayne said. "I'm working on getting it updated, but Bruce—"

"What are you two talking about?"

Duke looked up to find Lisa standing there, both hands on her hips. He jumped to his feet and swept his cowboy hat off his head for some reason. He felt like he'd lost his dang mind. "Hey, Lisa. I just brought your dad some pie."

She switched her frowning gaze from him to her father. Something softened there, and Duke could see and feel the love she held for her daddy.

"Sit down, princess," Wayne said. "Take the glaring down a notch. This fine young man knows what I like." He grinned and took a bite of the apple pie this time.

"You're going to go into a sugar coma," Lisa said, taking the spot Kelly had been sitting in. "Belinda and Marge are making pie right now too."

No wonder Duke had been met with some icy stares from the kitchen upon his arrival. Duke put his cowboy hat back on his head and sat down, hoping Lisa wouldn't think too hard about how he'd jumped to attention upon her arrival.

"There's always room for more pie," Wayne said, his watery eyes moving to his daughter.

"Hmm." She crossed her legs, and Duke noted the dirty blue jeans tucked into her rubber work boots. She'd clearly been outside working on the ranch, and he wondered what chores possibly needed to be done in mid-afternoon on Thanksgiving Day.

She met his eye, but Duke had no idea what to say to her. "You didn't bake these, did you?"

"No, ma'am," he said.

"Don't have any hidden skills in the kitchen?" She cocked her eyebrows and folded her arms. She was so closed off, and Duke wondered what it would take to get her to open up.

Surprised by that thought, he couldn't speak. He simply shook his head and said, "No, ma'am," again. He was decent enough in the kitchen when he had to be. He could make anything out of eggs, and he knew exactly when to take the bacon out of the pan so it wasn't too crispy or too fatty.

He knew how to make a couple of hearty stews and soups, and he could sear a steak like a pro. She didn't need to know any of that right now.

"You're in my spot," Kelly said, returning to the living room.

Lisa got right up and surveyed the furniture as her half-brother took the place where he'd been sitting previously. He held a plate with a piece of pecan pie on it, and it felt like a challenge to Duke.

"Kelly," Wayne said. "Did you offer anyone else any pie?"

"We called from the kitchen," the man said, though Duke hadn't heard anything. "No one said anything."

Bruce entered the living room with a plate of pie too, along with who Duke assumed to be Belinda and Marge. They took the rest of the couch and the other chair, leaving Lisa standing in the middle of the room.

She looked around at them. "Looks like the pie is ready."

"Oh, did you want some?" one of the women asked in a falsely kind voice. "You didn't say anything."

"No one asked," Lisa said, striding away. She called over

her shoulder, "Duke? What kind do you want? You'll stay for pie, right?"

Duke looked at Wayne, who shook his head and sighed. He felt very much like Daniel entering the lion's den, but he didn't know how to get up and leave now.

Lisa paused and faced him, her eyes full of desperation and hope. They pleaded with him to *please stay. Don't leave me here alone with them*, and Duke couldn't do such a thing.

He didn't even want to, which said a lot about his feelings for the brunette who'd always annoyed him a little bit.

He got to his feet, his pulse acting like a big bass drum as it boomed in his chest. "I'll come get some," he said. "What kinds have y'all got?"

CHAPTER 26

Lisa fumed in the kitchen, her humiliation burning as hot as her fury. How embarrassing that Duke Chappell had witnessed her half-brothers' obvious snub. Their wives were no better, and Lisa knew in that moment that she'd never fit in with them.

She'd tried. Lord knew she'd tried.

For them to leave Daddy out of the pie party was ten times as infuriating, and Lisa threw a stabby glare in the direction of the living room. Daddy did have a bunch of pie in front of him, but that wasn't because his sons had lovingly doted on him.

That had been Duke Chappell.

Lisa cast a glance in the man's direction, his presence in the house as welcome as it was upsetting. "What were you and Daddy talking about?" she whispered as she picked up a knife to cut herself a slice of pecan pie. "And what kind of pie do you want?"

"I'll take the pecan," he said, his voice just as low as hers. "And we weren't talkin' about anything bad, Lisa."

"What was it?" She sliced cleanly through the pie and used the serving spatula to lift the piece out and onto a plate.

"Honestly, I'm not sure," Duke said, but his tone suggested he did.

Lisa straightened and looked him dead in the eye. "I have enough people lying to me right now," she said evenly. The house was so big that the others wouldn't overhear unless she yelled, especially with the way they were now horse-laughing in the living room. "I don't want one of them to be you."

"He said he's real sick," Duke said, swallowing. "You kids have taken over the ranch, and your brothers think you're meddling, and he's updating his will." He actually backed up a step. "That was when you came in."

Pure horror moved through Lisa. Daddy had been telling Duke all the family secrets. She supposed he didn't think they were secrets. Only Lisa had a problem with things the way they stood right now. Legally, if Daddy died tomorrow, she'd get nothing.

She'd always worked here at the family stud farm. Bruce and Kelly had not had a problem with her when she shoveled out stalls or gassed up vehicles. They hadn't had a problem with her taking over their accounts payable. Literally, anything she wanted to learn and do, they'd let her. They liked taking their paychecks for doing a couple of things around the farm while they really worked on their outdoor apparel company. She was the one who worked with the horses, kept their studs in peak physical condition, and drove studs to their appointments come covering season.

It hadn't been until Daddy had fallen ill that they'd started acting like Lisa wasn't welcome around the farm. Her nerves quivered on the edge of a knife, and she had to look away from Duke before she burst into tears.

"I didn't know your father was quite this sick," Duke whispered. "I'm sorry, Lisa. It must be hard for you. How are you feeling?"

"You have no idea what's hard for me and what's not." She sliced the knife through a small sliver of pie and put it on a plate. She gave him a glare before marching back toward the living room.

Lisa knew how to push people away. That was something she was very good at, having watched her mother do it for years before she'd finally left Daddy and Lisa at the stud farm in favor of a younger man. She'd pushed him away too, and everyone else in her life.

Mama had walls a mile tall, and it took something and someone extraordinary to get over them. Lisa hadn't figured out how to do it yet, and she'd learned over the years that walls like the kind Mama had protected her.

Lisa wanted to be protected too. She didn't want to hurt all the time, and she'd started building her own walls.

Unfortunately, in the living room, the only option for a place to sit was on the other half of the loveseat Duke had been sitting on. She took that spot and watched as the handsome cowboy from Bluegrass Ranch approached at a much slower clip than she had.

He took the spot next to her, filling the rest of the loveseat. Truth be told, he filled a lot of empty places in Lisa's life. He was one of her only friends, and he'd been a listening ear when she'd shown up in his office weeks ago to apologize.

Tears gathered in her eyes, and she blinked them away quickly. She would not cry in front of her half-brothers, and she definitely would not cry in front of Duke Chappell.

"Did your family eat Thanksgiving dinner already?" she asked, ignoring the other conversation around her. That was what her brothers and their wives did to her—ignored her. She'd thought that was what she'd wanted until she'd realized that they planned to continue doing that after Daddy died.

Worse, they'd cut her out of her own heritage completely if they could. Worry ate through her as she took her first bite of pie and looked at Duke.

"Yes," he said. "Mom served it at one o'clock, and in my family, if you're a minute late, you're an hour." He grinned and shook his head. "No one likes Mom's wrath, so we're always on time."

Lisa plastered a fake smile on her face and took another bite of the pie. It tasted like cardboard, and her stomach actually rebelled against it. On the inside, she was a huge mess, with everything she held so tightly coming unwound and near to exploding out of her.

On the outside, she was calm, cool, and collected. She

would eat this whole piece of pie and make small talk for as long as she could. Then she'd retreat back to the farm and the horses she loved. She'd feed the chickens and tell them all of her fears for the future. She'd make sure the goats had fresh water, and she'd check her to-do list for the following day.

No one would talk to her or bother her, which Lisa usually preferred. Lately, though, she'd only been feeling lonely when she was alone, not like she had the world in the palm of her hand, and all she had to do was take the next step and she'd conquer it.

Now, the world felt like it would fall. On the way down, she'd be crushed, and she'd leave the family farm bruised, battered, and broken, without a dime to her name.

Her name wouldn't mean anything anymore, and she once again prayed with all the energy of her soul that Daddy wouldn't die for a while yet. At least until he had the will and estate all ironed out.

Duke leaned closer to her and asked, "Did you get an official diagnosis on your daddy?" She'd told him he was sick before, with an elevated white blood cell count, but he hadn't heard much more than that.

"Cancer," she said quietly. "He's been declining since summertime."

"I'm sorry," he said again. "If there's anything I can do to help, you'll let me know?"

She nodded, struck by his kindness and concern. His fork scraped his plate as he took another bite of pie.

"He's working on a new will," she whispered, barely

moving her mouth. She couldn't believe she was going to tell Duke any of this. Somehow, the man had scaled her walls or knocked them down. He'd used a kindness battering ram, and if there was something Lisa needed more than anything else, it was kindness from another person.

"Bruce is claiming he's not of sound mind right now," she continued without looking up. Around her, her brothers continued to talk, and they weren't paying her any attention. "It's not going very fast or very well, and if he dies without a new will, that's it for me."

She met Duke's eyes, and his compassion swam in the dark depths of them. He put his hand on her knee for a moment. A quick touch that left almost as soon as it landed.

He'd taken another bite of pie by the time Bruce asked, "Are you two seeing each other?"

Lisa jerked her head up and met her brother's eyes. "No," she said with a scoff.

"What are you talking about then?" he challenged.

"I was just telling Lisa that I think this pecan pie is better than my mother's," Duke said, sailing in with the perfect statement. "I was worried about how I'd break the news to her." He grinned at Bruce and stood up. "I best be gettin' back to Bluegrass. You finished?" He reached for her plate, and Lisa relinquished it to him.

He walked into the kitchen, and it wasn't until he set their plates in the sink that she blinked. The weight of every eye in the house landed on her, and she hated all the staring. Someone would think she'd grown an additional head once Daddy had been diagnosed with cancer.

She got to her feet and said, "I'll walk him out." She met him at the mouth of the hallway and let him go first. He opened the front door and stepped onto the porch, and the freedom of the outdoor air called to Lisa to join him.

She did, wishing she'd put her jacket back on first. He paused at the top of the steps, and she stepped to his side. After a long, deep, cleansing breath, she said, "Sorry about that. Everything is really messed up right now."

"You don't need to apologize to me." Duke didn't look at her, but his fingers slid down her arm and right between hers. "I meant it when I said you could let me know if you needed anything." He squeezed her hand. "*Anything*, Lisa, okay?"

She nodded, her voice trapped somewhere beneath the ball of emotion in her throat. *Trapped* was the perfect way to describe Lisa's whole life. She'd never felt more trapped in her life, and the need to break free and get away seethed somewhere in her chest. She couldn't breathe properly, and she couldn't think beyond her flight instinct. Yet, she didn't move.

"My office is always open too," he said, releasing her hand. "If you just need somewhere to come sit for a while."

She couldn't quite meet his gaze, but she managed to nod again before Duke went down the steps and sidewalk to his truck. She stayed on the porch and watched him until she couldn't see his vehicle anymore.

Only then did she release everything she'd been holding hostage inside her, and it all came spilling out in the form of horrible, gut-wrenching sobs.

CHAPTER 27

Mariah swept the floor in her rental house, moving the broom along the grain of the wood. Her house had never been cleaner, and she still didn't know what to do about Lawrence. Her temperature rose, and she had to consciously calm herself down.

Technically, he hadn't said he'd call. He'd said he'd talk to her later. It had been seven days since the disaster at The Dance Barn, and she hadn't heard from him yet.

She'd cleaned windowsills yesterday, and she'd wiped down all of her cabinets and put in new liners. Now her bowls and plates sat on pristine, blue-flowered shelves. Mariah didn't have anything else to clean, but if she didn't stay busy, she might go insane.

The holidays sat right around the corner, and she'd started to imagine having a date to all of the parties and dinners that came with them. In her mind, they'd wear matching ugly sweaters to her office party, and she'd take a special Christmas treat to Reid, the horse she'd ridden many times now.

She pulled back on the tears, because her relationship with Lawrence was about a lot more than just having a warm body next to her for an office party. Her heart pulsed in her chest, because her relationship with Lawrence had become very, very serious to her.

She hadn't lied when she'd said she'd thought about a future with him. She hated how she'd described it, because he was more than "good enough" for her. He was perfect for her. Tears filled her eyes, and this time, she didn't hold them back. She let them quietly roll down her cheeks as she used a dustpan to clean up the dead grass and twigs that Phantom had tracked in earlier that day.

Her phone chimed from its spot on the kitchen counter, and she swept the debris into the trash can before checking it. Alicia had texted to remind everyone about brunch at her apartment in the morning.

You all need to be on your best behavior, her younger sister had said. *Malcolm will be there.*

"I've met Malcolm before," Mariah grumbled to herself, but she confirmed that she would indeed be on her best behavior at brunch the following morning.

Are you going to bring Lawrence? Alicia asked. *It's our bring-everyone brunch.*

You should, Mya, Dani said. *I know Daddy would love to meet him.*

Mariah very nearly threw her phone across the room as everything in her mind went white. Desperation filled her, choking in the back of her throat. She breathed in, held it, and then blew her breath out. She repeated that action a couple more times, and she started to calm fully.

She hadn't told either of her sisters about what had happened at The Dance Barn. She hadn't told Jane. She'd been suffering in complete silence, and she wasn't sure if she preferred that, or if her sisters could give her some advice.

I haven't heard from Lawrence since a really bad date a week ago. Mariah sent the text, her fingers gripping her phone tightly.

Oh no, Alicia said.

Mariah drew in a breath, waiting for the phone to ring. Dani wouldn't text in response, and sure enough, Mariah's phone rang, and her older sister's name sat on the screen.

"Hey," Mariah said after answering the call.

"I can't believe you haven't heard from him," Dani said, not bothering with a greeting. "You guys are so cute together. You're *perfect* for each other. What happened?"

"He doesn't think he's interesting enough," Mariah said. "He thinks I deserve someone better than him."

Dani sat there for a moment, clearly thinking about what Mariah had said. She sighed, and said, "Mya," and nothing else.

"What?" Mariah asked.

"Why does he feel like that?"

"I don't know," Mariah said. "I've done nothing but tell him how amazing he is." And he was amazing. He was handsome, and smart, and attentive. He hardly ever ran late, and he was an accomplished horseman. Maybe he didn't have the loudest voice of all the Chappells, and maybe he wasn't the one everyone looked up to. In Mariah's opinion, there was nothing wrong with being quiet and dependable.

"Did you...maybe say something to him?"

"No," Mariah said, frowning. "I didn't say anything to him."

"Tell me what happened a week ago."

Mariah had been over that night a million times in her mind. She didn't want to relive it for Dani, but her sister would needle her relentlessly if she didn't. So Mariah started talking, and before she knew it, the whole story had spilled out.

"So he's already sensitive about not being interesting," Dani said. "And then you called a different man interesting..."

"I didn't mean it to sound like he *wasn't* interesting," Mariah said, all of her defenses firmly in place. "Those two words didn't mean I wanted to date someone else."

"I know that," Dani said. "You know that. Lawrence isn't in the best of places already, and it sounds like he spiraled a little."

"Obviously," Mariah said. "Dani, what should I do?"

"How did you get him back last time?"

"I drove past his ranch for a week before I finally went to pick peaches."

"What?"

Mariah waved her hand, though her sister wasn't there.

"It doesn't matter. I can't do that again. I'm not going to just bump into him."

"So drive out to his ranch and talk to him. Tell him you don't need more time. That you love him and you want him in your life and that he's the most interesting man you've ever met."

Mariah rolled her eyes. Dani made things sound so simple when they weren't.

"I know," Dani said, and the lightbulb above her head could be heard in her voice. "Invite him to brunch tomorrow."

"How does that help me?"

"You want to introduce him to your family," Dani said. "You haven't done that since Robert."

"Yeah, but…" Mariah hadn't told Lawrence that yet. She sighed. She wanted Lawrence in her life, but they did have more to talk about. She wanted to have those hard conversations with him, because a relationship with him was the only thing she wanted.

"I can't," she said. "I feel like he has to reach out to me first. Maybe he just needs a little time to think. I know sometimes I need some space—not that I can get any of that with you."

"Hey," Dani protested. "That's what big sisters are for."

"Yeah, yeah," Mariah said. "What's happening with your baby?"

Dani hesitated, and Mariah wasn't sure if that was a good sign or not.

"I'm sorry," she blurted. "You don't have to tell me."

"It's good news," Dani said. "Doug and I were going to tell everyone at brunch tomorrow."

"Oh, Doug's coming?"

"Yes," Dani said. "It's our holiday brunch. Significant others invited. That's why Alicia's lecturing us about being on our best behavior."

Mariah pressed her eyes closed. She'd completely forgotten that significant others had been invited to this brunch. She'd talked to Lawrence about it a while ago, and she wondered if he remembered. Could she text him and ask if he'd be there or not? Maybe that would spur him into either breaking up with her officially or opening the lines of communication again.

"Phantom is flipping out about something," Dani said. "Call Lawrence, Mya." The line went dead after she heard the loud, booming bark of Dani's dog, and Mariah let her phone fall to her lap.

She wasn't going to call Lawrence. He'd said he'd talk to her later, and *he* was the one who'd walked out a week ago.

* * *

"You've got to be kidding," Mariah said, lifting her foot off the accelerator as the text from her sister popped up on her screen. She pulled to the side of the road and picked up her phone from the console. "I'm already late."

Her fingers flew across the screen to answer her younger sister. *Fine. I can go grab the croissants.*

How Alicia didn't have one of the main components of brunch was a mystery to Mariah's organized, planner-focused mind. She'd have had a list of groceries she needed three weeks ago, and she'd have edited it four times before actually going to the store. Then, she'd have checked, double-checked, and triple-checked a few times before the grocery stores closed last night.

Thanks so much! We probably need a dozen. Alicia sent, and Mariah flipped on her blinker and checked her rearview mirror before pulling back onto the road. She turned around and went back toward the main part of town.

"Hey," she muttered to herself. "At least now you'll have a reason for being late, and no one will know you almost didn't come."

She made it to the grocery store, which was busier than she'd like for this Sunday morning. A sigh pulled through her body, because even the self-checkout lines would be long with this many cars in the parking lot.

She went inside, and she actually enjoyed the hustle and bustle of a busy store. The energy pouring from the very air brought something dormant inside her to life, and she took a few moments admiring the other pastries in the bakery section of the store. She finally selected a tray of a dozen croissants and turned toward the front of the store.

On the way there, she snagged a small package of crumb doughnuts, and she'd eaten a couple of those by the time she made it to the checkout. After that, she got back on the road to Alicia's apartment.

Twenty minutes later, Mariah pulled up to the building, now forty minutes past the time she should've arrived. Relief flowed through her as she walked toward the stairs to get to the third floor, because she'd likely missed all the small talk. She'd enter the apartment, greet everyone, and Alicia would rush everyone to sit down and get started.

She went up the steps, glancing out over the parking lot every time she faced it. A black truck sat in the lot, and something triggered in her mind, causing her to stumble. She'd already started to turn to go up the last set of steps to the third floor, and when she put her foot down, it didn't land on anything solid.

She grunted and threw her hand out to grab onto the railing so she wouldn't fall. Once she was steady, she spun back to the parking lot. From the landing two and a half floors up, she could clearly see the huge, hulking black pickup truck.

She knew that truck. She'd ridden in that truck many times.

"Lawrence is here," she whispered, squinting to see inside the truck. Was he sitting inside the cab? Had he made this march up the stairs to her sister's apartment? If he had, why hadn't he called or texted her first?

Dani and Alicia hadn't either.

Mariah's heart pounded, her adrenaline rushing through her at the speed of light. Above her, a door opened, and Dani said, "I'll call her. Just a sec."

Mariah pressed her back into the stone, knowing her

sister wouldn't see her unless she came to the top of the steps. She just needed a moment to catch her breath and figure out if she was going to go inside, face everyone in her family, and see Lawrence for the first time in eight days.

Unfortunately, her phone rang, the ringtone splitting the silence surrounding her. Mariah's pulse pounced again, and she cursed under her breath as she hurried to dig in her purse. She plucked the device out at the same time Dani appeared at the top of the steps and said, "There you are."

"Is this you?" Mariah asked, though she knew it was.

"Yes." Dani removed the phone from her ear and tapped. The phone stopped ringing, and Mariah looked up the ten steps to her older sister. She could feel her heartbeat in her throat, and she couldn't swallow past it.

Dani smiled at her and gestured for her to continue coming up. "Come on," she said. "We're just waiting for you."

Mariah couldn't move, and Dani's smile slipped. She came down a few steps, asking, "What's wrong?"

"Is Lawrence here?" Mariah asked, watching her sister's face for any sign of the truth. It flashed right there through her eyes, and Mariah's legs felt much weaker than before.

Dani joined her on the landing and took her by the shoulders, her fingers surprisingly strong for such a small woman. "The man is in love with you."

Mariah scoffed and shook her head, her tears instant and unable to be contained. She swiped at her eyes, because she'd dreamt of having a good man fall in love with her. Everything she'd wanted in her first husband was present in Lawrence, and she couldn't believe she'd messed everything up with him with only a few words.

"Come on," Dani said gently. "Come see for yourself."

CHAPTER 28

Lawrence's eyes kept darting to the front door of the apartment, which Dani had left partially ajar when she'd gone outside to call Mariah. His very bones ached with how tightly he held his muscles, but he couldn't relax.

He couldn't believe he was even here, and he couldn't believe that Mariah's family—including her father—had been so kind to him. He couldn't believe he'd answered a call from an unknown number last night, and he'd had to make his way to the couch and sit down when he'd heard, "Hello, Lawrence. This is Dani Finn, Mariah's sister. Remember me?"

Of course he remembered her. He'd been thinking about Mariah and the embarrassing way he'd walked out on their date for eight solid days and nights. He could barely concentrate, and that wasn't great for the beginning of a new month. He needed all of his wits about him to make sure all of the invoices went out to the right people, for the correct amounts.

He'd been sending texts willy nilly, and thankfully, he'd only made a few mistakes. For Lawrence, though, who normally didn't make *any* mistakes with his reminders and invoices, he felt like a complete mess.

Right now, he couldn't even swallow, so he had no idea how he was going to eat anything at this brunch. He'd eaten breakfast already, because he'd already put in three hours of work on the ranch before returning to the homestead to shower and get over here on time.

It had taken every ounce of courage he had to come up three flights of stairs and knock on the door by himself. When he met Mariah's father, he'd imagined that she'd be standing at his side, her hand gripped in his, and her joy to be with him up in the stratosphere.

As it had happened, he'd whipped his cowboy hat off his head and said, "Good morning, sir," before shaking the man's hand. Dani had introduced him to Ralph and then Alicia. Her boyfriend had shown up only a few minutes after him, and he'd met Malcolm too.

"What's going on?" Alicia asked, her voice full of a growl. She stomped across the room to the front door and whipped it open. "Dani?"

Lawrence met Doug's eyes, and he offered him a smile. "I'm sure she'll be back in a minute."

What if she can't get Mariah to come in? Lawrence wondered. This was such a bad idea, and frustration built inside him. He should've called her last night after he'd gotten off the phone with Dani. He could've at least texted to let her know he'd meet her here this morning. He could've shown up at her house with the flowers he'd brought here, made up with her in private, and then shown up on the doorstep to meet her father the way he'd originally imagined.

He'd done everything wrong—again.

"Maybe I should go," he said almost under his breath.

Doug looked at him and lifted his coffee mug to his lips. "I don't think that's necessary, but you do what you think is right."

"I should've talked to her in private."

"Their family is very important to them," Doug said. "They're small, and they like getting together."

Lawrence nodded, and while he wanted to leave, he couldn't get his feet to move. In the next breath, the door widened, and Alicia walked back in, this time carrying a plastic grocery sack with something inside.

"She's here," she said, smiling around at everyone. "Give me two minutes to slice these , and we'll eat."

Lawrence couldn't acknowledge anything she'd said, because he couldn't look away from the sunlight pouring in through the doorway. Dani filled it, and then Mariah entered the apartment last.

A rush of relief poured through him, and he found himself striding toward the front door without even telling himself to do it. "Mariah," he said, and she looked up from putting her purse on the side table near the door.

"I'm so sorry," he said, swooping into her personal space and embracing her. The watery nature of her eyes registered with him, as did the stiffness in her body. A moment later, though, she melted into him and put her arms around him too. "I'm sorry," he said again. "I'm *so* sorry. Please forgive me. I love you, and I'm such an idiot, and I can't stand not being with you."

He pulled away and stroked both of his hands through her hair and down the sides of her face, searching it for any sign that she might actually forgive him. She was crying, and Lawrence felt like such a fool.

He also didn't know what else to say.

Someone stepped next to him, petals and leaves rustling, and Lawrence looked at Dani. She carried the bouquet of wildflowers he'd brought with him, and she smiled encouragingly at him as she extended the flowers toward him.

He cleared his throat and took them, murmuring, "Thank you, Dani." He focused on the flowers and fixed a couple of them before looking at Mariah. "I know you like flowers, and these looked like something you might wear on one of your printed dresses." He smiled as she wiped her eyes. "Is there any way you can forgive me? Can we try again please?"

She looked from the wildflowers to his face. "Do you really love me?"

"Completely," he said, and it sounded like he was the most miserable man on the planet for doing so. "Everything that happens, I want to tell you about. You're the first person I think about in the morning, and the last person I'm thinking about before I fall asleep at night. I hate that I haven't been able to talk to you every single day lately, and I

know it's my fault. I'm willing to do whatever you want—
the yoga or meditation. I'll go on that food tour you
mentioned. Anything."

She still hadn't said anything, and Lawrence was seriously going to go insane if she didn't speak soon.

"Can we find a field somewhere," she said. "Where no
one else will bother us? And we can just lie there and look at
the sky and breathe in and out together."

Joy exploded through Lawrence, and he nodded. "Yes,"
he said. "Yes, we can do that."

"That's what I want," she said. "I don't need fancy
things, Lawrence, though I think *you* think I do. I don't
want a big, grandiose life. We can find a house for us that will
be the perfect place for us to raise our family. Maybe that's
on your ranch, and maybe it's not. I don't care." She took a
big breath. "I just want to be with you—and only you."

"I can hardly believe it," he whispered.

She took his face in both of her hands and brought him
closer to him. "Start believing it, cowboy, because it's true.
I'm in love with you too."

Lawrence grinned, and the only reason he had to stop
was because Mariah pressed her mouth to his and
kissed him.

Cheering sounded throughout the apartment, and
Mariah broke the kiss with a giggle, tucking herself against
his chest. Lawrence held her tightly, both arms around her,
and pressed his eyes closed.

Thank you, Lord, he thought. *Thank you for allowing
her to forgive me.*

"Come on, now," Alicia said behind him. "This is going to be a lunch instead of brunch."

Mariah stepped out of Lawrence's arms, but she secured her hand in his. "That's because you didn't even have croissants, Lish."

Lawrence met Alicia's eye, and she looked away quickly.

"Alicia," Mariah said, plenty of warning and accusation in her voice. She glanced at Lawrence and then Dani. "What's going on?"

No one answered, and Mariah appealed to her father. "Don't ask me," he said, lifting both hands into the air as if in surrender. "I don't want to be in the middle of this."

"Lawrence was running late," Dani finally said. "So we made up an excuse to delay you until he could get here."

Mariah's eyes flew to his, and he gave her a one-shouldered shrug. "Sorry," he said. "We had a horse kick down a fence this morning, and I had to rebuild that."

The others started pulling out chairs and settling down at the table Alicia had set and decorated for Christmas. "So what you're saying is your life is exciting and unpredictable," Mariah said.

Lawrence chuckled and pulled her chair out for her. He took the wildflowers and set them back on the kitchen counter, then he took the last remaining seat at the table. He looked around at the six other people—Dani and her husband, Doug. Alicia and her boyfriend, Malcolm. Mariah's father, Ralph. And finally Mariah—and he felt like he belonged here with them.

"Life on the ranch is a little unpredictable," he said.

"Animals have a mind of their own." He smiled as he took the orange juice bottle from Dani and poured himself a glass.

"Mariah seems to have one of those too," Ralph said, smiling at his daughter. Lawrence smiled too, and he poured her juice for her as well. The food went around, and Lawrence took some of everything, from the sausage breakfast casserole to the fresh fruit.

"Well, we have news," Alicia said once everyone had food and all the big dishes were back on the counter. She surveyed the group at the table, her eyes sparkling like the stars in heaven. "Malcolm and I are engaged."

She squealed and held out her left hand, which definitely hadn't had a diamond ring on it earlier but did now.

"Oh, my word," Dani said, the statement made of air. She grabbed her younger sister's hand and stared at the ring. "This is gorgeous. Well done, Malcolm."

He grinned at her and put his arm around Alicia.

"Congratulations." Mariah sounded happy for her sister. She wore a smile on her face. But her nails dug into Lawrence's leg, and he wondered what was going through her head. Was she jealous? Didn't she know her own engagement was coming soon?

"We have news too," Dani said, meeting Doug's eyes. Hers turned glassy, and she cleared her throat. "Jordan chose us to adopt her baby." She sniffled and wiped her face. "I swore I wouldn't cry, but I can't help it."

"Oh, Dani." Mariah jumped up from her seat and went around Lawrence to hug her sister. She embraced Doug, and before Lawrence knew it, the whole family was out of their seats again, hugging everyone and offering congratulations.

He stood out of the way, and when they started to sit back down, he did too. Everyone looked at him, but he didn't know what he was supposed to say. He looked at Mariah, but she was looking at him too.

"I don't know what's going on," he said.

"Do you two have any news?" Ralph asked, stabbing a piece of pineapple and popping it into his mouth.

"Uh..."

"We've started talking about our future," Mariah said smoothly. "Kids, marriage, where we'll live. That kind of thing." She gave Lawrence a small smile that said so much more than she'd said out loud. "You're going to have to wait for more official news from us, though."

"Fair enough," Ralph said. "My news is that all my paperwork is in for my retirement."

"Great news, Daddy," Dani said, and the other girls gave their assent to that as well.

"And, uh." He cleared his throat. "I've started seeing someone."

A pin could've dropped in the room and caused a huge clatter for how silent everyone went. Not a rustle. No scraping of silverware against plates. Not even the hum of the furnace filled the air.

"What?" Dani finally asked, glancing at her two sisters. "Who?"

"Her name is Linda Little," Ralph said, his face turning

a dark shade of red. "It's pretty new, and we've been out three or four times."

Another pause while the disbelief seeped through the room. Then Mariah, who sat beside her father, reached over and covered his hand with hers. "That's great news, Daddy. It's about time you started dating."

She beamed at him and then around the table, and the warmth from her smile seemed to thaw everyone else, and both Dani and Alicia agreed that their father had done a good thing by starting to see Linda.

He enjoyed brunch with her family, contributing his laughter and words to the conversation. Near the end of the meal, though, he caught Mariah's eyes, and she nodded toward the front door.

"Can we take a walk for a few minutes?" she asked.

"Sure," he said.

"Ten minutes," Alicia said firmly. "Remember my neighbor is coming over with his camera to take our picture? It's for the Christmas cards, and he's doing it for free." She glanced at the clock. "Ten minutes."

"Ten minutes," Mariah promised, and she stood up and put her napkin on her plate. Lawrence copied her, nodded to everyone, and followed Mariah toward the door.

CHAPTER 29

M ariah swung her hand in Lawrence's, the sun that was out this morning so much brighter than it had been an hour ago. "Everything went okay with meeting Daddy?"

"Yes," he said. "He's a great guy."

"So are you, you know," she said, looking up at him.

He ducked his head and kept walking. "I'm working on not comparing myself to others," he said. "I signed up for this mobile therapy app, and that was one of the things the counselor said." He looked up and into her eyes. The kiss of fresh air on her face reminded her of the sloppy kiss she'd shared with him in Alicia's apartment. In front of everyone.

She definitely wanted to talk more about their future together, and she didn't want to do that in public. She wanted to kiss him again, and really let him know that she'd meant what she'd said—*I love you.*

"It doesn't matter that I'm not Spur. Or Cayden. Or

that I can't get every woman I meet to go out with me. I'm me—I'm Lawrence—and I have value too."

"Of course you do," she said. "For the record, I wanted to go out with you the very moment I met you."

"You did?" He chuckled and shook his head. "Was that before or after you sniped at me for how far you had to drive?"

She burst out laughing, tipping her head back and really letting the sound fly from her throat. Lawrence joined her, his hand sliding along her lower back and bringing her against his body. "I love you, Mariah," he said, and the moment turned stone cold sober.

She paused and turned toward him. They looked at one another, and Mariah simply enjoyed the power of the love moving through her. "I've messed up every relationship I've ever had, Lawrence, and I thought I'd done it again." She reached up and ran her fingers up the side of his face and across his forehead. "I love you. I say stupid things sometimes, but you have to know you are not only 'good enough' for me." They breathed in together, and Lawrence let his eyes drift closed.

"You are *perfect* for me," she whispered. "We belong together, and I don't care if our life is simple or not. With you, it'll be exactly what it's supposed to be."

Several moments of silence passed, and she added, "I love you, Lawrence."

He kissed her then, and while it started slow, it quickly turned into a passionate kiss where they could both pour exactly what they were feeling into the action.

He pulled away first, leaving Mariah breathless and wanting more. He took her hand again and turned her back toward Alicia's apartment. "What kind of wedding do you want?" he asked.

"Something country," she said. "Outside."

"So not in the winter."

"Spring would work," she said. "You have that big ranch. Blaine got married there."

"Spur too," he said. "Cayden's getting married at Sweet Rose, and Trey's done everything at Beth's."

"Makes sense," Mariah said.

"Spring is only four or five months away," he said.

"Oh, honey, I'm an event planner who's used to crushing deadlines." She laughed. "I can handle my own wedding in four or five months."

He nodded and grinned at her. "We should go look at diamonds this week. Do you want to?"

"Absolutely," she said, unable to contain her smile. "Name the time, baby, and I'll be there."

"After this, we can go to my office and look at my schedule."

Mariah sighed as she leaned into him, those feelings of peace and comfort that she'd so often craved and couldn't find so prevalent with Lawrence Chappell. Yes, she loved him, and she couldn't wait to be his wife.

* * *

Lawrence smoothed down the tips of his bow tie, everything about Cayden and Ginny's wedding prim and proper. And expensive. The venue where they were getting married probably cost fifty thousand dollars to rent, but Ginny actually owned it.

When Lawrence had arrived for the rehearsal dinner last night, he'd simply stood in the doorway of the great hall, which today would hold enough chairs for one thousand people.

One thousand. Lawrence could name the people he'd invite to his wedding on his fingers, though he did know more people than that.

He simply didn't care if they all came to his wedding or not.

He knew Cayden and Ginny didn't care either, but with the prominent standing she held in the community, combined with the fame of Bluegrass Ranch, and they were putting on an event that made Lawrence a bit sick to his stomach.

The good news was that he only had to wear the tuxedo and stand in the right pictures today. No one would be watching him to make sure he didn't step on his new wife's feet. The spotlight would shine on someone else, and as Lawrence looked at himself in the mirror and swept his hair to the side, then covered it with his cowboy hat, he determined to enjoy himself that day.

"No matter what," he said.

"Talking to yourself again?" Spur asked, poking his head

into the room where Lawrence was nearly finished getting dressed.

"Yes," Lawrence said, turning to his oldest brother. "It's not a mistake to ask her to marry me today, right?"

Spur came all the way into the room and let the door close behind him. It had been hung on hydraulic hinges that made no noise and slowed the door down as it approached the doorjamb. "No, I don't think it'll be a mistake to propose today." He clapped Lawrence on the shoulder and drew him into a hug. "I'm so glad you found her, Lawrence. The two of you seem to fit together perfectly."

Spur looked at him, searching for the answer to his unspoken question, and Lawrence could only nod.

He and Mariah had gone shopping for diamonds, and she'd found one she liked very much. He'd bought it and had it sized for her, but he hadn't told her that. They'd spoken more about the future they wanted together, and while they'd shared a meal with Cayden and Ginny at the homestead, Mariah had mentioned leaving behind the marketing firm and doing more event planning.

Ginny had offered her a job at Sweet Rose on the spot, saying that she'd hired an event coordinator, but the job was simply too big for one person. Ginny had done so much for Sweet Rose, and she hadn't even realized she was doing the work of three people.

Her event coordinator knew it, and Ginny had worn wide eyes as she'd spoken with Mariah about coming to work at Sweet Rose.

Nothing had been ironed out yet, but Mariah talked

about it every single day, and Lawrence believed the New Year would bring new changes for her. He certainly hoped an engagement would be one of those changes.

Lawrence reached into his pocket and touched the perfectly round band of the diamond ring. His pulse kicked up a notch and shot out several beats in the space of one.

"You're doing this today," Spur said, smiling. "It's the right time, and she's the right woman."

"You're right," Lawrence said. "How close are we?"

Spur checked his watch. "You've got twenty minutes before you need to be in line—with Mariah—ready to go."

"Twenty minutes." Lawrence reached up and pulled at his collar. "Maybe I should wait until I'm wearing a normal shirt."

Spur chuckled and shook his head. "Go get it done, cowboy." He turned and opened the door, gesturing Lawrence through it ahead of him.

Lawrence took in this bigger waiting room, and even it was a nicer space than most people got married in. Plush couches lined the walls and created columns in the room. It was tastefully decorated in a western theme, and there were actually refreshments in the room for all of the groomsmen in the wedding party.

Ginny's brothers mingled with Lawrence's, and they'd brought in their sons too. Some of her cousins had come from Georgia, and if they were in any way related to her or Cayden, they had access to this room.

Lawrence avoided talking to anyone, though Duke, Cayden, and Daddy all caught his eye. He ducked out of the room and took a deep breath of the cooler air out in the hall. He pushed the air out and then breathed in deeply through his nose, imagining the oxygen going all the way into his brain and making his thoughts clearer.

He turned left and faced the hallway that led to the women's reception room. Mariah would be there with the other wives and girlfriends, and anyone else Ginny had given access to. Lawrence had heard several stories about her mother, but he hadn't actually met the woman yet.

He walked with purpose down the hall and knocked on the door. No one came right away, and Lawrence had just raised his fist to knock again when the door opened.

A white-haired woman stood there, and simply by the way she held herself, Lawrence could tell she was royalty. Rich royalty.

"What do you want, young man?" she barked.

"Now, now, Wendy," Mom said. "I'm sure this fine young man has a reason for knocking on the women's door." She grinned at Lawrence and hooked her arm through Wendy Winters'.

The older woman looked like she might claw off Mom's face, and she delicately removed her arm from Mom's. "This is one of your sons."

"That's right," Mom said. "I'll get Mariah, son." She turned and left him with Wendy, who glared at him from the top of his head right on down to his cowboy boots.

"Are you older or younger than Cayden?" Wendy asked.

"Younger, ma'am," he said.

"Married?" She squinted at him, and Lawrence almost

started laughing. He supposed she could be formidable in certain situations, but her firing questions at him like she cared about the answers and would use them to determine his worth was quite funny.

"No, ma'am. Hoping to change that this year, though." He nodded to the room behind her, noticing that Wendy Winters was not moving out of the way to let him enter.

Mariah came to Wendy's side, first looking at her and then him. "What are you doing here?" she asked, still trying to pin something in her hair. "I'm not quite ready, and I think we have fifteen more minutes."

"I was wondering if you'd take a walk with me."

"A walk?" Her eyebrows went up. "It's freezing outside. What are we going to do? Roam the halls in our formal clothes?"

"You want to talk right here? We can talk right here." Lawrence noticed movement behind her, but he'd committed now. He reached into his pocket and pulled out the engagement ring.

Holding it up, he said, "I went back to that jewelry store where you found this ring. I liked it a lot too, but I know you loved it. Since I'm in love with you, and I'll literally do anything in my power to make you happy, I thought I'd get it for you."

Mariah pulled in a breath and covered her mouth with one hand. Olli crowded in behind her, as did Ginny, Tam, and Beth. Mom practically elbowed her way through them all to stand right beside Mariah, whose sisters were both in the room too.

"Wait," one of them yelled, and Mariah half-laughed as the first of her tears ran down her face.

Dani arrived, and she held up her phone. "Did we miss the best part?"

"Not yet," Mom said.

"Shh," Olli said. "He hasn't even asked yet."

Lawrence swallowed, and had he known he'd have the whole engagement recorded, he may have insisted Mariah leave the room. Even just asking her in the hallway without the audience would be better than this.

"Get down on your knees, baby," Mom whispered in a stage voice that everyone could hear.

Annoyance sang through him, and he glared at his mother. "Mom," he said. "It's a miracle I've managed to get myself dressed this morning."

She held up both hands in surrender. "Sorry, sorry."

Lawrence took another breath and focused on Mariah. Only Mariah. The woman he'd first met through glass, when she was spitting mad at him. He could see her walking toward him to pick peaches, and he could still remember the very first time he'd kissed her.

"I love you," he said again. He did get down on both knees, and he held up the ring. "I know we don't have all of our plans worked out for the future, but I can't stand the thought of calling you my girlfriend for even one more day. Will you do me the great honor of becoming my fiancée?"

"That was so perfect," Olli said with a sigh.

"Really perfect," Ginny said, beaming down at Lawrence.

"Yes," Mariah said, and that caused a squealing eruption to happen among the women. She stepped forward and took Lawrence's face in her hands, something he absolutely loved, and kissed him.

Her lips trembled against his, and the kiss didn't last long. He slid the ring on her finger, and she held her hand out to examine the glinting gem. "I do love this ring." She showed it to all the females in the near vicinity before turning back to him. "And I do love you, Lawrence."

He got to his feet and took her into his arms. "I love you so much," he whispered in her ear while the group applauded and whooped as if they were cowboys and not the ladies that would walk down the aisles with them.

He grinned at his mother over Mariah's shoulder, and then her sister. They engulfed the couple in a hug too, which caused everyone to laugh. Finally Lawrence disentangled himself from all the embracing, and he slid his arm around Mariah's waist. "Could I really get sixty seconds alone with you, please?

"Yes, let's take a minute." She herded him out into the hall, as if she was the one who'd wanted to take a walk the first time. The women around them chatted as they started back toward their mirrors and makeup.

The door closed, and Lawrence didn't take another step. He wrapped his fiancée in his arms and kissed her, this time letting himself go a little further than he had while the camera was rolling.

She finally broke the kiss with a giggle, and she pressed

her forehead to his bowtie. "I'm going to have to redo my makeup now, cowboy."

"Worth it, though, right?" he whispered, enjoying the shape and feel of her in front of him.

She looked up, her bright blue eyes sparkling at him like stars. "Totally worth it."

Keep reading for a bonus sneak peek of the next book in the Bluegrass Ranch series, *ACQUIRING THE COWBOY BILLIONAIRE*. **It's available in paperback.**

Sneak Peek! Chapter One - Acquiring the Cowboy Billionaire

Duke Chappell stood in the line to walk down the aisle, one of Ginny's second cousins on his arm. He glanced at the woman, but he'd already forgotten her name. That was saying something for a man like Duke, who'd learned long ago how to memorize names —especially female names—because he was always ready to ask someone out if they interested him.

The problem was, no one interested Duke half as much as Lisa Harvey.

She wasn't at today's wedding, because she had no reason to be. He wasn't dating her, despite the tender moments they'd shared on Thanksgiving Day, a little over three weeks ago now.

He couldn't stop thinking about her, though, and his feet shifted as if he'd leave his brother's wedding and drive to her farm to make sure she was okay.

She hadn't stopped by his office at all, and she hadn't texted him beyond the business they needed to talk about.

Frustration built inside him as the music started. Everyone in line perked up a little, and Duke was eternally glad in moments like these that he sat at the end of the Chappell family and not the beginning.

Being the youngest hadn't always been easy for Duke, but he'd grown into the role. At some point a year or two ago, he'd realized that he didn't have to be the loudest or best to be valuable, both on the ranch and in his family. He didn't have to ask every woman for her number, and he didn't have to go out with them all either.

He'd dated enough now to know what he liked, and he knew he gravitated toward a woman with dark hair and dark eyes, as they held more mystery for him than blondes. He liked women who could talk to him without being awkward, and he didn't say no to a woman who knew how to cook, dance, and make him laugh.

He didn't think he'd put in too tall of an order with the Lord, but he sure hadn't had much luck finding someone he wanted to walk down the aisle with. Not the way Cayden and Ginny had. With Lawrence announcing his proposal on the family text only minutes ago, Duke's collar felt far too tight in a way that wasn't all physical.

He still reached up to try to loosen it, swallowing when he had a little bit more room between his Adam's apple and his bowtie. Cayden and Ginny's wedding was extremely formal, which didn't fit either of them all that well. But it fit their outside personas, and every groomsman wore a full tuxedo with tails.

Duke felt like a complete idiot, because he was about as far from a tuxedo as Pluto was from the sun. When he got married, he wanted to be in jeans and a plaid shirt, riding a horse, with his bride on a horse at his side. He didn't care what she wore, and he wanted to ride past his friends and family while they cheered and let off balloons.

Then the pastor would marry them, and he and his new bride would ride into the sunset and live happily-ever-after.

The whole thing would take a week to prepare, and about a half an hour to execute, and then he'd be done.

Duke didn't have the patience for a long engagement and huge, drawn-out celebration. He believed in marriage, and he did want to get married. He just didn't understand the show behind it. To him, it was a colossal waste of time, energy, and money, and all of those were finite.

He turned to the woman on his arm, and she wore a sparkly, gold dress that fell all the way to the floor. All women wore heels with a dress like that, and he gave her a smile. "I've got you, okay? You ready?"

She smiled back at him and nodded, her nerves plain in her eyes.

Duke had been in three weddings now, and he'd made this walk before. He put a smile on his face and took the first steps when he needed to, glad he'd worn his black cowboy dress boots with his tux. He, Ian, and Spur were the only ones who'd refused to trade out their boots for shiny loafers. Daddy too. The man hadn't worn anything but cowboy boots for fifty years, and it didn't matter if it was literally the biggest wedding the entire state of Kentucky had ever seen.

The aisle went on and on, and the faces started to blur after the first three steps. Duke kept going until he reached the altar, where Cayden stood in his tuxedo. He didn't look nervous at all, but he had a special way of stuffing everything away where no one could see it.

The music switched from the frilly, classical sounds that had been twinkling through the hall to the wedding march. Duke turned his attention to the back of the room where he'd tromped into the hall, expecting to see Ginny.

She didn't appear, and her father had died years ago. She'd asked Daddy to walk her down the aisle, and Duke's father had been riding that high for months now. He didn't have any girls of his own to walk down the aisle, and Ginny had literally made all of his dreams come true with a simple question.

The crowd grew somewhat restless, which honestly wasn't hard to do when a thousand people needed to be entertained and catered to.

Then a murmur rose up, and that turned into a cry. Duke saw several people pointing, and he too craned his neck to look up.

A part of the ceiling had detached and was slowly sinking toward the floor.

Ginny rode on it by herself, holding onto a pole to keep herself steady. She wore a snow-white dress that clung to her curves in a way that only custom-made clothing can do.

Lace covered the bodice and ran up past the white fabric

that covered her to her shoulders and down to her wrists. Her skin could peek through that lace, and she looked like an angel descending from heaven to marry her cowboy.

Duke could admit he was impressed by that, and he couldn't stop smiling as the platform reached the ground and Ginny reached for Daddy. He'd somehow appeared right where he needed to be, and he grinned at her as they started a limping step toward Cayden.

The platform had brought Ginny two-thirds of the way to the altar, so they didn't have to walk far. Daddy pressed his cheek to Ginny's and then passed her to Cayden, who kissed her against the corner of her eye and faced the altar.

Duke's relief soared through him as he got released from his brotherly duties of standing in a rainbow around the altar. He took small steps as he shuffled with everyone else, finally taking his seat on the end of the front row, on the far right. He could barely see Cayden and Ginny because of the width of this place, but he was determined to pay attention to his brother's nuptials.

He'd been making a conscious effort to stay off his phone more, because it was seriously his default for anything. Standing in a line at the store? He was on his phone. He'd just finished a class? Time to check his phone. Talking to Lawrence in the office they shared? He could scroll social media or answer texts at the same time.

Sometimes he hated his phone, and he hadn't even brought it into the hall for the wedding.

At the altar, the pastor gave a sweet speech about relying on each other and finding ways to show love for one another on a daily basis. Cayden and Ginny were the perfect example of relying on each other, as Duke had observed Cayden making the thirty-minute drive to Ginny's rental house whenever she needed him. He'd pack up his work and take it with him, because he wanted to be the safest, softest place for the woman he loved.

Duke wanted to be that man for someone too, and his thoughts went right back to Lisa. He frowned at himself as Cayden turned toward Ginny, and she started reading her vows.

"Cayden, you captured my heart long before I was even ready to give it away. You've always been there for me when I needed it, and I love that I can depend on you for anything, at any time." She smiled at him, and the power of it filled the entire space from top to bottom. She really possessed a strong spirit, and Duke had always liked her.

Ginny and Cayden had told him and Lawrence not to plan on moving out of the homestead. It was a huge space, with six bedrooms, and they didn't mind sharing two of them upstairs.

Duke really didn't want to live there with them alone, and depending on when Mariah and Lawrence got married, he might have to make some new living arrangements in the very near future.

"I love you with my whole heart today," Ginny said. "It only grows with each passing day, and I promise to be by your side for all of the steps of your life. Good days, and bad ones. All the pretty things, and all the ugly ones too." She beamed at her husband-to-be, and Duke had the distinct thought that Cayden was the luckiest man in the world. "I'm thrilled I get to be your wife, and bear your name."

"Wow," the pastor said. "I don't know how Cayden is going to top that."

The crowd twittered with laughter, and Duke's mind took a moment to catch up. He laughed a little bit too late, and he cut off his voice when everyone else started to as well. He didn't need his loud voice echoing in this hall during his brother's wedding.

"Virginia," Cayden said, lifting her hands to his lips. "You are the love of my life, and I've known it almost from the moment I met you. I would do anything for you, and I can't wait to experience our life together."

He turned back to the pastor, his promise short and sweet. Even getting him to say his vows into the microphone had not been something he'd wanted to do, but he'd spoken the truth when he'd said he'd do anything for Ginny.

The pastor used the powers vested in him from God above and the state of Kentucky, and he pronounced Cayden and Ginny man and wife.

The crowd surged to their feet, and Duke was once again caught off-guard. He did stand and start clapping, but he didn't join his loud cowboy voice to the rest of his family on the front row. Several of them whistled through their teeth —something Duke could do too—but he didn't do that either.

Cayden dipped Ginny right there at the altar and kissed her, which only prompted more and rowdier cheering.

Then they turned toward the crowd and lifted their

joined hands. They walked down the aisle, running the last few steps to the platform. They both got on this time, and with one hand secured to the pole, they waved with their free hand to everyone gathered in the hall.

The life in the party left with them, and Duke turned to Lawrence. "That was pretty amazing."

"Spectacular," his brother agreed.

"Are you going to do something like that for your wedding?"

"I doubt it," Lawrence said, smiling at Duke. "You?"

"I can't even imagine getting married inside," he said. He didn't make it a well-known fact that he'd thought about his wedding day, because that apparently wasn't something men did. He just knew he didn't want a big fuss.

"Let's go get something to drink before the luncheon," Lawrence said, leading the way down the aisle.

Duke followed him back to the reception room, where the refreshments had been replenished. He took a moment to pick up his phone from where he'd placed it in the windowsill. His heartbeat caught in his throat when he saw Lisa had texted him.

Not only that, but she'd called too.

He tapped on her name to read her text, and she'd said, *My daddy has gone into the hospital. Can you call me when you get a minute?*

He glanced around, wondering if this was the right minute to introduce this emergency into his life. Should he call now or wait until the wedding festivities were over?

He hurried over to Daddy and showed him the phone. "Should I call her right now?'

"Yes," Daddy said. "Duke, there's one thousand people here. If you need to leave, no one's going to miss you."

"The most important thing that needed to happen today," Mom added. "Has happened." She linked her arm through Daddy's and leaned her cheek against his bicep. "Poor Wayne. I hope he's okay."

Duke knew he wasn't okay, and as he dialed Lisa, he prayed with all the energy of his soul that Wayne Harvey had had enough time to update his will.

Sneak Peek! Chapter Two - Acquiring the Cowboy Billionaire

L isa Harvey stood in the back of the microscopic hospital room, thinking that everything she'd seen on TV movies about the health care system had been wrong. There were no beeping machines assuring her that Daddy was still alive. The rooms weren't big enough to host families. The lighting was super harsh—none of this low lighting where female patients fell in love with handsome doctors.

In fact, the last three doctors that had been in the room had all been at least a decade younger than Lisa. At least. The last guy—a urologist—looked like he was barely fourteen years old. And none of them had been tall, dark, and handsome.

They also didn't wear white coats with stethoscopes around their necks, and Lisa scoffed under her breath as she glanced toward her two half-brothers. Kelly and Bruce had huddled near the door of the room, and with their heads bent together, Lisa folded her arms and scowled in their direction.

They were likely talking about her. She wanted to talk to them and find out why they'd turned vitriolic toward her the moment Daddy had been diagnosed. That was the only thing that had changed in their family, and Lisa didn't understand the sudden shift.

It had happened to everyone—the brothers and their wives. Even the three nieces and nephews Lisa loved had turned somewhat cold toward her.

If she didn't love Daddy with her whole heart, and she didn't enjoy working with the horses quite so much, Lisa would leave Dreamsville. Her dreams certainly weren't coming true here, and she stood to lose everything she'd spent the last thirty-four years of her life working toward.

Familiar desperation swirled within her now, and no amount of swallowing and throat-clearing would make it go away. She'd been so desperate thirty minutes ago—*so* close to tears—that she'd texted Duke Chappell.

Her phone currently sat in her back pocket, and she'd left the notifications on, vibrations and everything. Daddy couldn't hear much without his hearing aids, and he hadn't turned them on that morning. There hadn't been time.

When Lisa had come in from her morning chores, she'd realized immediately that something was wrong. It was the lack of the scent of coffee hanging in the air. Daddy adored coffee, and he brewed his specialty grounds every morning by seven, no matter what.

Except there was a "no matter what," and it was that

Daddy hadn't been able to get out of bed that morning. Lisa had instantly gone down the hallway to his bedroom, calling his name. She could admit she'd hesitated at the closed door, wondering if she was going to find a breathing body on the other side...or one that wasn't.

She could still keenly feel the pinch of helplessness and the way her heartbeat had become a living, breathing, physical entity reverberating through her whole body. It had settled back into something she didn't even think about or detect, but for a few painful seconds standing in the hallway outside Daddy's bedroom, her pulse had consumed her.

He'd been alive, obviously, and he'd managed to get himself sitting up. He hadn't been able to get his right leg to move, though, and that meant he couldn't stand, couldn't walk, and couldn't make coffee.

His lack of caffeine had made him extremely unpleasant, and he'd barked at Lisa that she didn't need to fuss over him. She'd barked right back that someone needed to, and Bruce and Kelly weren't going to do it. Instant regret had filled her —still did—and she'd apologized profusely before calling both of her brothers to come help her.

Daddy was a big man, with a big personality. He'd been a cowboy his whole life, and he knew the value of hard work. Everything he had, he'd built.

Getting him to come to the hospital in an ambulance had been terribly difficult, and in the end, it had been Lisa who'd helped him see there was no other way.

You can't walk, Daddy, she'd said. *You know there's some-*

thing wrong. Something we don't know about yet. Why can't we go to the hospital and find out what it is?

She knew why he was resistant to doing such a thing.

Fear.

Fear was a very tangible being in Lisa's life, and it had been for the past seven months. It could coil around her heart and start to squeeze before she recognized it. It could seep under the cracks in the doors she'd been slamming closed for months. It could sneak up on her while she worked with a horse or shoveled out a stall, when everything had been sunny and perfectly fine only the moment before.

Right now, fear had a chokehold on her, and Lisa could barely get enough air into her lungs.

Her phone buzzed and zinged out a loud chime, drawing the attention of both brothers and Belinda, Bruce's wife, who sat in the only chair in the room. The three of them frowned at her simultaneously, as if receiving a message in the hospital was the worst possible crime on the planet.

"Who is it, baby?" Daddy asked. "Is it your momma, askin' 'bout me?" His words slurred slightly, and while Lisa couldn't see his face from her position in the back corner of the room, she didn't think he'd have his eyes open.

She also had no idea what to say. Her mother had left Dreamsville when Lisa was fifteen years old. She'd packed two suitcases and set them in the kitchen Lisa still used each morning. She'd gone about her day, making breakfast and weeding a flowerbed. When Daddy had come in from his chores, she'd announced she was leaving.

She hadn't offered to take Lisa with her, and Lisa

wasn't sure what she'd have done. In the first few months after her departure, Lisa had missed her terribly. Daddy had too. The two of them had clung to each other, and with Bruce and Kelly so much older than her, it had just been the two of them at the stud farm, working and grieving.

"I don't know, Daddy," she said quietly, pulling her phone from her pocket. She quickly pushed the sliding button up to put the device on vibrate-only, because she didn't need six eyes latching onto her and trying to fillet her alive. She also didn't need more questions like the one her daddy had just asked.

She hadn't heard from her mother in about five years now, and the only reason Darla had called last time was to tell Lisa that she'd gotten engaged to someone else. Her third marriage. Lisa had not attended the wedding, and she hadn't heard from her mother since.

The message was from Duke, and Lisa's heart grew a tiny set of wings. The man had some serious power over her, and she wasn't even sure when she'd opened the door and invited him into her life. They'd never gotten along all that well, but she suspected that was because of her saltiness toward him. He reflected it back to her, and she couldn't really blame him for that.

Sorry, he said. *I was in Cayden's and Ginny's wedding. I'm free now. I can call anytime. Tell me when.*

Lisa had forgotten about the wedding of the year, and foolishness filled her. She'd been disappointed and she'd started to see things through jade-colored glasses when Duke didn't pick up. He'd said she could call him and ask for anything, but he hadn't picked up.

She distinctly remembered scoffing and wishing she could take back the notification that would tell him she'd called and texted.

He'd been in a wedding, and Lisa swallowed the forming lump of embarrassment in her throat. There were going to be a lot of awkward and uncomfortable things she'd have to deal with in the near future. How she'd privately reacted to Duke not picking up her call was probably the smallest one.

She stepped over to the bed and gazed down at Daddy. "You're okay here for a minute, Daddy? It's Duke, and I need to call him back."

His eyes opened, and they looked like a newborn's eyes —unfocused and slightly watery. Daddy smiled and tried to reach his hand toward her. Lisa went most of the way and curled his fingers through his. "You rest," she said. "I'll be right back."

"Love you, baby doll," he said, his eyes drifting closed again. The moment froze, and Lisa was so glad there wasn't a horrible hospital machine beeping in this new memory. Daddy had always loved her, and after Mama had left, he'd tell her every night that they could get through hard times.

"Together, Lise," he'd said. "Me and you can do this. It's hard, and sometimes I want to raise my fist to heaven and ask God why this happened. What I did wrong."

She could still picture him shaking his head, such sorrow in her eyes. Then he flipped the chicken breast he'd been cooking and turned back to her. "But I love you, baby doll. At least she didn't take you from me too."

He'd become more affectionate after Mama had left, and Lisa hadn't hated that. He hugged her more often, and he'd put his arm around her and told her he was proud of her dozens of times since then.

She made it past the glaring bodyguards at the door and stepped into the hall. Relief hit her like a wall of water, and she stopped and blinked, trying to process so much in such a short space of time. She didn't want to go too far in case one of the doctors or nurses came back with news.

They'd sent Daddy for an MRI about forty minutes ago, and that was when Lisa's anxiety had overtaken her and she'd excused herself to call Duke.

As she dialed him now, she realized she just needed to hear a friendly voice, and his was the first she'd thought of. She just wanted someone who was on her side to tell her that she was a worthwhile human being.

She took a few steps away from the door and settled against the wall opposite of Daddy's room, tears already gathering in her eyes.

"Lisa," Duke said, his voice somewhat breathless. "Are you okay, honey?" He let the last word drip out of his mouth the way honey did, slow and sweet and delicious.

Lisa actually smiled, though she normally disliked terms of endearment that made her feel small or less-than who she was.

"Where are you?" he said. "I can change and be at the hospital in maybe thirty minutes."

She found she couldn't speak, not without revealing the emotions tumbling through her. *Would that be such a bad thing?* she wondered. She didn't let anyone in, except Daddy. He wasn't going to be with her much longer; she could simply feel it.

She drew in a deep breath, and said, "It's your brother's wedding, Duke. You can't just run out." Her voice was too high and somewhat strained, but every word she said helped her feel a little stronger.

"You'd be doin' me a favor," he said. "Everyone understands emergencies."

"This is *my* emergency," she said. "Not yours."

"Lisa," he said, but he didn't present another argument.

She looked down the hall, wishing the Lord would paint the words she should say on the stark walls. Maybe then she'd know how to talk to a man. Duke, specifically, she thought. Help me talk to Duke specifically.

"I'm okay," she said, pressing her eyes closed. "Daddy couldn't move his right leg this morning." The story poured from her in only a minute, and she took a long, shuddering breath when she finished.

"I'm so sorry, Lisa," Duke said, his voice soft and full of that caring compassion she'd seen on his face on Thanksgiving. "I'll come as soon as I can, okay?"

"Why?" she asked. "I haven't asked you to come."

He said nothing, and Lisa watched Daddy's nurse stand from the station down the hall. Her pulse bumped against her ribcage, and she straightened from the wall.

"I'm sorry to bother you on Cayden's wedding day," she

whispered. "Please forgive me. I just needed to hear a friendly voice, and yours was the first one I wanted to hear."

She had no idea what she'd really said between those words, but in that moment, she didn't care. "I just wanted someone to be on *my* side."

"I'm on your side," Duke said. "You don't have to do this alone, honey. I really will come."

She smiled. "I know," she said. "Thank you, Duke. The nurse is coming, and I have to go."

"Text me what you find out," he said. "I love your daddy too."

"Okay," she said, and armed with that knowledge that Daddy was loved by more than his family, Lisa stepped across the hall to arrive at the door of her father's room at the same time the nurse did.

She gave Lisa a smile and let her go in first. Lisa squeezed past Bruce and Kelly and returned to her spot near the back window. The cold air emanated off of the glass, and Lisa seized onto the sensation and let it move through her.

"The doctor just got the MRI scan," the nurse said. "He's on his way over. He shouldn't be long, but maybe another twenty minutes." She smiled at Daddy and went about her work checking things. What, Lisa didn't know.

She left the room again, and it was back to hurry-up-and-wait. Everything in the hospital happened on a molasses time schedule, with only microbursts of activity.

She re-pocketed her phone and sank into the counter.

The minutes passed slowly, and Lisa actually closed her eyes and rested her head against the window. The next time the door opened, a knock preceded it and then Duke Chappell's voice said, "Oh, this is the right room."

He entered without waiting to be invited in, and Lisa dang near fell down in her haste to straighten.

His eyes caught on hers, but Duke took a moment to say hello to her brothers, shaking both of their hands and saying he'd heard about Daddy and wanted to come see what the family needed.

He stopped at Daddy's bedside and leaned down to say something to him. Lisa couldn't hear anything through the fog that had enveloped her upon Duke's arrival. He wore a pair of blue jeans, a very shiny pair of black cowboy boots, and yellow polo that pulled across his chest. He'd covered that with a black leather jacket, and he was pure perfection in a cowboy hat.

Lastly, he turned his attention to her, taking the three steps past the bed to the tiny alcove which led into the even smaller bathroom. The sink was outside the bathroom, in the counter where Lisa had been attempting to doze.

"Hey, honey," he said quietly, sliding his arm around her waist and bringing her flush against his body. His touch melted all the icy pieces inside her. His care for her made her weep. She clung to him in a way she'd only done to Daddy before, and she allowed him to hold her up for several long moments while she couldn't do it herself.

"It's okay, now," he whispered, using one hand to stroke her hair. "I'm here now, honey, and you'll be okay."

She wasn't sure she believed him, but she wanted to. She seized onto the words and used them as a life preserver in this vast new ocean where she'd been trying to swim alone since May.

The door opened again, and Duke released her, both of them turning toward the door as the doctor entered. He took in the group of people, and even Belinda stood from the recliner, worry on her face.

The very room seemed to inhale and hold its breath while the doctor said, "We've got quite the crew in here." He smiled and looked at Daddy. "How are you feeling, Wayne?'

"I've been better," Daddy said, and Lisa couldn't hold back the half-sob, half-laugh.

"I'll bet you have," the doctor said. "Let's pull up your scan and see what you're dealing with."

Lisa couldn't see the computer screen from behind it, so she edged out, stealing Duke's hand so she could stay grounded. He went with her, and they moved to stand behind Daddy's bed, in the tiny space between it and the wall.

"Can you see?" Lisa whispered to Duke.

He shook his head and said, "It doesn't matter if I see, Lise. Can you see?"

She nodded, because the doctor had pushed the screen back so it was almost flat against the wall. She pulled in a breath and held it, then reached her free hand over the bed and put it on Daddy's shoulder.

He covered her hand with his, and they waited for the doctor to put the scan on the screen. Duke's hand in hers was tight and warm, and Lisa really liked it. She'd told him he shouldn't come, but he had anyway, and she liked that too.

She had to admit that she simply liked Duke Chappell, and maybe it was time to stop fighting the feelings that had been pinging at her for months now. She glanced at him, and when their eyes met, the charge that zapped between them could've revived Daddy's heart had he needed it.

She smiled, and Duke did too, and suddenly, Lisa could handle whatever image came up on the screen. Just like she'd had Daddy at her side when Mama had left, she now had Duke in her corner.

"Finally," the doctor said. "Here it is."

Lisa leaned over the bed a little more, as if getting closer to the screen would help her understand the image starting to form there.

"I'm afraid it's not good news," the doctor said, pointing with his pen. Lisa blinked, and the room turned white. The only thing anchoring her to the Earth was Duke's hand in hers.

I can't wait to see what will happen with Duke and Lisa in *ACQUIRING THE COWBOY BILLIONAIRE.* **Now available in paperback.**

Bluegrass Ranch Romance

Book 1: Winning the Cowboy Billionaire: She'll do anything to secure the funding she needs to take her perfumery to the next level...even date the boy next door.

Book 2: Roping the Cowboy Billionaire: She'll do anything to show her ex she's not still hung up on him...even date her best friend.

Book 3: Training the Cowboy Billionaire: She'll do anything to save her ranch...even marry a cowboy just so they can enter a race together.

Book 4: Parading the Cowboy Billionaire: She'll do anything to spite her mother and find her own happiness...even keep her cowboy billionaire boyfriend a secret.

Book 5: Promoting the Cowboy Billionaire: She'll do anything to keep her job...even date a client to stay on her boss's good side.

Book 6: Acquiring the Cowboy Billionaire: She'll do anything to keep her father's stud farm in the family...even marry the maddening cowboy billionaire she's never gotten along with.

Book 7: Saving the Cowboy Billionaire: She'll do anything to prove to her friends that she's over her ex...even date the cowboy she once went with in high school.

Book 8: Convincing the Cowboy Billionaire: She'll do anything to keep her dignity...even convincing the saltiest cowboy billionaire at the ranch to be her boyfriend.

Chestnut Ranch Romance

Book 1: A Cowboy and his Neighbor: Best friends and neighbors shouldn't share a kiss...

Book 2: A Cowboy and his Mistletoe Kiss: He wasn't supposed to kiss her. Can Travis and Millie find a way to turn their mistletoe kiss into true love?

Book 3: A Cowboy and his Christmas Crush: Can a Christmas crush and their mutual love of rescuing dogs bring them back together?

Book 4: A Cowboy and his Daughter: They were married for a few months. She lost their baby...or so he thought.

Book 5: A Cowboy and his Boss: She's his boss. He's had a crush on her for a couple of summers now. Can Toni and Griffin mix business and pleasure while making sure the teens they're in charge of stay in line?

Book 6: A Cowboy and his Fake Marriage: She needs a husband to keep her ranch...can she convince the cowboy next-door to marry her?

Book 7: A Cowboy and his Secret Kiss: He likes the pretty adventure guide next door, but she wants to keep their relationship off the grid. Can he kiss her in secret and keep his heart intact?

Book 8: A Cowboy and his Skipped Christmas: He's been in love with her forever. She's told him no more times than either of them can count. Can Theo and Sorrell find their way through past pain to a happy future together?

TEXAS LONGHORN RANCH ROMANCE

Book 1: Loving Her Cowboy Best Friend: She's a city girl returning to her hometown. He's a country boy through and through. When these two former best friends (and ex-lovers) start working together, romantic sparks fly that could ignite a wildfire... Will Regina and Blake get burned or can they tame the flames into true love?

Book 2: Kissing Her Cowboy Boss: She's a veterinarian with a secret past. He's her new boss. When Todd hires Laura, it's because she's willing to live on-site and work full-time for the ranch. But when their feelings turn personal, will Laura put up walls between them to keep them apart?

ABOUT EMMY

Emmy is a Midwest mom who loves dogs, cowboys, and Texas. She's been writing for years and loves weaving stories of love, hope, and second chances. Learn more about her and her books at www.emmyeugene.com.

Printed in Great Britain
by Amazon